RANSOMED

A CASEY CORT LEGAL THRILLER

AIME AUSTIN

AIME AUSTIN
www.AimeAustin.com

LOS ANGELES, CALIFORNIA

ALSO BY AIME AUSTIN

Judged

Caged

Disgraced

Unarmed

Kidnapped

Reunited

Contained

Poisoned

Abused

RANSOMED

A CASEY CORT LEGAL THRILLER

AIME AUSTIN

Ransomed

This edition published by
Moore Digital Media Inc.
1125 N Fairfax Avenue
Unit 46071
West Hollywood, CA 90046
www.aimeaustin.com

Copyright © 2015 by Sylvie Fox as Under Color of Law
ISBN 13: 978-1-64414-042-0
eISBN 13: 978-1-64414-041-3

Cover Designer: Wicked Good Book Covers
Cover images © Depositphotos, Shutterstock

Ransomed/Aime Austin. — 3d ed.

"The fact that obscene conduct by males in the workplace and sexual harassment in our society generally has become the object of special opprobrium and public scorn does not turn the defendant's outrageous conduct into a federal crime."

–JUDGE GILBERT MERRITT—August 14, 1997

1

"What was that noise?" Greg Salazar asked. My across-the-hall neighbors, Greg and Jason Corry were in my apartment helping me assess my wardrobe...or maybe my life. Decisions about both loomed large in my head right now.

"It was my stomach," I admitted. The growl echoed off the walls of my bedroom. In my defense, it was a small room, with bare walls in a thousand square foot prewar apartment.

"When's the last time you ate?" Jason asked. He was a doctor who tended to ask about people's health outside of the hospital.

"Who knows?" I shrugged. Since my ex had called, anxiety had replaced hunger.

"You're losing weight," Jason said. Then dead silence between the three of us in my bedroom. "Not that I'm making any kind of statement about your health or wellbeing," he offered. Jason was a doctor, so I took it in the spirit offered. "It's just that bodies need nourishment. Crash diets aren't a good idea."

I had to admire his ability to walk the fine line between saying I was curvy and saying I needed to eat.

"Then my mind needs less stress," I countered.

"What exactly happened?" Greg looked genuinely perplexed. "You're going to your ex-boyfriend's parents' house for a party for his uncle judge? That's a lot for someone you haven't spoken with in—what is it—seven years?"

He had a point. I think I'd been too shocked by Tom Brody being on the other end of my phone to ask all the questions they were asking now. I didn't want to answer those, so I punted.

"It's an opportunity to mingle with the right people," I said plainly. "Judges who can assign me cases. Maybe look on me a little more favorably when I'm in court."

"The *right* people?" Greg pressed.

"The legal community in this county is very insular. I used to be on the inside, now I'm on the outs. I want to be back in." I could hear that it sounded like the Mafia.

"Into Tom's arms too?" Jason came at me obliquely.

"No. Yes. Maybe. I don't know."

"You don't know?" Greg's voice was full of incredulity he was taking no means to hide. "He dumped you when the water got too hot. That's not the action of a true partner."

"We were twenty-one, twenty-two. It's been years. We're in our thirties now." If I'd been naïve, then Tom could be excused for his immaturity as well. At least that's what I was telling myself.

"Did he apologize?" Greg asked.

"When?"

"When he called you out of the blue to ask you to this party."

"No. Maybe he wants to do that in person. Speaking of. I need to be there in an hour. It's going to take at least that to get across town. Can you help?"

Greg opened the closet door, did a quick survey, and pulled out a black wrap dress.

"A little black dress can never do you wrong. Diane Von Furstenberg created something truly for women. Can't say that of a lot of designers."

I had no idea who Diane was and didn't have time to ask. Instead, I took the clothing suggestion and shooed them out. I didn't want to be too late. This party was the kind I'd gone to when I'd been a summer associate at Morrell Gates. Shaking hands with judges never hurt. They were more likely to remember me sober, though.

Dressed, I ran down four flights to North Moreland Boulevard bypassing all the cars next to my building, including Greg's and Jason's. My ancient Honda was in a garage under another building my landlord owned, a block and a half from the apartment.

I never wore high heels, but my sandals certainly kept me from picking up speed as I tried not to move too slow or sweat too much. The ground was wet, but at least it wasn't raining or a late summer swelter.

Once I got to the car and got in, I turned the key.

Nothing.

I tried not to panic, but sweat was starting to pool under my crucifix and in my push-up bra. Saturday night was not the time to need a mechanic or a new starter motor. My repair shop was in Cleveland Heights and my mechanic seemed like the kind of guy who took time for his family.

I took a deep breath, gave the car a little bit of gas, then turned the key again.

Success.

The engine sputtered to life. At least I'd make it to Lakewood. What would happen on the other end, I'd worry about in a few hours. Maybe after I put something into my stomach. It was Cleveland, at least I knew there'd be food. I heard in New York or Los Angeles, food wasn't guaranteed at a party.

In the hour it took me to drive from Shaker Square to Lakewood, I replayed my entire relationship with Tom Brody in my mind. From feeling grateful that he'd asked me out and dated me of all the other well-off and well-connected kids in our law school class at Cleveland Marshall to the not-so-great ending.

Tom and I had almost moved in together, almost gotten engaged. I wasn't angry exactly, but more perplexed as to why having strong ethics and morals had been a dealbreaker.

I'd reported plagiarism in a law review article by a kid named Ted Strohmeyer to the law school Dean as outlined in the school's policy. One each and every one of us had to sign.

Now, of course, I could see my naivete. Strohmeyer was very rich—Bill Gates rich—former student. The Strohmeyer family—yes, the 'You'll be a high flyer when you drink Strohmeyer' Strohmeyers. Yes, the ones who owned the brewery that employed every tenth person in Cuyahoga County until half the operation had moved to Mexico.

Yes, the Strohmeyers who also own the professional football team—in a football town. Yes, I was fully aware of my folly. That lovely family made sure I couldn't get arrested in this town, much less find gainful employment. I lost my very prestigious job at the law firm of Morrell Gates, and I also lost Tom.

To this day, I don't know the real reason Tom broke up with me. But back then, with my world crashing in on me, finding 'closure' wasn't at the top of my list.

Instead, I picked myself up, dusted myself off, and started my own law practice. The Strohmeyers couldn't keep me from hiring myself. Although it was a rocky start, to say the least, things were going much better.

Better being a relative term, of course. Now, I could pay my bills and not worry about imminent bankruptcy every month. Things made a turn for the better when I lost my most famous case. Yes, losing turned me into a winner. I'm not the first loser turned winner. Look at F. Lee Bailey or David Boies. I bet you can't name a case that they've won. F. Lee famously lost the 'Boston Strangler' case and the Patty Hearst matter, but he's still featured on court TV every other time I flip by. David Boies represented Al Gore and Napster. He was on the losing side of two of the most famous cases in history, but I bet you he's still busy.

Two years ago, I'd met Sheila Harrison Grant. At the time, she had been a federal judge. The county Department of Children and Family Services had removed her daughter and put the girl in foster care. Up until then, I had been churning juvenile court files at two hundred fifty dollars a pop. And I wasn't closing enough cases to make a decent living. Then Judge Grant plunked twenty-five hundred big ones on my desk and I was in business.

I did my level best to defend that woman against charges that she was a verbally abusive alcoholic. I'd mounted a defense of the kind never seen in Cuyahoga County juvenile court. I had called witnesses and hired experts. I had even used the Johnnie Cochran tactic of focusing on the agency's racial bias to distract the court from the allegations.

But Sheila Grant was one of those clients who had sabotaged me at every turn, and I lost spectacularly. I went down in flames. So I appealed her case because I should have won. I'm proud to say that I snatched a Pyrrhic victory from the jaws of defeat. But I guess Judge Grant didn't trust me. She took justice into her own hands, allegedly kidnapping her daughter and fleeing from the jurisdiction. The court took judicial notice of this and dismissed my winning appeal.

Now I understood why certain trashy celebrities believed all publicity was good publicity. Judge Grant was good for me. With my name in the papers, my phone started ringing off the hook. A few mentions in The Plain Dealer were worth more than two bus benches and a year's worth of advertising on the back of the phone book.

People now paid me the going rate of two hundred smackers per hour for their child-related matters in Juvenile and Domestic Relations court. I wasn't getting rich, or even grasping at middle class. But I had enough money to pay my bills and make the minimum payments on my student loans and credit cards. That was why I was able to sit on my futon pawing through shopping bags.

Out of the blue, Tom asked me to come to his parents' house. I was so surprised that he had my phone number, so surprised to hear his voice on the phone, that asking him why there was a party hadn't occurred to me until long after he'd hung up.

I hadn't been to the big manse in Lakewood in over eight years. It would have been a godsend if I could have lost fifty pounds by cocktail hour, but miracles like that didn't happen for me. Instead, I'd be the sturdy-looking girl straight from peasant European stock among a group of skinny Irish folks. Resigned to my fat fate, I got going.The nearly hour-long drive across town was long and boring. None of the radio stations I dialed up in the Honda could distract me from my nervousness, fear, or worry. I had no idea what I was in for tonight.

"Ma'am." The valet nodded obsequiously as he took my keys and undoubtedly hid my car somewhere its hoopty cooties couldn't infect the German and Japanese luxury cars ostentatiously displayed in the motor court.

It was chilly by the lake, and I congratulated myself on having the presence of mind to bring a faux Pashmina wrap. With it thrown over my shoulders just so, I hoped I didn't look like I was playing dress-up in my mother's clothes.

I sighed with relief when Tom appeared. He came down the wide granite steps that spilled from the back of the house.

"Gosh, I missed you," was all he said before wrapping me in a bear of a hug. I should have been swept away by the embrace, for which I'd waited so long. "I'm so glad you could make it." He hauled me back and scrutinized my face. Then he grabbed me by the shoulders and bussed me on the cheek.

"Hey," I said. Seven years of advanced education and it was the best I could come up with. I felt like someone had kicked me in the gut. It had been eight years since I'd seen him up close and personal, but there he stood. Age had been kinder to him than me. Tom looked like the young, dashing assistant county prosecutor he was. His dark blond hair hadn't receded, and his eyes were the same warm brown that I remembered, with maybe a new little crinkle at the corners.

Almost before it was gone, I caught the brush of lips and the slight scratch of stubble against my cheek. Clearly, hanging out with my gay neighbors was not enough male contact to satisfy me. I hoped Tom didn't notice that I was a little wobbly on my feet after one brief encounter.

"What's going on tonight? I didn't know what to wear."

He looked me up and down dispassionately. "You're fine. I didn't tell you what's up?" he asked offhandedly. "My bad. It's a celebration."

We walked across the back lawn toward the house. I tried to keep up with him, pulling my heels out of the quicksand-like mud and grass every two or three steps.

"It's a barbecue." I watched the red-jacketed valets and the white jacketed waiters weaving through the throng of guests. Some barbecue. "We're celebrating the investiture of Uncle Eamon," he continued.

"Investiture?" I mentally flipped through the county bar association's judicial roster. "But he's already a judge at Probate."

"And this is why I invited you." He stopped suddenly ten feet from the house and the bustle of the caterers, and looked at me. "You know how there's been an opening at juvenile since Judge Conti resigned?"

I nodded in response. The exact reasons for Judge Conti's resignation were unclear, but the result had been that the other judges' dockets were busier than ever. What had already been slow justice had become molasses-like. Speculation on who the governor would appoint was rampant.

"Uncle Eamon is assuming that seat."

I felt my eyes grow wide with surprise. This was an unexpected turn of events. I had only been to Probate once when the mother of one of my minor clients wanted to change the daughter's last name to the stepfather's. My single matter had ended up in front of another judge, so I'd never encountered Eamon Brody in person. The possibility of a judge who might be just that little bit favorable to me in a court I was in every day gave me a little thrill. This was *good*—worth squeezing my back fat into a sturdy bra good.

Tom held the back door open and I walked in ahead of him, hoping the Pashmina's fringe covered my wide expanse of ass. Tom's father, Judge Patrick Brody and a few other old white men came out of the house's spacious study smelling of scotch, the half-smoked Cuban cigars still smoldering in their hands.

"Casey." Judge Brody pumped my hand like the politician he was. "Good to see you after all these years. You're the girlfriend from law school, right?" He looked at his cronies, chuckling. "I can't keep up with Tom's revolving door. He just broke up with the beautiful Lizzy Cofrancesco last week, I think it was. Good thing we were able to get those wedding deposits back." He thumped me heartily on the back as he and his friends stepped outside.

"Nothing like being second choice," I murmured to Tom. The older I got, the harder it was to keep my feelings inside, or my mouth shut. Oddly, I felt jealous of the beautiful Lizzy Cofrancesco. Though after eight years I had no right to feel any way about anyone in Tom's life.

"Look, I'm going to be honest here. I broke up with Lizzy Cofrancesco a couple of weeks ago, but that's another story altogether. I know that you work over on Twenty Second and I thought it would be beneficial for you to talk to my uncle. It's a good idea to befriend the lion in the jungle, I think."

Fortunately, a bunch of cars began arriving, and Tom had host duties, so I could wallow in the misery of being the platonic acquaintance—alone. I took myself over to the bartender and had a margarita or two. I needed some Dutch courage to get me through this embarrassing evening. If I were a better person, I'd have downed the two tequila-heavy drinks that came my way, and maybe a third, then shaken every hand I could. Tom had provided the grease. I needed to take advantage of this moment.

There were more power brokers scattered across the Brody acre and a half then at a Massimo political fundraiser. But I wasn't a politically motivated, glad-hander. If I was, it wouldn't have taken a scandal to jump start my practice.

After nursing my second margarita until the ice disappeared, Tom's father and his cronies broke up their meeting and started circulating among the group. I turned around after a hand landed on my shoulder.

"We haven't met before, have we?" Liam Brody said.

We had, but I didn't contradict the man. "I-I'm Casey Cort," I stuttered with my re-introduction. "A friend of Tom's."

"How do you know my nephew?"

"We went to law school together, sir."

The hand that had never left my back, patted vigorously. "Another CSU Viking. Good to know. Don't meet as many down in Columbus." Although Liam didn't remember me, I remembered him. He had served as the Cuyahoga County prosecutor forever. Tom's uncle had recently run for, and won, the office of Attorney General.

"How is the AG's office treating you?" I couldn't wait to go home later and marvel at my sparkling conversation.

"Good, good. I'm doing what I can for the citizens of Ohio. But enough about me. Where do you work?"

"I'm in private practice," I said. The euphemism for loser solo practitioner. "Primarily, I practice in Juvenile and Domestic Relations court."

"Good for you then, being here tonight. Let me introduce you to my brother." He clasped my shoulder tightly and led me over to the other musketeers. As we made the short trip across the back yard, under the vine-covered trellis, I marveled that I'd made so little impression on Tom's family. We'd gone out more than two years, and I'd thought we were pretty serious, but Liam didn't even remember me. Maybe he was in the early stages of dementia. Ohio voters elected Brodys because of their name, not because of their intellect. Tom excluded, of course.

The men had exchanged their scotch and cigars for beer—and in the case of those ignoring the surgeon general's decades old warning—cigarettes. Liam clasped my left hand in his and held our interlocked arms, folded at the elbows, tight to our sides. These Brodys were certainly touchy-feely today. With my free hand, I shook Judge Patrick Brody's again, and then Liam turned me over to soon-to-be juvenile judge, Eamon Brody.

"Nice to meet you, Casey did you say your name was?"

I nodded.

"You can just call me Judge Brody," he said with a straight face.

"Don't you get confused with your brother—the *other* Judge Brody?" I asked. Alcohol brought out my snark factor, not to mention my witty repartee.

"I'm older. I was judge first. There's no confusion." I mentally kicked myself. Why was I involved in such a stupid conversation, when what I really needed to be doing was ingratiating myself to this man?

"Well...I don't know if Tom mentioned, but I primarily practice in Juvenile Court. I work in Domestic Relations as well—you know, the family arena," I said in my best ass-kissing voice.

He patted my hand paternally, and steered me toward a more secluded area of the property, away from his cohorts. "I've barely moved into my chambers. Maybe you can stop by some day next week. I could use a woman's eye while I'm hanging pictures, decorating."

Now he was being a chauvinistic ass. Albeit the ass controlling the purse strings. I put on my prettiest smile and said, "I don't want to intrude on Mrs. Brody's turf," trying to remember if there *was* a Mrs. Brody for Judge Eamon. They may all think of themselves as Judge Brody, but I needed to distinguish them, and their Christian names were suitable as long as I remembered not to say them out loud.

"Moira hasn't driven downtown in twenty years," he said, waving his hand dismissively. "I need a younger woman's eye, anyway."

A friend in court, especially one behind the bench, was never a bad thing. If this was the price of admission, so be it. "I'll give your chambers a call after the holiday weekend."

He patted my arm perilously close to my boobs. Maybe his eyesight was going as well. Old age didn't treat the

Brody family well. "Good, good. Now tell me why our Tommy isn't married to a nice girl like you?"

I didn't exactly want to bring up my law review debacle, so I faked.

"Tom and I took some time off after school to figure out what we wanted. He just broke up with the beautiful Lizzy Cofrancesco, though. And I'm free. Who knows what the future holds?" I hoped I didn't sound as desperate as I felt saying those words.

Judge Eamon turned around to face me. His smoky alcohol breath hit me in the face. He was that close. I had never been a fan of intoxicated men. As a fixture of my parents' church-based social circle, they could always be counted on to misbehave. He brushed a stray hair behind my ear. "Tommy would be a fool to pass up a girl like you, a second time."

I wanted to step away from him, I really did. But my parents had raised me with good manners requiring me to respect my elders—no matter how badly behaved. And there was the not so little matter of a prickly boxwood hedge poking into my back. Somehow, Judge Eamon had trapped me into a corner of the gardens when I wasn't paying attention.

"Well that's up to him, I guess," I said. My words were a little slurred, though I felt as sober as—well—a judge.

His meaty, sweaty hand trailed down from my face and cupped my breast as he pretended to wrap me more tightly in my Pashmina. I was horrified when my nipple peaked under his manipulation. I don't know if it was too much alcohol blunting my inhibitions or if I was just plain hard up. A leering grin passed over his flushed face as he catalogued my reaction.

Thank goodness, a white-jacketed server came to our remote corner of the world, offering some kind of fattening cheese appetizer. "J-judge Eamon," I stuttered. Crap, I did the very thing I meant not to. "I mean Judge Brody, it's been good seeing you again. I'll be sure to call you next week. I have to use the ladies room. If you'll excuse me." I pulled my Pashmina over my shoulders, resisting pulling it over my head like my mother's babushka and strode away as fast as I could with pointy heels and quicksand-like mud.

2

I tried not to think about Judge Eamon for the next three weeks. Fortunately, I didn't have any cases before him coming up for hearing soon. Plus, judges were so busy with juvenile crime that any case involving my clients' seemingly petty could-lose-my-child-forever grievances would likely end up before some apathetic magistrate. The past weeks had been a battle between moving my career forward and the ick factor the judge had aroused.

While I wasn't thinking about Judge Eamon, my land line rang, its ancient jangle startling me.

"Is this Casey Cort?" a gruff voice asked.

"This is she speaking," I answered just like my mother had taught me as a child.

"This is Judge Brody. *Eamon* Brody."

"Good, um…afternoon Judge Brody." I fumbled with the phone, the cool molded plastic awkward and bulky compared to my new cell.

"Well hello there, girl. Long time no hear. I've been waitin' for your call. The walls of my new chambers are still bare."

"I've been busy…" I lied. Why was I making excuses? I was not some servant to be summoned at will.

"Tom said that you've moved up into some bigger cases. I've got a pesky one that's come to my attention. I was thinking you could maybe help?"

My ears perked up. This sounded far more intriguing than wallpaper and carpet samples. "I'm listening."

"Marisa and Ian Ellingwood have called it quits."

All my senses went on high alert. The Ellingwoods were only second to the Strohmeyers when it came to celebrated families in Cuyahoga County's most elite circles. Circles that I did not travel in, but the Brodys did.

"Do they need divorce attorneys?"

"No, dear. It's even better than that. They were never married."

"I thought…"

"So did they. It was my sad duty to inform them that common law marriage was outlawed in Ohio in nineteen ninety-one." How come Judge Eamon's sad tone sounded gleeful? Gripping the phone tighter to my ear, I kept listening. "Poor things just learned that their children's fate is to be left up to the vagaries of us folks down on Twenty Second Street," the Judge said as if he'd been in the trenches at Juvenile forever, instead of a few weeks.

So *why* was he calling me? Hope bubbled in my chest. "Are they represented?" I asked, trying to keep the longing from my voice.

"The husband, *excuse me*, alleged father has hired Gerald Popovic. And Marisa has asked me for an attorney recommendation. She said she is far too distraught to interview a bunch of lawyers and would strongly consider my choice. Naturally, I thought of you."

I hoped my gasp of surprise was inaudible. I wouldn't even have to line up for the cattle call. I knew how women in these tense situations acted. Most of the time, they would hire the first lawyer that landed in their path. Visions of a ten thousand dollar—twenty five hundred dollars no longer got me jazzed—retainer check danced before my very eyes.

"So, you're interested, I gather?" Judge Eamon prompted into the silence.

"Very much," I said, grabbing the ballpoint pen and small pad of sticky notes I kept in my hallway phone nook.

"I'll see you in my office, first thing Monday morning. Nine-thirty?"

"Can't you just give me her number, and I could give Mrs., um Miss..." I realized if Marisa Ellingwood wasn't married, she wasn't really Marisa *Ellingwood,* but I didn't know her maiden name. "I could give Marisa a call this weekend and set up an appointment with her in my office first thing Monday."

Exasperation cut through Judge Eamon's congeniality. "I haven't got all the particulars here at my home, Ms. Cort. I would think for such a big piece of business, you could make your way down to my chambers for a minute or two," he huffed, the loud expulsion of breath explosive over the phone. "So, can I expect you, at say, half past nine?"

I can't make it. But my voice belied my intuition. "Of course. I'll be there, Judge Brody. Thanks for thinking of me."

This was the second time I'd said yes to a Brody this weekend against my better judgment.

Tom had called me earlier that afternoon and asked me out to dinner. I was embarrassingly gleeful. And as ill-advised as I knew it to be, I said yes. I didn't know if it was a 'date' or not, and I'm not sure I care. Truth be told, I could fall for him again in a heartbeat.

At the end of the day, though, he was probably going to get back together with Lizzy. Although my monthly perusal of the Celebrations section of the *Plain Dealer* hadn't revealed anything so far. But a girl could dream, couldn't she? I looked down at the weekend schlub clothes that I'd put on that morning to clean my apartment. Time to change. At least I could look good while I searched for that elusive 'closure.'

By the time the buzzer sounded, I had showered and changed into white jeans and a white faux cashmere sweater. Someone had once told me that monochromatic dressing would make me look thinner. I couldn't see any difference in my full length mirror, but I hoped the advice was sound. I wiped my clammy hands on my jeans, grateful that Simba's white cat fur would be invisible, for once.

I hit the button that would unlock the front door and heard Tom's steps become louder as he ascended the four flights of creaky wooden stairs to my pre-war flat. He knocked on the door. I took a breath to calm my screaming nerves and opened it. Oh-so-coincidentally, my neighbors Jason and Greg were taking out their garbage, together. As if lifting one plastic bag was a two-person job.

I surreptitiously waved at the boys and then greeted Tom. My ex standing at my front door brought back so many good feelings, but the sound of impatiently clearing throats interrupted my trip down memory lane.

"Tom, you should meet Jason and Greg," I said. He shook their hands, his handsome face perplexed for the shortest moment. If I hadn't known him so well, I might have missed it. "Jason and Greg are partners," I explained.

"Nice to meet you both," Tom said somewhat stiffly.

"So, where are you kids off to tonight?" Jason asked unfazed.

Along with my neighbors, I looked expectantly at Tom.

"I made reservations at Charley's Crab," he said. This was good. The Beachwood establishment was one of the most upscale restaurants on the Eastside.

"Am I underdressed?" I asked nervously, mad at myself for caring.

"No, you look wonderful," Tom said. *Wonderful* was far better than the *fine* I'd gotten three weeks ago. I'd been upgraded to compliment two point oh. Maybe I hadn't gotten my hopes up in vain.

Jason looked like the father of a teenage girl, ready to launch into interrogation mode.

I pointedly looked at my watch. "Well, I think we'd better get going then." I locked my door and started down the stairs, not checking to make sure Tom was following me.

As far as I could remember, Charley's Crab hadn't changed much from the one time I'd been there years ago. Before I got fired from Morrell Gates, I'd come to a dinner here with associates and partners from the firm. We'd had a designated limo driver, and I'd won the night's drinking game, so my memories were a bit hazy. The restaurant had the same sort of feel, though, dark wood paneled rooms festooned with tasteful nautical paraphernalia. Tom helped me with my coat and the host held out a chair. The diners were the usual eclectic mix of Cleveland, from old dowagers with diamonds and pearls to young affluent couples in five hundred dollar designer jeans.

After the busboy had poured us water and left a breadbasket, Tom spoke. "So, how have you been? I feel like we never cross paths in the justice center."

The justice center was the main court building downtown. The thirty or so judges stationed there handled all the state criminal and civil cases in Cuyahoga County. In addition to the family law work, I used to do a few low level criminal cases there. But it takes a lot of grease on the palms of judges to get appointed to those cases. With my income, I've never had grease, so that part of my practice had died an untimely death the year before.

"I'm focusing on family and juvenile law," I said. "I can be a better lawyer if I just focus on one or two specialties."

"Man, I haven't been up to Twenty-Second Street in years. Not much has changed, I bet," Tom said. I guessed Judge Eamon hadn't summoned any of the Brody boys to his chambers—no one assumed *they* had an eye for decoration.

He was right about the court's stagnation, though. The two buildings that house juvenile court on Twenty-First and Twenty-Second Streets hadn't changed since he'd worked there. Young prosecutors were required to rotate through every division before they could move downtown to felony prosecution. For most, that rotation lasted as long as two or three years. With Tom's connections, I was surprised that he'd had to work there the two or three months he did. By the time I started getting appointed to a significant number of cases, he'd been long gone.

"It's the same," I said. I wasn't the most loquacious girl in the world, though I was a bit more chatty than this normally. What does a thirty-three year old woman say to the man who so unceremoniously dumped her eight years before? Tom was lazily buttering his second slice of bread, not looking the least bit worried about our stuttering conversation.

"Are you hungry? What are you going to order?"

I wasn't hungry. An entire flock of butterflies—are butterflies a flock or is there some totally weird word for a group of them like 'clutch' or 'school'?—decided to perform for Cirque du Soleil in my stomach. I couldn't imagine trying to stuff a slice of bread, much less a dinner down there too.

"I'm going to have the Australian lobster," I said. I'd picked the most expensive item on the menu. It was really juvenile of me, but there it was, my master plot of revenge by crustacean.

Tom closed the menu that had obscured his face. "I'll probably have the surf and turf. It's usually good here."

"What did the beautiful Lizzy Cofrancesco usually order?" Did my childish behavior know no bounds? She was probably some wisp of a thing who couldn't possibly finish a *whole* salad much less a lobster.

"I don't remember," Tom said with finality. Well, I guess the subject of the beautiful Lizzy Cofrancesco was closed, for now.

The waiter came for drink orders. I asked for a white Russian. I needed a little—no, a lot of—Dutch courage. If there was one thing I'd always hated, it was lawyers with no figurative balls. If we couldn't stick up for ourselves, I didn't believe we should be in the business of advocating for others. After a sip or two, or three, of my drink, I decided to break the silence.

"Why did you invite me here?" I blurted.

"Wow. You get to the point, don't you?"

"When you get this close to forty, you don't have the luxury of time," I said matter-of-factly. Yes, I knew thirty-three was *not* forty, but my birthdays seemed to come every six months, not once a year like they used to. "I wouldn't be exaggerating to say I was surprised to hear from you after...oh...an eight-year hiatus." Not that I'd been counting.

He had the good grace to look a little uncomfortable. It was very Hugh Grant of him or would have been if only he'd grown his hair a little longer and had acquired an irresistible British accent. "It doesn't feel like it's been that long."

Men have no sense of time. When my father said fifteen minutes, it was always an hour, at least. Maybe eight years felt like two to Tom. Being a lawyer had taught me when to speak and when to listen. This was one of those times when I should keep my mouth shut. So I did.

After a beat, he continued. "I've missed you." He ducked his head again. Even in this low light, I could see his cheeks coloring. "I was kind of hoping we could...you know...maybe...see each other again?" His voice did a little uptick at the end.

Thank God, the waiter came to take our order. I didn't know what to say—how to answer—if indeed there was a question. This was the last thing I expected when he'd called last night. I was too busy being mad that he expected me to be available on such short notice and spending money I didn't have on this, the second new outfit I'd bought in a month. Did I say something about good lawyers having balls? Um, I wasn't talking about myself. I backed away from his statement like an anorexic getting away from the dessert table.

"So, how's work?" I asked, feeling better on the *terra firma* known as the law.

"Things are okay," he said.

Good, he wasn't going to talk about going out again. His answer registered. Things were okay? 'Okay' was *not* going to satisfy my rabid curiosity. Prosecutors were hard to investigate, for good reason. They didn't seem to like criminals stalking them. But it made ex-girlfriend type snooping difficult. I wanted my answers, now. "Exactly what section are you in? What kind of cases are you handling?"

"I did a bunch of assignments, but I've settled in the Major Trial Unit," he said without embellishment. Had I been handling major trials myself, I would have known this. Despite my modest success of late, I still existed on the fringes of the Cleveland bar.

"I'm not surprised you're in the elite squad. I didn't imagine you'd be biding your time in real estate foreclosures or the tax unit."

"Those guys do some great work," he said judiciously. "But I like the excitement of regular jury trials. I get to put bad guys away for rape and murder every day. Makes sleep come easy."

"How's your family? I didn't really get to talk to anyone at the party." I didn't mention that these nameless souls either hadn't recognized me or had avoided me like the plague at Judge Eamon's barbecue.

"Mom's okay. She's still doing work for the children's hospital, but not as much running around as she used to.

She's spending more time with her sisters. They travel together, and then make scrapbooks about their vacations. They did a few weeks working on a family tree in Nairnshire this year."

Wherever the hell that was. "What about your dad?"

"I'm sure you know he's now the presiding judge in general division." I did know, but didn't want to look like I cared.

"I guess you're not trying any cases before him?"

"Nah, none of us can." Of course Tom's two older brothers, Simon and Andrew were attorneys in Cleveland as well. "Though I'm sure he gets an earful about us from the other judges."

"How's your uncle Eamon settling in?"

"You still haven't been to see him? I think he'd give you a whole slew of cases, if you asked."

I didn't mention the invitation to help 'decorate' Judge Eamon's suite, or the Ellingwood case that might never materialize. Eamon seemed like the type whose aid came with strings. I didn't want to be a marionette. I changed the subject slightly.

"No one ever said. Why did Eamon leave Probate?"

Something flitted across Tom's face. This was the second time tonight his thoughts had made him uncomfortable. A lot had changed over the years, his haircut was smarter, his clothes more sophisticated, but I could still read him like an open book.

"I don't know. I think he just got bored. I mean how exciting can dead people be? Fights over money, again and again. But I think you should make an effort to get to know him—especially if you continue to practice there. He's going to be at a family dinner next weekend—if you're game?"

I pushed my food around the plate some more. Next weekend? Tom seemed serious about this getting back together thing. During the rest of dinner we gossiped about our fellow law school alumni—who'd gotten married, divorced, hired, and fired. Then dessert came. Tom had taken the liberty of ordering my favorite while I'd gone to powder my nose. And no, I didn't have any powder; I really peed. But who wants to hear that? My mom always used that euphemism in public and I vowed to carry on the tradition.

It took two people to place dessert on the table. The waiter described the huge brown concoction as some kind of chocolate truffle cake with a molten chocolate center. It had *Frangelico crème anglaise* and vanilla ice cream, topped with crumbled Heath bar crunch. It looked and sounded more like a truffle bomb with its molten lava center shooting out caramel and little igneous heath bars. Thank God, he'd only ordered one.

Tom reached across the table. I thought he was going to pick up one of the big spoons laid on clean napkins to help himself to the heaving pile of chocolate. Instead, he grabbed my left hand with his right. Clearly, I was not as immune to him as I had pretended to be all through dinner. I looked at all that chocolate gooey goodness and figured I'd never be hungry again. I had finally found my diet solution, lust.

My soon-to-be not ex cocked his head to one side in a way I remembered he did whenever we were going to talk about anything serious. "I meant what I said earlier." He didn't need to remind me which something he was talking about.

An internal debate raged in my head. The good angel said I shouldn't be snookered so easily. The bad angel had me undressed and in bed with Tom within the hour. I deflected as best I could. "I need time to think about this. I can't just go from zero to one hundred in a few hours. Seriously, I think we have a lot to talk about before I can even consider us." Not the least of which was whether he was truly ready to give up on the beautiful Lizzy Cofrancesco.

"Like what?" he asked. I almost lost my courage then. This could all be so easy. We could slip back into a comfortable relationship. I could finally get semi-regular sex. Maybe we would get married. All would be as it was supposed to be those many years ago. In the back of my mind though, I just couldn't get over the niggle of doubt. Damned good angel.

She reminded me that Tom had left me. Cold. No easy break up. No soft landing. One day he was there and the next day he wasn't. And I was left to deal with the aftermath of my law review/lost job/career implosion by my lonesome. That angel put her tiny hand in my ear and snapped me out of my idle fantasies. I don't know if I should ever seriously think of making a 'for better or for worse' commitment to Tom. He certainly hadn't been there when things were worse for me.

Balls. *Cojones.* A girl lawyer's got to have big ones, right? With two White Russians warming my belly, I gathered my courage and asked the big question. "Why did you dump me in law school?" The proverbial elephant had farted in the living room.

The ice cream slid down the side of the chocolate bomb, melting in a pool atop the *crème anglaise.* Tom's double take told me that he wasn't expecting me to be so blunt. He'd grown up into a big bad prosecutor who wasn't challenged by many. But I'd grown up too.

He slipped his dessert spoon into the cake and took one big bite then another. "You having any?" he asked me.

"Do I look like I need to be at the dessert table?" I asked.

"Casey," he started giving me a long, and what I vainly hoped was an appreciative glance. "I still think you're very pretty. You'll always be that lost girl I met in the parking lot that first day of orientation."

If I had been vanilla bean ice cream, I would have melted. All the smart girl fight went out of me. If I'd ever had any *cojones* at all, they must have shrunk to the size peas.

I didn't probe the break-up question any further. I took a couple spoonfuls of the gooey chocolate dessert—and it was good, better than sex good, but then I remembered how I'd looked under the unforgiving fluorescent lights in the Ann Taylor Loft dressing room this morning and put the utensil down.

Since my rabid feminism was on a vacation, I let Tom pay without a token protest on my part. He helped me with my coat and then to his car. I tried not to be jealous of his Acura—a very upscale version of the hoopty Honda I was still driving, eleven years after my parents bought it for my college graduation. You push the little 'H' together at the top and, BAM! It's a luxury car. Well, that and a whole lot of leather and chrome and wood and gadgets.

Tom had the radio down low on the drive back to my place.

"Where are you living these days?" I asked. During law school, he'd had a little place in University Heights near where I was now. My curiosity about the minute details of his existence overcame my reticence to become involved in his life again.

"I'm just off Edgewater," he said. "I think you'd like it. It's a lot like your building—old with those fuddy-duddy details you admire—molding and stuff."

He pulled into the driveway next to my building and turned off the car.

"I know this was a little weird—me asking you out of the blue like this—but I've been thinking about it a long time. I made a huge mistake at Cleveland Marshall. I can admit now that I was scared of losing my place in the world and of embarrassing my family." When I started to speak, he waved me off. "No, it was dumb. You did the right thing, and everyone else did the wrong thing." He angled closer to me, leaning over the center console. Tom laid a surprisingly warm hand against my cheek. "Give us one more chance, Casey."

Then his face blotted out the world as he kissed me. People always say you can't go back. They're wrong. His lips dragged me back eight years. And I wasn't exactly kicking and screaming. For the first time in a long time, I felt like I had a future.

3

Claire Henshaw
September 21, 2003

I stood on my front steps, tapped my foot and glared at my watch, willing its precise Swiss movement to be wrong for once.

"What's the matter, Mommy?" My four-year-old son Luke looked up at me, his big brown eyes far too serious for his young face. I wanted nothing more than to kiss his little oblong head like I did when he was a baby. It was tucked into the faux fur-trimmed hood of his mini puffy coat, just begging for my touch. But I held myself back. I didn't want to make him into a little sissy.

His father was late. The more important the appointment I had to get to, the later Darius Gaines seemed to be. I had told him, I don't know how many times, that I needed to work on the third Sunday of the month, every month. It never changed. And every third Sunday without fail, he was late. I don't know if his behavior should be classified as passive or aggressive or both, but either way I was damned tired of it.

A black Nissan skidded to a stop along the curb in front of my townhouse on Chester Parkway. Darius jogged to where we stood, not bothering to close the driver's side door. A scantily clad woman gesticulated and yelled into the bottom half of a clamshell cell phone, barely detectable through the darkly tinted glass. I dug half moons into my palms, holding my razor sharp tongue in check. Now was not the time to get into anything with Darius.

"Hey Little Darius, you ready to go?" my ex asked.

The biggest mistake I'd ever made was to allow this man to name my son after him. I'd started calling him by his middle name as soon as we came home from the hospital. He would always be Luke to me.

My baby got that unsure look he had whenever his father and I were within five feet of each other. Silently I tried to assure him that his parents would not fight today. I'd promised myself this morning in the shower, there would be none of the usual drama that accompanied our handovers. I relented and gave into my urge to kiss him on the top of his little oval head and pushed him toward his father's outstretched hands.

"Bye, baby. Have a good time with your daddy. Be my good little man. I'll see you in the morning, okay?"

My son nodded, the weight of the world pulling down his little shoulders.

As soon as Darius and his hoochie-mama-of-the-moment pulled away, I jumped into my car. Under no circumstances did I want to be late to my meeting. A few times a month I lead a class for women with kids caught up in the foster care system. I taught the same class at the Northeast Pre-Release Center on weekdays and in the rec room of my office at the Uama center one Sunday a month.

Rather than lecturing from the standard two-hour curriculum that I used on the ever-changing faces at the prison, my Sunday group had evolved into an ongoing session where I helped the women navigate the juvenile court system. I wish I could have given more help to the prisoners, but there was too much turnover at Pre-Release and some serious time constraints.

Several women and children were milling around the back door when I eased along the cracked pavement of the Uama parking lot, trying to avoid the crater-sized potholes that never got fixed. A microcosm of this broken down city.

"Sorry ladies. Baby daddy drama," I explained. "You know how it is." The women nodded knowingly. A number of 'mm hmms' and 'yeah girls' floated my way. Normally I didn't share my business with clients, but these women, better than any others, knew what I was dealing with.

Hastily I arranged the plastic folding chairs into a circle and threw an old blanket and some toys onto the middle of it for the few kids there. I clapped my hands to stop the chattering and get the moms' attention.

"Ladies. First I want to let you know that Kyanna is missing today because her little Jayden came home this week," I announced. The women clapped and hooted like we'd just closed the curtain on a successful musical. As I waved my hands to quiet the noise, I saw Rhonda cut her eyes at me and whisper to another woman. I didn't allow backbiting or sniping in this group. Not that I got my advice from television personalities, but I'd once read a piece in Oprah's eponymous magazine about her 'no gossip' policy and it resonated. I'd quickly adopted it.

I held firm to the mission of Uama. Our tagline, written in Kiswahili stated, 'Mkono moja haulei methali,' *a single hand cannot nurse a child.* Former first lady Hillary Clinton might have made 'it takes a village' cliché, but the sentiment still rang true. The sooner these ladies realized that they were more formidable working together rather than apart, the better. Nothing decimated the black female community quicker than divide and conquer. My group was not going to descend into a rowdy episode of Maury Povich on my watch.

"Rhonda, is there something you wish to share with all of us?" I asked, sounding like a scolding Sunday school teacher, even to my own ears.

"I was just sayin' the system ain't ever changed. Kyanna did a little somethin' somethin' to get her baby back." She made a crude gesture, pumping her fist in front of her mouth to emphasize her point.

I didn't have any kind of training in group counseling, but I knew I couldn't let this assumption stand.

"Rhonda, please don't be unfair just because you don't have your own children back in your custody. I started this group so that we could share legal strategies and information on helping all women in the group get their kids out of the system."

Another mom, Min-ji piped in. "We don't mean no disrespect to you, Claire. All of us—" She gave a quelling look at anyone who dared disagree with her. "—appreciate your help. Our lawyers and the guardians don't give us the time of day. It's been good having you help explain the papers to us and stuff. But Rhonda's right. Everybody's saying that if you do right by Judge Brody, he'll do right by you and can get your kids back."

The women started talking amongst themselves again. Without the help of prison guards at my other location, it was like trying to keep a class of sugar-high post-snack second graders quiet.

"Ladies, please." I directed my question to the most vocal of the women. "Are you saying that Kyanna performed sexual favors for Judge Brody to get favorable treatment in her case?"

"You can gussy it up all you want with that fancy lawyer talk, Miz Henshaw. But bottom line is that she opened her mouth, took in a little jizz and her baby came home just that quick," Rhonda said, snapping her fingers to underscore her point.

The ladies started talking amongst themselves again, but I didn't stop them this time. The sheer audacity of the allegations shocked me. My legal experience might have been limited to years of anonymous document review, working for a now disgraced federal judge, and serving as the legal outreach director at Uama, but surely, no judge would have the nerve to do what Rhonda was saying.

Every lawyer, even an inexperienced one like me, knew that juvenile court was a nightmare. If you were unmarried and had kids or were a minor in the kind of trouble that poor people always seem to get themselves into, then you could well end up there. From what the women here and at the prison tell me, it's the epitome of a bureaucratic nightmare—Dilbert times ten. Court never started on time. The staff was less than professional, losing files and sometimes children in the vast system. That was the only reason I regret not marrying Luke's father.

If Darius and I ever had a serious disagreement over custody, we'd end up in juvey hell. I'd put up with almost anything from his black ass to avoid East Twenty-Second Street.

I looked at the clock guiltily. With my mind wandering, I'd let the break go on too damn long. I clapped my hands loudly and everyone quieted. Even the little kids playing on the blanket with the carefully selected afro-centric toys looked my way.

I called the meeting to order. I always started with a progress report. Without prompting, the women sometimes forgot to update me on the important changes in their lives. Developments that could profoundly affect their court cases.

"Rhonda, why don't you go first?" I suggested. I hoped that keeping her focused on her own kids would keep her mind and mouth out of the gutter.

"My PC hearing is coming up in two weeks," she said. Rhonda was the toughest one in the group. She'd just as easily cut you up as kiss you, so I was shocked to see her chin tremble for just a second.

I reminded everyone that if the court awarded the county permanent custody of their kids—they would have no legal right to them ever again. "Have you talked to your lawyer?" Sometimes these women tried to hide the sunshine with one finger.

"She don't give me the time of day. I did what you said. I left her messages on her voicemail saying I needed to set up a time to prepare for trial. That's what you said, right?" I nodded my head in a gesture that said 'more or less,' prompting Rhonda to continue. "When that heifer finally called me back, she said that she was the lawyer and she didn't need me telling her what her job was. She would take care of the legal stuff. All I needed to do was show up sober. This ain't nothing but a jive mess."

Admittedly, Rhonda's tale discouraged me. All the juvenile lawyers I'd ever met at bar association functions lamented the lack of their clients' participation. I had told the group if they did what they were supposed to do and were open with their lawyers, then they would have the best chance of getting their kids back. Obviously, I hadn't considered territorial asshole lawyers.

"Rhonda," I said, impatient, not with her, but with the *system.* "Don't give up. Just give her another call. If you want, leave my name and number. I'd be more than happy to speak with her on your behalf." I cringed inwardly. This kind of intervention was very outside of my job description. My *job* was to provide education and outreach to women in the community on juvenile court, foster care, and guardianship issues.

The executive director at Uama had *not* hired me to provide direct representation or advocacy of any kind. She had been crystal clear about that before I took this job. When I started, ninety percent of the job was prison outreach. I had asked for and reluctantly received permission to extend my position to include community outreach. In fact, I was here on the weekend on my own dime. I couldn't convince the board to enhance my modest salary to include these extra sessions.

"Min-ji, do you have anything to report?"

"The good news is that the foster mom is letting me come over a few days a week to see McKenna. So I think she's starting to learn that I'm Mama. I bit the bullet and moved back in with my parents. I'm in the apartment over the garage."

"How's that going?" I asked tentatively.

"They're not charging me any rent or anything, so that's good. But they're talking like they want to take over custody of McKenna if she comes back. They're still treating me like I'm an irresponsible teenager."

Min-ji had come the farthest of the women I had counseled. Of course, she had started out with the most. Her parents, Korean and West Indian immigrants, had raised her in the comfortable bosom of suburban Cleveland Heights. And that's now where she'd returned.

"I know your parents' interference can be hard to deal with. But it's probably better that little McKenna be at home rather than with that foster family, no matter how nice they are."

"I don't know. I think they're going to hang the past few years over my head, no matter what."

"Why don't we work on getting McKenna home then deal with your parents later." I knew my answer was cursory, but if we got too deep into the women's personal lives, it turned into group therapy, another thing I wasn't qualified to do. "How about you—"

A ringing phone echoed off the walls of the rec room. For a few disoriented seconds my gaze darted around the room, trying to figure out who could be calling the center on the weekend and why the answering machine hadn't intercepted.

The woman I had started to call on next pointed at my large tote bag. "I think it's you."

She was right. Since Darius had become more involved with Luke, I'd gotten the cell phone for emergencies. Darius thought every parenting dilemma was an emergency. Luke didn't eat breakfast. The phone rang. Luke wouldn't get dressed. The phone rang. Luke cried. The phone rang. Darius needed parenting classes more than my Uama clients did. I excused myself, grabbed the phone and my tote and moved into the narrow hallway where our offices were located.

I flipped open the phone and pressed the green talk button, still awkward with the gadget's tiny buttons.

"This is Claire."

"It's Darius." My ex sounded breathless. No doubt Luke had tired him out and my little man was ready to come home to his mama. "Don't freak out, but something's happened."

My pulse sped into heart attack zone as every maternal nightmare flashed before my eyes.

"Where's Luke? Is he okay?" I yelled, or more likely screamed into the phone.

"He's okay. He's with me."

"And where is that?"

"The emergency room at Hillcrest Hospital."

4

Miles Siegel

September 21, 2003

"So Miles, how's Claire?" my mother asked over the phone. "When will we get to meet her?" She was undoubtedly perched on a stool at the breakfast bar, her favorite spot in the kitchen.

"Don't 'we' me, Linda," my father piped in on the extension. He was, I knew, in his study seated in the Pottery Barn club chair my mother had bought for him—his leather slippered feet propped up on the matching leather ottoman.

My parents' house could be summed up in two words: animal hide. Somehow they'd gotten the idea that leather was durable. So everything was cow hide from coats to shoes to furniture. For otherwise environmentally conscious people, I'd always wondered how they justified killing all those cows.

I faked a cough covering my laughter. Whenever my father wanted something done around the house, he pronounced, 'we' should do this or that. Roughly translated, it
meant me or my mother. But now he's Tonto disclaiming
the Lone Ranger.

"I don't know, Mom." And I didn't. I'd been seeing Claire
for a few months, but the idea of taking on a ready-made
family and all its baggage intimidated the hell out of me.

Claire and I were nowhere near the stage where my parents needed to fly out from Philadelphia to meet us for dinner. We might never be at that stage, but that's something I
wanted to mull over without my parents' advice.

"Oh dear. Is she not good in bed, Miles?"

I loved my mom. I did. But the woman had no bounda-
ries. I called her every week like clockwork because if I
didn't she'd light up my answering machine like nobody's
business. And for a black woman, she could lay on the Jewish guilt like you wouldn't believe. That, I think, she got
from my father.

"You don't have to answer that," said my father, his
voice crackling over the ancient cordless phone.

"I'm not." The call waiting beeped. "I have another call,
excuse me." Grateful for the interruption, I switched over
before my mother could launch into her usual diatribe
about the inherent rudeness of call waiting.

"Miles Siegel," I answered like it was my work phone.
Bad habit.

"Miles, it's Claire," my girlfriend's voice cut in and out.
Speak of the devil.

"Are you calling me from your cell?" She'd gotten the
mobile phone for child-related emergencies. I hoped that
wasn't the reason for the call.

"Yeah, I need..." she said. The rest of her words were lost in the static. Though I thought I heard Darius' and Luke's names. Any sentence with those two names screamed emergency.

"I can't hear you. Let me get off with my parents and I'll call you back." I switched back to my parents who were, predictably, having a heated conversation with each other through the phone about call waiting. I was born well into their marriage, and they'd always had a weird symbiotic relationship that didn't include me.

"Mom, Dad. It's Claire," I interrupted. "She sounded a little weird. I have to go. I'll talk to you guys next weekend okay?"

"That's fine," my mother said and continued to argue with my father about something else, their conversation having veered off on another tangent. I hung up, wondering how long they'd talk to each other before they noticed I was off the line. I'd give it twenty minutes at least.

I called Claire a couple of times. Voice mail. She must have turned her phone off. I stepped out onto the small brick patio of my third floor apartment and watched the weekend traffic stream along Euclid Heights Boulevard in fits and starts. I lived near Coventry, an eclectic shopping area in Cleveland Heights that attracted weekend visitors from the Heights. Parents pushed strollers. Case students jogged along. Although it wasn't at all like my hometown of Philly, the hustle and bustle made me feel like I still lived in a real city.

I ran back into the living room, and the phone rang again. This time Claire's signal was crystal clear. Her little boy was hurt. She was speeding her way to Hillcrest Hospital and wanted me to meet her there.

Dutiful boyfriend that I was, I threw on some old Chuck Taylors, buttoned my jeans and made it over to the Hillcrest in record time.

Even if I hadn't known Claire for months, she would have been easy to spot. I found her smooth brown skin and pouty lips very attractive. She was what black people called, 'that color.' That color was somewhere between light enough to pass and too dark to be considered pretty—not that I followed these narrow definitions, mind you, it's just the shorthand that I'd grown up with.

No matter when I saw her, she was always well put together—hair and makeup just so. Though today she'd lost a little of her usual composure, her hair wasn't smoothed into its usual shiny bob, and she'd nibbled off her lipstick. Claire stood by the empty nurses' station, worriedly shredding tissues.

I pulled a handkerchief from my pocket—a vestige of my environmentally minded parents—and handed it to her. She accepted it gratefully and dabbed at her swollen eyes.

"What happened? Is it Luke?" I asked, bewildered by her tears. I never knew what to do when a woman cried.

Though it felt somewhat awkward, I put my arm around Claire's shoulders. In answer to my question, Claire nodded, unable to speak.

"Is his father...Darius...here?" I asked. It was difficult for me to get the name of her ex-lover past my lips. It wasn't that I was jealous. I just didn't like the man. All our lives would have been so much better if he were an absentee father like so many other brothers—then I chastised myself for the uncharitable thought. Especially as I wasn't too eager to take on the role of Luke's father myself.

She dabbed at her red-rimmed eyes again, and noisily blew her nose. Claire was an attractive woman, but not a pretty crier. "I haven't seen him yet. I just got here." She fished in her huge bag for something and pulled out her cell phone. Before she could dial, a heavyset woman robed in pink scrubs rolled up to the counter, the gray office chair's wheels groaning with the effort.

"Can I help you?" she asked, eyes darting between the two of us.

Claire caught her breath and cleared her throat before she spoke. "I think my son may have been admitted. Luke...I mean, Darius Gaines, Jr."

She looked from me to Claire and back again, assessing. "Are you the parents?"

"I'm just a friend," I answered too quickly,—and unnecessarily.

"I'm his *mother*. Claire Henshaw," she said, glancing my way, a frown creasing her normally smooth features. The woman looked at us, eyebrow raised slightly, judgment clouding her face, before typing into the terminal in front of her.

"I have a Darius Gaines, Junior admitted. He's in the last bay on the right. The doctor is taping—" I missed the rest of the sentence because Claire had already hightailed it in the direction the nurse or orderly had pointed, pulling me along in her wake.

When we got behind the curtain, Luke was having his right arm taped up. He had a death grip on a Blow Pop in his left hand. The doctor was pasting the last strip of the plaster cast in place when Luke noticed his mother. Seeing her tear-stained face, his little one screwed up and he started crying. Darius, looked up at Claire in sheepish acknowledgement.

The doctor looked around the crowded area and gathered his tools on a roll-away metal table. "I'll be back in a few minutes with some care instructions for you all," he said, his South Asian accent soft and lilting. He pushed the table aside and quickly took his leave.

"Darius, you only left my house a few hours ago. What in the hell happened?" Claire's voice was tight with barely suppressed fury.

"Freya was watching little Darius and he fell from the living room window," Darius Senior said far too matter-of-factly for my taste. But I kept my opinion to myself. I was simply an observer here.

"What do you mean Freya was watching him? Who exactly *is* Freya? Is she that little hoochie from this morning? Where were *you*? You're supposed to be the parent here."

"I just stepped out for a minute to talk to Kevin and we went for a little ride. Then we saw Shawn and 'em and I was out a little longer than I thought."

"You were out with the boys?" Self-consciously I looked around as Claire's voice veered off into screech range. "This is your son, who you talk about spending time with." Uh-oh, she had her hand on her hip, the other was gesturing a derogatory talking motion, poised like a clucking chicken. "Who you desperately wanted and you leave him with some whore so you can spend time with the *boys*."

"Freya is not some whore and I don't appreciate you talking about my girlfriend that way. And who are you to say anything—so concerned about when I was going to show up? You said you were working, but I see you're with your light-skinned boyfriend here."

I threw up my hands in surrender. "Hey, I'm just here to lend moral support." I let the insult about my color roll off my back like I've had to do for more years than I can count. I'm as black as the next guy, but with the genes of my Jewish father, I don't exactly look like some gangsta rapper. Rather, I look like what I am, a guy from integrated northwest Philly. While they argued some more, I backed out of the room and took a seat on the nearest couch, upholstered in a scratchy, sticky synthetic fiber.

Hearing the commotion, a nurse swiftly entered the bay I'd just left and escorted the bickering parents to a small room off the waiting area. That little guy had to be hurting in there. I walked to a play area I saw segregated in the corner of the waiting room and picked up a few magic markers no one would miss. Without invitation, I pulled back the curtain and poked my head in.

"Luke?" I asked. The little boy nodded, looking like he was on the brink of new tears. The old tears had barely dried, leaving grainy white streaks of salt on his brown face. "I'm bored waiting out here all by myself. Can you keep me company?"

The little boy nodded again, less tentative this time. I pulled up the lone plastic chair in the area and sat at his bedside.

"Do you know what's special about having a cast?" I asked, my voice filled with as much wonder and awe as I could pack in. Luke shook his head. "Well. Everybody you know gets to sign their name. That way, when you're going to sleep at night you can look at the names of all your friends." Luke's eyes no longer brimmed with unshed tears. Instead, he looked at me with fascination. "Here, let me sign my name first." I penned my John Hancock with as much flourish as I could muster on the cast's rough surface.

"So who's your favorite cartoon character?"

He didn't respond, instead looking at me with silent inquisition.

"Okay, what do you like better, SpongeBob SquarePants or the Rugrats?"

"Rugrats," he said so quietly, I almost didn't hear.

"Do you want Tommy Pickles or Chuckie Finster?"

Luke's reticence disappeared in his growing excitement. "Chuckie," he cried in the unmodulated manner of a child.

"Chuckie it is." I did a quick, passable sketch of Chuckie, with emphasis on his flaming hair and purple, square glasses.

When I gently moved Luke's arm back to his own tiny lap, his eyes widened. Children were so easily impressed with adult's motor skills. "Wow, it's Chuckie. Can you put Tommy on there?"

My Tommy Pickles was better than my Chuckie. I took liberties and added a striped scarf around the character's neck because that beret seemed so lonely without it.

"Can you draw a dog?" he asked.

"Why don't we leave space for your mom and dad and friends to sign their names, okay?" I answered, hoping his mother wasn't upset I'd taken the liberty of christening the cast.

Luke nodded, reluctantly.

Claire came back in, mercifully alone as I capped the pens.

"The doc says you can go home in a little bit, 'kay baby?" Luke's face scrunched up like he was going to cry again.

Claire hoisted herself up on the bed and gave him a hug, murmuring something to him about big boys not crying.

I excused myself to put the magic markers back in the kids' toy basket, and sat in the thankfully empty waiting room. I had no desire to see Darius or his woman of the week. Luke's father treated me like the competition and never missed an opportunity to indulge in a game of one-upmanship. No offense to Darius, but he was playing a game he could never win.

Fiddling with my BlackBerry, I checked my messages. Of course, there was something from my parents. After the abrupt end to our conversation, they were wondering if everything was okay. There was nothing from anyone from work. My current job as an Assistant United States Attorney was by far more of a nine-to-five job, than I'd ever had during my years on the Philly police force.

I closed my e-mail, and played a little Pong with the tiny PDA keys. I tried not to keep looking at the time, but I liked to play a few video games, maybe bag a few hoops on Sunday afternoons, unless I was getting laid, of course. And it was clear *that* wasn't happening today.

I put the phone away, and looked over toward the hospital bed. Claire caught my eye and levered herself down from the bed, leaving the little guy, who'd fallen fast asleep, no doubt exhausted from all the excitement. My girlfriend had her concerned mommy face on, not the face of the sultry woman I knew she could become under cover of darkness. She sat very close to me on the roughly textured couch, and her warm hand gathered my free one.

"Thanks for coming by this afternoon. I was beside myself when I found out Luke was in the hospital," she whispered quietly. If she was worried about Luke waking up, she needn't have whispered. Between the endless paging of doctors over a very loud speaker and the beeping of monitors, it was a wonder anyone could ever sleep in this place. But he had, so the two of us whispering probably wouldn't rouse him.

She squeezed my hand. I was embarrassed that my groin tightened in response. Mommies and sex just didn't mix. I knew intellectually that sex led to motherhood sometimes, so they were inextricably connected, but still.

"I'm glad I could come," I said, pulling my Blackberry from my pocket and fingering it with my free hand.

Claire frowned, but didn't say anything about my smartphone addiction.

"I think you'd make a really great dad. Not like this trifling Darius," Claire said, leaning against my shoulder. I resisted the urge to shrug her off. Don't get me wrong, I liked Claire well enough. It was just that I wanted to keep our relationship casual and light. I wanted to maybe go to dinner, a movie, hook-up—then get back to moving myself up the career ladder. I wasn't ready to be anyone's daddy. I couldn't tell her that now, but I knew I shouldn't wait too long.

5

I took each of the worn stone steps as slowly as I could, trudging up the stairs of the ancient juvenile court building like a recalcitrant child. Judge Eamon would definitely be sober this morning, so I couldn't quite justify the dread that pooled in my stomach as thick and unyielding as tar in winter. The entrance was bereft of the usual carnival atmosphere. Nine-thirty in the morning was a few hours before the throngs of humanity would arrive for the afternoon child-abuse dockets.

I endured the usual demeaning security check that skipped over city police, county workers and prosecutors, but put us defense lawyers through the wringer each and every time. When I'd passed through the metal detectors and reassembled the shambles made of my briefcase and purse, I made my way to what had been formerly Judge Conti's chambers.

Weak light spilled from the narrow opening of the door to the anteroom, and when my admittedly tentative knock went unanswered, I poked my head around the doorjamb. I was surprised to see the room empty, but I figured Judge Conti's bailiff was no longer welcome here and Judge Eamon's crew was waiting for a transfer from Probate court. I stood in the wood-paneled, but otherwise bare room uncertainly. Universally, judges did *not* appreciate unannounced visitors. They liked to get their robes on before lawyers stepped in their chambers.

I cleared my throat loudly, announcing my presence.

"Is that you, Ms. Cort?" Judge Eamon called from inside his chambers.

"Yeah …yes," I stuttered.

"Glad you could make it." Judge Eamon's voice was somewhat muffled behind his partially open office door. I made no move to come in, cooling my heels on the worn parquet floor, not wanting to violate the sanctity of his chambers without a formal invitation.

In what was no doubt a power play, he took his sweet time coming to the anteroom. He was, of course, enrobed, though I could swear I saw some bare leg between the hem of his robe and the top of his thick black socks. But as I walked to the bailiff's desk, I tried not to look too closely.

Before setting down my bag, I shook the proffered hand and stumbled over my own tongue trying to get to the point of my visit.

Purposefully, I pulled back and opened my briefcase, a leather shield between us. I pulled out what I hoped was an official looking canary yellow legal pad and the silver Cross pen that my parents had predictably bought me for graduation. I twisted the pen so the point extended from the barrel and leaned slightly toward the desk, eager to get my referral information and get out of there.

Too late, I realized that by leaning over, my now substantial, fat enhanced cleavage jiggled in my snow-white wrap blouse. It had looked very professional with my conservative navy pinstriped suit and heels when I stood before the full-length mirror that morning. With tiny pearl studs in my ears and a faux pearl pendant lying against my chest, I had hoped to put my best foot forward. Instead, the fake pearl bounced against my breasts and wedged itself between my cleavage, drawing attention to the wrong part of my body.

I pulled up quickly and oh-so-casually laid my pen on the desk, trying to channel the seasoned attorney in me, though my heartbeat had surpassed heart attack range. The silver pen promptly rolled off the utilitarian metal desk and onto the floor, undermining my credibility in a heartbeat. As I bent to pick it up, I felt my skirt ride up, exposing the back of my bare thighs. Despite my attempt to be professional, I wasn't wearing stockings. When I'd gotten heavy, I'd given them up because they were either so tight they constricted my breathing or they rolled down making yet another unattractive bulge around my waist.

Thankfully, I was able to grab the pen before it disappeared under the desk, sparing me from an even more undignified posture.

"So, you were going to tell me about Marisa Ellingwood," I prompted.

Judge Eamon glanced at the clock on the wall. "Why don't we retire to my office where we can sit and chat?"

I hated when people were stingy. Judge Eamon reminded me of one of those kids in elementary school who promised you forbidden candy. But to get it, you had to jump through whatever sadistic hoops they could devise.

Despite my limited success of the last few months, I was still a very hungry lawyer, and a case like this could move my career to the next level. I wouldn't have to go to high-paying potential clients and benevolent judges, hat in hand, grateful for whatever scraps they doled out. Playing the poor cousin was a tiring role.

"That would be lovely," I said in my polite voice. The kind I reserved for old people, children, and bureaucrats I wanted to maim.

I gathered up my things and followed him to his office. Again, my eyes were drawn to the strip of white skin that started where his robe ended and stopped at his black socks. I checked my watch to make sure I hadn't come early and interrupted him in the middle of—whatever he would be doing that would require him to go without pants.

As Judge Eamon rounded the massive oak desk and took up position in the throne-like chair, I realized that the inside of his office was preternaturally quiet, like we'd walked into a dead zone. The endless bustle of the juvenile court had receded to a quiet hum, sounding more like the inside of a seashell and less like the final stop for delinquent and abused children.

"What do you think of the office?" he said. "I think I need something to gussy it up."

I looked around at the dark room lined with ancient oak panels that had been waxed by dozens of hands over the last hundred years. Admittedly, the office was kind of plain. Not the kind of place I'd want to spend eight plus hours a day.

Most judges 'decorated' their chambers with drab earth tone prints of ducks, or eagles, or something patriotic alongside pictures of cherubic children photographed barefoot, robed in requisite white oxfords and blue jeans.

In contrast, Judge Eamon had nothing—not even artwork from his chambers in the Probate court. It was as if he were starting anew, not continuing a long career on the bench. The only break in the unadorned wooden monotony of the walls was the window overlooking the dusty courtyard. I knew it had been a play area for children when this had been a detention center as well as a court. That window and a washroom door were the only adornments. Judges didn't deign to share a bathroom with us mere mortals.

"I don't know what you need in here." I hesitated. "Maybe some paintings of wildlife, a little Americana. Some family photos would be nice." The irony of my lack of originality was lost on him.

"What do you have hanging in your house?"

In my mind's eye, I cataloged the mostly bare white plaster walls of my apartment. While I had always meant to decorate, I just didn't have the flair for it. Jason and Greg's perfect apartment, its floor plan a mirror of my own, constantly mocked me. Their casually elegant décor was what a home should feel like—which is why I spent so much time there.

"I've hung a few impressionist posters," I replied, embellishing the truth. "I haven't really done any decorating."

"What about your bedroom?" Judge Eamon asked, leaning forward. "I'm sure a single girl like you has an interesting boudoir."

Boudoir? Who used that word? "It's a small room, and with my canopy bed, closet doors, and windows, there's not really any space for prints. And art is not in my budget. But I would like it to be," I prompted.

"Well, my dear, age does have its advantages. It is in *my* budget," he said, sitting back and steepling his fingers. With an expansive motion of his hands encompassing the room, he spoke again. "If you had all the money in the world—what would you put up here—really?" He winked conspiratorially. "The county will foot the bill."

I was color challenged, decoration challenged—well, just plain challenged when it came to making a home, or an office, or even myself look good. If I ever got enough money together to buy a house, or met someone who could buy one, I figured I'd hire a decorator. But that's not what the judge wanted to hear. Marisa Ellingwood—that's why I was here. I just had to remember that I was playing the game to get to the prize.

"Why don't you bring the room up to your level, then?" I asked, my question rhetorical. "If money were no object, I'd bring in a big oriental rug, put up red velvet curtains with brass rods and heavy gold tie-backs, and maybe put some nice brass sculptures on the bookshelves. Oh, and I'd take out some of the books. Who's researching cases from books anymore now that there's Lexis? And I'd get some Brasso in here, make the place shine." I smiled in smug satisfaction at the picture I'd painted. No reason for him to know I'd plucked the room right out of The Sims.

"See now, that wasn't so hard, was it? That's what I was looking for." He banged his fist, gavel-like, on the desk. The metal fittings rattled, a dull thud against ancient wood. "I'm going to do exactly what you say. Now let's get down to brass tacks about Mrs. Ellingwood."

I put pen to paper and scratched out copious notes as he told me more about the family and the situation. I was glad that I'd cleared my morning calendar, because he'd set up a meeting with my potential client for eleven-thirty at the Union Club. I wasn't a member, but assumed the reservation was under the auspices of the client. I just hoped I didn't have to spring for lunch because private dining was not in my budget.

I'm not sure what I'd built up in my mind, but the meeting with Judge Eamon hadn't been so bad. I'd scratched his back with cliché decorating ideas and he'd virtually put thousands of dollars in my pocket with this referral. I wasn't even feeling bad about my earlier clumsiness or the decision to wear a blouse with no buttons or a skirt with no hose.

I plopped my briefcase on my lap, slid the pen into its loop and placed the pad in the center section. I rose, and was about to shake Judge Eamon's hand when I heard a noise behind me. A small black woman had pushed open the office door. Her eyes darted around nervously. Looked like Judge Eamon was getting a lot of decorating help these days. I squeaked a thanks and took my leave.

I pulled the office door; then the chambers door closed firmly behind me. That woman certainly didn't look like a lawyer. I wondered what she was getting from him. I cursed myself. It was none of my damn business. I sat down on one of the empty benches in the hall and looked in my briefcase.

I pulled out my pad, poised to make a few more notes. Marisa's case was the kind I needed. I didn't want to fuck it up by fumbling like an idiot. I placed the legal pad on my lap and reached for the Cross pen. It wasn't there. Damn it. I was sure I'd placed it firmly through the loop back in Judge Eamon's office. I pulled everything out of the bag, but my hands couldn't find the smooth grooved barrel, its coolness eluding me. I'd probably dropped the damned thing again. The skinny pen never stayed in its place. Which is why I never used it. But I'd wanted to appear professional. And my parents had been so proud of that gift. How much could it cost to replace? It didn't matter because I probably didn't have it.

I could go back in. It was no big deal. I took a deep breath and pushed open the door to chambers. How weird was it that there were no bailiffs or court clerks to keep the riffraff out of the judge's chambers? Weren't judges who took kids away and put yet more kids in jail just a little bit worried about their safety? Whatever. I didn't have a lot of time between now and my client meeting. Best to get in, and get the embarrassment of being a loser klutz over with.

Neither the judge or his visitor answered my knock. Taking one deep breath, I turned the cool brass knob and pushed open the heavy wood door. The room suddenly seemed much smaller than it had before. Both Judge Eamon and the woman were behind the desk. For a short moment, I wondered what they were doing back there. Then it registered.

The scrape of his fingernails again the satin of his robe, the buzz of the zipper.

"Bend over, Rhonda," the judge said.

The woman, whose naked brown flesh was out of place in this office, became visible when her elbows hit the desk. I may not have had sex in a long time, but I knew an erect penis when I saw one.

Judge Eamon finally noticed me, our eyes locking. "Judge Brody," I croaked. "I forgot…"

Rhonda saw me then, and her already dead looking eyes sunk a little further into her head. "I don't think…"

"You don't need to think, girl," he said, almost breathless. "You give me something now and I'll help you." The judge grunted, pushing Rhonda into the desk one last time. The pen lost all importance. I gathered my briefcase and bolted from the room, not bothering to look back.

6

After giving him the prescription painkillers and a lot of hot chocolate, I'd finally gotten Luke comfortable enough to sleep. I pulled his door nearly closed and walked down to the kitchen. I tried to pour myself some juice, but my hands were too shaky. Liquid spilled everywhere.

"Damn it!" I covered my mouth far too late. I crept halfway up the stairs, but Luke was out cold, if the snoring coming from his room was anything to go by. I came back down and sponged off the mess. Too bad I didn't drink anymore. I could have used a stiff shot of Courvoisier.

The knock at the door was faint, but persistent. Miles had come by to check on me. This buoyed my hopes. For some reason I thought Miles was going to break up with me. But that was just my self-esteem taking a hit. I smoothed my hair, buttoned the front of my jeans and pulled my sweat-shirt down.

And in a single second, the air went out of my sails.

"Darius. What are you doing here?"

"I wanted to check up on my son."

"I have a phone."

"Didn't want to wake him up. They gave him Tylenol with that stuff to knock him out, right?"

"Codeine."

"You gonna let me in? Your heat's runnin' out the door."

"It's not that cold."

He turned those pleading eyes on me.

"Fine."

"It's a torus fracture."

"When are you going to do something with that certificate?" Darius hadn't completely lied to me when we met. He wasn't exactly in college, but in a radiology tech program. He'd finished, but hadn't taken advantage of the job placement the school offered.

"I'm looking."

"You've been saying that for years."

"Aw, dream girl. Let's not do this. Why are we always fighting? We used to be so good together. I remember that day we met. It had started out so cold, but by that night we were keeping each other warm."

That term of endearment always took me back. It hadn't been all bad, Darius and I. I told my parents one thing, but I'd really loved him. The day I'd met him, my life had taken a hard left turn. I had never expected to wake up one day as someone's Baby Mama. Nor did I plan to spend every weekend embroiled in Baby Mama Drama. For years, I'd hid as much of this as I could from my family because I didn't want to hear them say, 'I told you so.'

Don't get me wrong, my family raised me right. I graduated from one of the best colleges in the country. Then I'd moved back home to go to law school and plan out my career. I had just gotten sidetracked along the way.

It had been one of those mid December days that made even the heartiest Chicagoans curse their hometown. A terrible Lake Michigan wind had pushed me and a few other shivering men and women into a tiny bus shelter while we waited for the Stony Island Express to pull up.

I'd shivered in my tiny Abercrombie jacket and Uggs. During the four years I was at school in Atlanta, I'd forgotten that a Chicago winter wind could cut through you like a knife. I looked at my watch and sighed with frustration, but I didn't have time to walk back home, borrow a warmer coat from my mother, and still make it to my international antitrust class on time. It was the last class of the semester, and I couldn't afford to miss any hints Professor Hermenegild may give about the final exam.

I felt a tap on my shoulder. Clutching my messenger bag reflexively, I turned around and noticed a nice-looking brown-skinned man pointing at my scarf. My mother had taught me better than to speak with strange men on the street. And for years, since I'd turned thirteen and started developing, I'd studiously ignored every come on and provocative gesture from a man. Whether he was some uncouth brother in a car or a construction worker enjoying his lunchtime beer, I gave them my back and the figurative finger.

"You might want to fix that," he said, pointing toward the ground.

In my haste to reach the bus and my class on time, I'd wound my orange and black scarf around my neck haphazardly. I hadn't noticed the striped fringe trailing through the graying slush.

I shook off the dirty ice and snow as best as I could and wrapped the knit around my neck a few extra times for good measure.

He looked me up and down appraisingly. I gave him my 'look'—cultivated over many years—meant to cut him down to size. He shifted closer to me in the shelter, undeterred. "You're a cute girl. But those colors don't exactly go with your outfit. Halloween was two months ago."

Like everyone else had been doing for the last ten minutes, I leaned out of the shelter, scanning the street for the bus. Nothing, not even a car sped down Hyde Park Boulevard. It was like all of Chicago had stayed home when the news broadcasted today's expected wind chill. But, I wasn't going anywhere. Might as well have a little fun.

"For your information, this scarf is from Princeton University, in New Jersey. It was a gift from my boyfriend."

"Would that be your ex-boyfriend?" the man asked, arching a nicely shaped brow.

"It was a long distance thing. Didn't work out," I said, hoping to cut off the conversation there. I turned away from him and did the lean again. Still no bus.

"What kind of school is this Princeton? Do you go there?"

I hadn't talked to someone unfamiliar with the Ivies in a very long time. "It's a well-regarded school," I said haughtily.

"Who would I have heard of from this Halloween school?"

I smiled inwardly. I'd always thought the Princeton Tiger colors *were* a little garish, especially when compared to the more mellow colors the other Ivy League schools sported.

"They've graduated a bunch of senators, governors and people like that," I said, grateful that the bus pulled up that instant. I boarded and retreated to the back row of seats near the overworked heater. It was a half hour bus ride, and I hoped to thaw out before I had to transfer. I'd just tucked my mittens in my pocket and pulled my brand new iPod from my bag, when the man from the bus shelter plopped down beside me.

"So, you from around here?"

I'd put the ear buds in my ears. But he wasn't put off by this obvious gesture.

I shrugged. "I live here in Hyde Park."

"Well, I'm just here in Chi town for a little bit, hanging with some friends." He thrust out his hand. "Darius Gaines."

I had too much training to ignore that outstretched hand, so I shook it, albeit tentatively.

"Is your name a secret?"

I reluctantly pulled the buds from my ears, feeling like a window seat airplane passenger held captive by the middle seat holder. Hopefully this trip would be far shorter than any plane ride I'd taken.

"Claire Henshaw."

"Where you on your way to?"

"I have a class at school."

"See, there? We got a lot in common. I'm in school too, in Cleveland," he said smugly.

Okay, I was surprised. He didn't seem like the kind of brother who was serious about getting ahead in life. I knew

I'd made a snap judgment, but he looked like he spent more time on his hair and clothes than on his schoolwork.

"You're not from Chicago?"

"Nah, I'm just here with my boys this weekend, doing a little partying now that school's out for the semester," he said. His wide smile and honest eyes beckoned me. When more people joined us on the already crowded bus, and pushed him closer to me, I wasn't as upset as I should have been.

"So you in school here? What you studying?" I wished he sounded more like a student, but after spending four years at an historically black college in Atlanta, I'd met plenty of black folks who seemed to graduate from high school with a diploma in Ebonics.

"I'm studying law at Northwestern. Today's my last class before exams," I said matter-of-factly. Though, in honesty I was waiting for the usual adoration I received when people found out I was at a top ten law school.

"You gonna work for the prosecutor or the defense?" he asked. The only lawyers this man had come into contact with were probably in the criminal justice system.

"I'm not planning to do either," I said. Though I hadn't landed a coveted spot at a large law firm like most of my classmates, I was hoping to use my family contacts to get something solid in government. I'd have to wait until I passed the bar, and I wouldn't be earning the big bucks, but hopefully it would be recession-proof work. While I was in law school, I'd already seen a wave of recent graduates laid off from firms during the dot com bust. The government may not be sexy, but I'd rather be the tortoise at the end of the race than kicked out of the race altogether.

"Cool," he said, satisfied with my answer. "My friends are goin' to Club Seven-twenty tonight, you wanna come?"

"I have to study," I demurred. "Since I don't have a job yet, my grades are still important."

Darius leaned against me, our shoulders brushing in a not unpleasant way. "It's only one night. You can study later."

We were near the stop where I would transfer. Half of me figured I should chalk this up to a public transportation flirtation and the other half was intrigued. I'd always dated the right boys from Jack and Jill or whose families knew my own. Darius represented a bit of danger and I was feeling dangerous.

I pulled my Palm Pilot from my bag and flipped the stylus from its holder. "Give me your number. I just might call you," I said, holding the tiny plastic pen over the screen.

He had taken the PDA from my hands and programmed in his number. After we had parted ways at the station, I'd dutifully gone to class and had dinner with my parents. But after they'd retired in front of the television, I'd decided, 'what the hell.' I dialed Darius' number and agreed to meet him and his friends at the club.

The club had been fun, the sex good. But when I'd found out I was pregnant, I'd nearly jumped from my parent's apartment building roof. My mom figured it out before I'd had the courage to tell her. No one in my family believed in abortion, so I'd made a go of it. Two unemployed people living in Cleveland was not a good idea. We moved south barely two months after Luke was born.

The seriousness of Darius' expression dragged me back to the present. "I caught a felony a few years ago," he said when he finally had my attention.

"What are you saying?" I asked, knowing I must have misheard.

"I pled out to a felony drug possession charge."

"When? You're dealing now? What kind of example—"

His hand on my arm stopped my mouth from running. "Claire, I don't deal—I didn't deal drugs. I was hanging out with some of the guys I'd grown up with. They picked up a delivery to drop off. We got profiled and I went down."

"Why are you telling me this now?"

"Because a black man with a felony has a hell of a time getting a job."

"Oh. Well. Oh." I got up and picked up the juice I'd left on the counter. I didn't have the energy for this. On the one hand he was irresponsible, leaving my baby with some girl from round the way. And then he slaps me with this stuff about the man keeping him down. I had a father. I knew how hard it was out here for a black man, much less one with a record. I tried to keep my sympathy in check.

I drained the glass and put it in the sink. I squeezed creamy blue detergent into the sponge and washed the glass carefully.

I flinched when those familiar hands squeezed up my arms to my shoulders. "I'm close to getting something. You're settled in and that Uana—"

"Uama." I'd heard that mistake too often. Uana translated into sex, not anything to do with the our mission of keeping families together.

"Our son needs his parents together. Maybe we can—"

"What about Freya?"

"What about her?"

I shook my head. He didn't take his commitments seriously. Not to me. Not to Luke. Not even to his woman of the moment. "I'm with Miles now."

"And that's serious?"

"I think so."

"You're kidding yourself. He's in a different world from you and me."

My insides burned with the idea that Darius lumped me in with him and his kind. I wanted to stamp my feet like Luke did when I refused to give him more candy. I was more like Miles than like Darius. I'd come from an intact family, gone to the right schools. And Darius, well, he was that other kind of black person my family had worked hard for me not to be.

"I think I need to head to bed. It may be a rough night and I want to get some sleep before—"

"I can—"

"Go."

"I don't want you to be mad at me."

"I'm not," I lied.

"If you're not mad, then—" Darius leaned in and brushed his lips against mine. Shock warred with remembered desire. Our sex life had never been the reason for our break-up. But as I lingered too long in the kiss, I remembered all the reasons we were very done. All the reasons I was with Miles, someone who would lift me up, not pull me down.

"Mom," Luke cried. His weak voice barely getting past the roaring blood pounding in my ears.

I squashed all sentimentality, took him forcefully by the arm and steered him toward the door. The last thing I needed was any evidence to fuel Luke's fantasy of his mommy and daddy getting back together.

7

No longer worried about my 'professional' image, I ran as fast as I could in my Cuban heeled slides. Someone must have been smiling down upon me because a Loop bus pulled up, and doors swung open. I got in and allowed the bus to envelope me in its fetid warmth.

I squeezed between two riders onto the molded plastic seat. Though I usually tried to keep my head down when I rode on public transportation, I looked around at everything and everyone, trying to take in something, anything that would wipe my mind clear of Judge Eamon's conduct.

"Does anyone—?"My voice broke and I could feel tears pricking at my lids. "Can anyone lend me a tissue?" I managed to get out.

An older black woman, very properly dressed in a lavender suit, snapped open the silver clasp of vintage purse and pulled a wrinkled tissue from its depths. Though it didn't look all that clean, it was unused and smelled like flowers as I dabbed my eyes. Carefully balling the tissue, I realized my hands were shaking.

My mind snapped back to Judge Eamon's chambers and the stunt he'd pulled. What unmitigated gall! What gave him the right to act like a teenage boy in heat? Didn't marriage vows or judge's robes mean anything to him?

I almost missed my stop, but hopped off the bus just in time to get out at Public Square. I stalked the rest of the way to my office in the Illuminating Building, up the long elevator ride and to my office. I slammed the door to the office I shared with another attorney and stormed into my office, batting away the messages in the outstretched hand of the receptionist and the entreaties from my part-time secretary.

I dropped my briefcase on one guest chair then sat on the other. Adrenaline pumped through my veins. Immediately, I popped up and stalked to my executive chair. My leg bobbed endlessly when I sat down.

Damn, what should I do? What did I see? I closed my eyes and took a calming breath. Once, when I was a kid kicking around the public library after school, I came across a book about adults going to the bathroom or something like it. I giggled for hours after paging through illustrations of teachers, police, and firefighters on the throne. Maybe I needed a book about sex like that. Teachers on their backs. Policemen getting blow jobs. Judges laying women over their desks. The same jag of laughter that caught me as a pre-teen girl started again. I was nearly in hysterics when I answered the tentative knock at the door.

"Come in," I called.

Letty stuck her head around the barely cracked door. She'd been my secretary through some very lean times. There were many bad weeks that she was paid and I took home nothing, and worse weeks where she took home I.O.U.s. Though her skills were somewhat limited, I felt a certain loyalty to someone who'd stuck with me through more thin than thick. I wished Tom understood that concept.

"You okay?" Letty asked. When I motioned, she came in and sat on a guest chair. She'd remembered to close the door behind her. I was thankful for her discretion. I didn't want my office mates to think I'd lost my mind. "You blew right through reception. I didn't have anything on the calendar for you this morning. Just that you were coming in late." She was fishing, but I wasn't taking the bait. I covered my remaining laugh with a hiccough.

"I'm fine," I lied. I did not want to think about Judge Eamon or talk about Judge Eamon to anyone. "I have a meeting with a potential client at the Union Club at eleven-thirty. I'll need you to run a conflict check on Marisa Elling-wood."

"*The* Marisa Ellingwood?" Letty was wide-eyed.

"Yes, that Ellingwood. Also, I'll need to get back to you with her maiden name as well," I said even though knew for a fact that none of my poor juvenile or criminal clients would have had the kind of dealings with the Ellingwood family that would prevent me from representing Marisa.

It was simply a task that got Letty out of my hair. She had that eerie intuition moms have, and would have figured me out in no time if I allowed her to stay in my office. With Letty on her way, I stole down the hall to the women's restroom. Furiously, I pumped a handful of the harsh industrial soap at the sink, and washed away as best I could what I'd seen. I came back to my office, put on moisturizer, lotion and perfume, and retouched my makeup.

I wasn't sure how I'd caused this morning's mess, but I was determined to put it out of my mind forever. No matter what carrot Judge Eamon Brody dangled, I would never walk into his chambers alone again. It was done, past, over. I vowed to banish what I'd seen from my mind forever.

With a single deep breath, I turned to my computer and typed Marisa's name into the search engine. My hands hardly shook. Banished, I repeated in silent entreaty, and clicked the links on the screen.

Given her in-laws' prominence, their marriage had made a big splash in the news. One click, and there in grainy digitized black and white were her engagement and wedding photos, as well as her bio. Marisa had been a minor Spanish television star when she gave it all up for love and moved to Cleveland. Thank goodness for the Internet. Even this limited information would give me a great leg up when I met with her in an hour. I was armed and ready for the meeting.

During law school, I'd accompanied a friend down to the BMV when she needed to turn in her Massachusetts driver's license for an Ohio one. When we'd finally made it to the first counter, the guy working there had asked if she'd come to Ohio for money or love. Money, she'd said without thinking. That was the standard answer any law student would have given, I thought. The BMV employee had laughed and flirted with her, and more quickly than I'd ever had, she received her newly laminated identification. I'd always thought moving for love, especially to Ohio would have been a more romantic answer. I imagined that's the answer Marisa Ellingwood, nee Gíl would have given.

I checked myself in my office's hidden full-length mirror one more time. Deeming myself professional enough and presentable, and assured by my brief call to MBNA that I had enough credit to cover lunch, I made my way over to the Union Club.

Marisa was already at the table when the Maître d' escorted me over. If I could die and be reborn to a completely different set of European immigrants, I'd want them to be Marisa's parents. In the gene pool lottery, she'd come up a winner. Not that she was pretty, exactly. With her dark hair and bold features, striking would be a more accurate description—no curly dishwater blond hair or childbearing hips on this one.

She stood from the table, clasped my hands in hers and bussed me on both cheeks in a typical European greeting style.

"It's nice to meet you," I said.

"Yes. Thank you. It is unfortunate we meet under such circumstances," she said, her husky voice softened with a Galician accent. Having grown up with immigrant parents, I always spotted people whose first language was not English.

"How can I help you?" I asked.

"The Brodys are, maybe were, family friends of my husband? But I did not know where else to turn?" she said, her uncertainty with the language making every sentence a question.

"I went to law school with Tom, Patrick's son," I said, trying to shore up my own flimsy family connections—then thought better of it. "But I'm not in that social circle. I mean,

I'm from a modest family, and I really work to serve my clients, not the elite of Cleveland. I think Judge Brody recommended me because I've been practicing in juvenile court for quite some time." I didn't mention that I would do anything in the world to get out of Juvey. Maybe this case would be my last hurrah.

"I need a lawyer," she said. "My children cannot be with *him.*"

"How old are they?" I asked, though I'd done enough research to know the answers. No reason to come out of the gate looking like a stalker, though.

"Carmen, my little Carmelita is twelve, and Zacharias is eight, God bless his soul."

"When did you guys get together? And why are you breaking up?"

"Break up? That's the term you use for boyfriend and girlfriend, *novio*, no? It is not like we had a casual relationship. I thought he was my husband."

"Didn't you have a wedding? I remember the photos in the newspapers," I asked, confused by the outward perception versus the reality.

"We met in Los Angeles," she said, pronouncing LA as if it were a Spanish name. "I was working on my acting. I was in the show Poseidon. You remember that?"

TVholic that I was, I remembered the show. It was about surfers down under. It was long on buff bodies and short on acting.

"It was filmed in Australia and New Zealand. Neither of us wanted to get married so far away from our families. When the show went on hiatus, I got pregnant with Carmelita, and it wasn't a good time to get married in a Catholic church, you know." I knew. Like her and like Tom, I'd been brought up in a fairly observant Catholic home. Though my family wasn't ultra religious, even I knew better than to show up to mass knocked up and unwed.

"After that, the time never seemed right. After little Zach was born, Ian had me sign some insurance papers, and said that it did not matter anyway because in Ohio, we'd been together a long enough time for the state to consider us married. I am not familiar with American laws so I believed him. The photographs you saw were all for publicity—for the show, for our families, whomever. I did not have any reason not to believe that we were husband and wife. We raised our children, bought a house. I volunteered at their schools. I am their mother. He cannot take them away. Can he?" she asked plaintively, her monologue winding down. Up until that last question, she had shown very little emotion.

There had been a time, twenty to thirty years ago when the court always presumed that a mother was a better parent. But the father's rights movement of the late 1980s took care of that notion. Now courts assumed that either parent was fully capable of taking care of the children. Even children of 'tender' years. Gone were the days when divorced fathers were 'weekend dads.' Ohio had adopted what they called shared parenting, but what my clients still referred to as joint custody. I didn't think it was the best idea. Now kids went back and forth from house to house once or twice each week. And if the parents lived in different school districts, *oy*.

"We'll do our best to keep them with you," I said in a way that I hoped sounded soothing.

I'd learned early in my career never to get a client's hopes up. Much of the 'practice' of law was managing expectations. But I did share with Marisa that she was at a small legal advantage. There was irrefutable biological evidence that she was the mother of her children. That wasn't the case for Ian Ellingwood, the putative father. Until the juvenile court established paternity, there was no requirement that Ian be allowed to see his children. She was in the driver's seat—free to use leverage to make whatever decision she liked.

Marisa was nodding in agreement and I was very sure my fortunes had just changed for the better. Something wet trickled down the back of my leg. I stood abruptly, the wooden chair falling none too softly on the threadbare carpet. Though it defied logic, I imagined that some of Judge Brody had somehow gotten on me.

"Get me a napkin and water. Do you have professional disinfectant?" I said to a passing busboy. My voice which I'd tried to modulate in these tony environs, got a bit too loud as my head filled with images from this morning. I couldn't shake the memory of Judge Brody's office or the idea of him doing to me what he'd been doing to that girl.

Dozens of gray heads turned toward me then quickly turned away. Mortified, my face flooded with warmth. The dining room was pin drop quiet. A waiter and a busboy stood by idly, no doubt discomfited by the first show of emotion in this place in a hundred years.

"What happened?"

I shook her hands off as politely as I could. "I'm fine. I'm creeped out at slimy things on my leg," I improvised. "Just a childhood fear."

I didn't know the name of the small dark-skinned man who spoke up, but I was eternally grateful.

"Ma'am, I deeply apologize," he said in some indefinable Caribbean accent, balling up a large rag. "I was just trying to clean off a serving tray and I splashed you. Why don't I bring you a warm towel?"

The maître d' who'd been absent from the quiet room suddenly appeared. Conversation ratcheted back to normal levels. "Ma'am, I apologize for Mr. Mabrey. Please let us rectify this situation by allowing the club to buy you lunch."

I nodded imperiously and placed the proffered napkin across my legs. I'd slipped for a moment, but I wouldn't let Judge Brody affect me again.

"Will you take my case?" Marisa said earnestly. As beautiful and sophisticated as she was, Marisa was still as self involved as most clients, and my speech on her superior parental rights had its desired effect.

"Yes, I'll be more than happy to help you," I said. "While I know it's crass to discuss money, it's necessary so let's get it out of the way. I require a retainer, in cases like this, of ten thousand dollars."

When Marisa penned a check with what I saw now was her inbred European flourish and handed it over without hesitation, I knew I'd charged a big client too little once again. I promised myself and my anemic bank account that I wouldn't make the same mistake a third time."

8

"Mom," I whispered fiercely into my work phone. "I haven't asked you guys for anything since Luke was born, but I need this, now. His safety's at stake." I blew out my breath in exasperation.

My parents sighed in unison. They were at work as well. I had roped them into a three-way call. Now that they had cell phones, they weren't tied to their desks.

"That's not exactly true, Claire Elaine." Uh-oh, the full name. "We made a substantial contribution to the down payment of that townhouse you're living in."

I felt like a chastised child who was asking for something new, having forgotten the gift they'd received just yesterday.

"But this is truly serious—a life or death matter, Mom. Dad, are you still there?"

"I'm here, baby," my dad said quietly. He was a high school teacher without the luxury or privacy of an office.

My mother was going to make this difficult. "What about us paying for you to go to Northwestern Law School? You said that you were going to stay in Chicago, but you got pregnant and ran behind that trifling man even after he said he wouldn't marry you. We never even get to see our grand-baby with you so far away." They made Chicago seem as distant as Cameroon. It was only three hundred and fifty miles, a day's drive or an hour's flight. I didn't challenge them on this, though, merely soldiered on.

"Mom, you were one hundred percent right about Da-rius. But this isn't about that. Luke's arm got broken yester-day when that man left my child with some girl he picked up who knows where. You know the kind, Mama—some 'round the way girl without the sense God gave her. I made a mistake with Darius," I admitted for the nine hundredth time. "But I need to get this fixed now."

"How much do you need?" my father asked.

"About seventy-five hundred," I said, knowing my father would round up to a nice even number.

"We'll see what we can do for you, baby," he said.

"Hmph," my mother huffed. In my mind's eye, I could see her crossing her arms over her ample bosom.

"Thank you. Thank you. I know this is hard on you guys, and I wouldn't ask if I didn't have to, but I can't leave my son in that man's custody any longer than I need to." I paused. Nothing came from their end in Chicago. "Well, I have to get back to work. I'll call you guys soon."

There wasn't really any work to get back to. I'd already done my class for that day, and there wasn't much else to the job. Sure, like any other teacher, I suppose, I could be in my office honing my curriculum. But like I'd learned from my dad, you put together a class that bureaucrats and administrators could agree on and you didn't make any changes that would rock the boat.

It'd worked for him for years, and it had worked for me here, so far. The only limb I'd gone out on was the Sunday sessions, and I hadn't even gotten any additional money or comp time for those. But I figured with my miniscule salary, Uama was getting exactly what they paid for.

I turned my attention, instead, to searching out family law attorneys on the internet. Other than a bunch of blinking banners and personal injury attorneys claiming to want my case for a mere forty percent, the web wasn't that helpful. As an attorney, I knew a lot of attorneys, but I'd worked mostly with the underemployed and unemployable, not a great source for referrals.

I pulled open my desk drawer and thumbed through my business card holder, past the handyman and the plumber, and pulled out the card of the one lawyer whom I knew practiced in juvenile court. I don't know why I hadn't thought of her at first. If she'd been good enough to recommend to the judge, then she'd be good enough for me.

"Casey Cort," I said in greeting, having dialed the phone. "This is Claire Henshaw. I have a child custody emergency. Can I see you today?"

***

Casey Cort looked plum worn out when I bustled into her office just after five o'clock. If I thought I'd been having a bad couple of days, Casey looked like a truck had hit her.

She put on her game face, though. "First, I'd like to thank you for the referral to Judge Grant." I couldn't tell if her gratitude was genuine. The case was probably a big one for her, but her client had ditched her in the end, leaving Casey holding all the worst cards.

"I got your note," I said. It was the first and probably last time, I'd gotten a hand written thank-you card from an attorney. She seemed to want to say something else, but thought better of it. I started to doubt my decision to consult with her. If her emotions came through like that in the courtroom, I wonder how she could successfully argue for a client in front of the judge—especially if that client wasn't the best parent. Well, that wouldn't make a difference in my case because I was surely in the right. She'd definitely have a problem, though, if she were defending Darius.

"How can I help you?"

"As you know I'm a lawyer, and now I'm even working in the juvenile arena, but I'm not familiar with representation of clients in court," I said, trying to justify my scant experience.

Casey looked upon me kindly. She had a mommy face—the kind of woman you'd want to hug and then gossip over coffee and muffins. "We can't all be experts in everything—especially with specialization in the law the way it is," she said. "So what's going on?"

I didn't want to talk about Darius or Luke just yet. I needed to feel her out—to see if she could represent someone like me. I glanced around the room meaningfully. "I don't see your diplomas. Did you go to school locally? You from Cleveland?" Although with her flat A's it was easy to tell she'd grown up in the Midwest.

"I'm local. Grew up on the west side, went to Ohio State and Cleveland State as well."

She didn't ask me where I'd gone to school. Those who went to fourth tier Cleveland State usually didn't. Even the other law school in town, Case, was in the second tier. Casey and her fellow alumni had a bit of an inferiority complex. But first and second tier lawyers didn't toil away twenty blocks from Public Square. I put my own superiority complex away for the moment, and dove in.

"Look, here's my issue. I have a son, Luke, and I never married his father." I watched her scratch notes on a pad and wondered if she realized that even though I sounded like the stereotypical black mother having a baby out of wedlock, I was the exception, not the rule in my family. But she wasn't a chatty one. "After we broke up, we went to court a year ago or so, and did a shared parenting plan. I wanted my baby's father to be in his life, even if he couldn't be in mine."

"How has that been working out?"

"The schedule and everything?" I asked. Casey nodded. "It's been fine, I mean he's late and stuff, but you know how thoughtless single guys can be. Anyway, I need to change visitation or do some kind of supervised visitation."

"That's kind of drastic," she said. "What changed?"

I tried not to cry, but pulled a couple of Kleenex from the box on her desk, just in case. "Darius broke Luke's arm."

Casey leaned forward in her chair, the first emotion she'd shown since I walked in. "Are you alleging physical abuse?"

"No!" I said emphatically then softened my response. "At least none that I know of. He left our four-year-old son with some woman he'd *just* met, to go play basketball with his friends. This woman was talking on her cell or doing something else but she definitely wasn't watching our son. He fell out of the first story window and broke his arm."

She rapidly scratched more notes. "When did this happen?"

"Sunday."

"How's Luke doing? What did the doctor say?"

"The doctor took an x-ray. It's something they're calling a buckle fracture. I think it'll heal in four or six weeks. But my little baby's wearing a cast. I have to put his arm in a plastic bag when I bathe him. It's ludicrous for any child, much less mine, to go through this for no good reason."

"When is his father's next scheduled visitation?"

"There's a mid-week dinner schedule on Wednesdays, but he's never done that. Next weekend is his next scheduled visit. Yesterday was just something we'd worked out because I work every third Sunday."

"Have you talked with the father—tried to work something out between yourselves?"

Obviously she'd never met Darius.

"I've compromised from jump. We're done with that. I'm a lawyer. He's not. It's time to use the court to hit him hard with a hammer—knock some sense into that big head."

Casey paused for a long moment. If she'd been standing, she'd have fallen over, she looked that exhausted.

"I've had a long day, and you're obviously a very competent lawyer in your own right, so I'll give you the short version. I can do my best to file an emergency action, but juvenile court moves like molasses. I can't promise that we'll be able to get a hearing in time to address your next visitation."

I nodded, hoping that I'd made the right decision to hire her and that she'd use whatever influence she had to bring pressure to bear on the court.

"I charge a retainer of five thousand dollars in these kinds of cases. My hourly rate is two hundred and fifty dollars. Are you going to have any problems with that?" she asked.

Grateful for my parents, I shook my head. "I'll messenger you a check with a copy of the retainer agreement. This was last minute for me, I didn't bring my checkbook." I failed to mention that the check would bounce from here to Cleveland Heights until my parents wired money into my account. They were as good as their word, however, so I wasn't worried about that part.

I gathered up my purse and my hip length black trench coat. Casey handed me a folder containing, I assumed, the retainer agreement. I made to leave, but then I turned back.

"That third Sunday I mentioned," I said, and she nodded wearily. "I host a group of mothers whose kids are in foster care. Anyway, I heard a strange rumor from the group that one of my moms got her son back after performing sexual favors for Judge...Brody, I think it was. Have you heard anything like that?"

Casey looked visibly shocked at my question, my same reaction to Rhonda at group. This is how vicious rumors got started, I knew. I didn't think this was as bad as a teacher falsely accused of sexual abuse, but it was probably pretty close.

"I've heard nothing like that," she said. "In fact, he's my boyfriend's uncle. I wouldn't repeat that to anyone else, if I were you."

She was right. I wasn't Oscar Wilde, did not want to end up penniless and jailed for a possibly false allegation. And I didn't want to find myself or my agency at the center of a slander lawsuit either. Embarrassed that I'd brought up a petty rumor, I hustled my butt out of there. I liked my job and my clients, but I had to keep focused on what was really important, Luke.

9

I'd progressed far enough in my practice that I'd hired a docketing company to file most of my papers in court. They charged by the week, instead of the hour like I did. My clients did not want to pay two hundred fifty dollars for me to stand in line at a government office, and for my non-paying clients, I didn't have the time to waste.

Despite my vow to avoid the hassle, I was standing in the filing line today at juvenile court. It was peppered with the usual assortment of humanity, most of whom had little idea what they were doing, and were, for the most part, unrepresented.

I watched as the overburdened and exasperated clerks explained to yet another plaintive parent that the papers they were attempting to file with the court were inadequate.

They handed out blurred photocopies of the Public Defender's address and phone number. Most of these people would find little help at the PD's office. The system was simply too overwhelmed. But court staff didn't mention it and neither did I. Pass the buck was the name of the bureaucratic game.

"Long time no see, counselor," Jenny said as I made my way to the front of the line.

"Quick Docket has been my new best friend, but I have a retained one here who needs her case expedited. So here I am." I handed the stapled and banded copies of my papers across the counter.

Stippled rubber thimbles covered her index finger and thumb, Jenny paged through my papers. "Motion to modify custody, child support, and a request for supervised visitation."

"I need a case number and judge assignment today," I requested. In any other court, the assignment of a judge and case number—used on all future court papers—would be immediate. In Juvenile, an attorney had to bring pressure to bear to get them within a reasonable period of time after filing. If I'd left it with the docket service, Claire Henshaw's papers would languish for weeks or months before anything happened. For my retained clients, part of what they were paying for was keeping their matter front and center at the court. And for an hourly fee, I was more than happy to provide that service.

Jenny nodded and stepped away from the counter, coming back with a Bates stamp and a thick pad of aqua construction paper sealed at both edges. She quickly adjusted the date then inked all of my documents with the next sequential case number.

"Ready for your courtroom assignment?" Jenny asked, pulling the stack of paper across the counter so it sat between us. This block, known as the judge stack, had pages printed with the judges' names on them, facing down. The stack was glued on both ends, requiring some kind of sharp instrument to separate one page from the deck every time the court assigned a case. The county instituted the stack when it became apparent that certain litigants were making an effort to pick judges friendly to their causes. The stack assured that the choice of judge was completely random and free of influence. Unfortunately, there were very few ways to change judges once the clerk assigned them—so this moment could mean the difference between fairness or injustice. Under the lip of the counter, I crossed my fingers that I wasn't assigned to Judge Brody.

Jenny sliced through the stack with a knife-sharp brass letter opener. She turned the paper over. I held my breath.

"Judge…Conti," she announced.

The air left my lungs in a whoosh of relief. I was spared from another encounter with Judge Eamon. Then it hit me.

"Okay," she started, her motions efficient, as she hand-wrote Judge Brody's names on my pleadings. "All Judge Conti cases will be assigned to Judge Brody until we get a new stack in."

Shit.

My only remaining hope was that Judge Eamon assigned my case to some overworked, overburdened magistrate with no side agenda. Magistrates in Juvenile and Domestic Relations court were for the most part politically connected lawyers who held near lifetime appointments at the court. They could hear evidence and make decisions in most cases with only cursory supervision by the court. I was not a fan of the magistrate system, as I didn't believe unelected individuals should have so much power, but for once, I knew I'd appreciate a political hack assigned to this case.

She handed me my two copies of the motions, complete with a date and case number stamp as well as her handwritten judicial designation. "Have you met Judge Brody yet?" she asked conversationally.

A flashback of our meeting came to mind. "I met him at the Brodys' Labor Day party."

"Ooh, fancy," Jenny said, looking at me appreciatively. I could see the question in her eyes, but chose not to answer how I was connected. "You're set here. If you want that ex parte motion granted, you'll have to walk this through." Which meant making my way to Judge Eamon's chambers and pleading Claire's case to him one-on-one. For a long moment, I considered putting my interests above those of my client. Then, I started the long walk from the administrative side of the building to the judge's chambers. A death row prisoner on their way to the gallows had more enthusiasm about their fate than I did at the moment.

When I approached Judge Eamon's chambers this time, the lights were on. A few straggling lawyers and a matronly looking woman I assumed was his new or old bailiff occupied his anteroom. Relief. I wasn't going to be alone with the judge. I wouldn't have to see anything like what I thought I saw last time.

I approached the gray haired woman and cleared my throat to get her attention.

"Yes," she said, sliding off and folding her neon blue cateye reading glasses, leaving them dangling on a chain at her chest. "Can I help you, dearie?"

I handed her a copy of my emergency motion and a copy of the judgment entry I'd prepared. A lawyer's suggested JE was always favorable to her client. Nine times out of ten a harried judge would sign them without alteration. "I'm walking this motion through."

She took it from my hand. "Have a seat, I'll put it on the judge's desk. Give us a half hour or so."

Gratified that I wouldn't have to encounter Judge Eamon or his latest conquest, I left my cell phone number and went outside. Soot, bus exhaust, and whatever other toxins a postindustrial city could throw at me filled the air. Despite the choking feeling grabbing at my throat, fall in downtown Cleveland was less toxic than the air in Judge Eamon's chambers.

Ten minutes later, my phone buzzed in my purse. The judge was paging me. I took a deep breath, gathered my resolve and presented myself to his bailiff.

"Casey Cort," she said, addressing me by name this time. "You should have mentioned that were a friend of the judge. I wouldn't have sent you packing. He's got your motion in front of him and will see you now."

For all the times I'd envied other lawyers and their chummy donation-fueled relationships to the judges, I'd have given anything not to be a *friend* of the court. I gathered what resolve remained, hefted my purse and briefcase and walked into his office, my head held high. Unlike the last time, Judge Eamon was robed and seated. He gestured toward a chair and obligingly, I sat. He put on reading glasses and looked at my moving papers with serious deliberation.

"I've read the affidavit of your client, Ms. Henshaw. I'm sympathetic to her cause, but don't know if the kid's broken arm, just one accident really, is sufficient to deprive the father of his unsupervised visitation rights."

I slumped back in the chair, visibly disheartened.

"Don't dismay, Ms. Cort. I'm not denying your request outright. Instead, I have a request."

"Yes, Your Honor," I said, beefing up the respect in my voice.

"Bring Miss—" He paused, scrutinizing my papers again. "Bring Miss Henshaw here. If you can get her here this afternoon or tomorrow morning at the earliest, I'll consider taking testimony in your ex parte motion."

I sat back, flabbergasted. Judge Eamon had either given Claire the chance of a lifetime, or he'd committed the biggest impropriety I'd ever seen from a judge. Court rules generally prohibited any judge from making a decision in a case without hearing both parties. The only time judges were allowed to hear only one party, ex parte, was when the party was likely to suffer an immediate harm. If time would only exacerbate the problem, a judge could make an immediate, though temporary, ruling in their favor. In my moving papers, I'd emphasized Claire's desperation and the seriousness of her son Darius Junior's injury. I felt a rare moment of elation. My legal skills seemed more artistic than functionary. My argument had worked.

"I'll have her here, Your Honor," I said. I walked from his chambers as quickly as propriety would allow, flipping open my cell phone as I moved from the building.

10

A solo audience with a judge was more than I could have asked for. I'm certainly glad that I hadn't represented myself. My knowledge of juvenile court was purely theoretical and not ready for prime time. Despite her fourth tier creds, that Casey Cort was able to pull it out when needed.

When I got to the judge's chambers, Casey was pacing outside while playing with her cell phone. What was it with people in my life and their incessant need to piddle with tiny buttons; first Miles, then her. They're all gonna die of tiny carpal tunnel syndrome—assuming there are carpal tunnels in their thumbs. My knowledge of anatomy was only second to my legal skills.

When the click of my low-heeled shoes penetrated her reverie, Casey looked up.

"Good. You're here." She quickly ushered me out into the corridor. "Let's strategize before we go in there."

"Where's Darius and his lawyer?" I asked in hushed tones. I may not have practiced much, but I thought it was a no-no for only one party to come before a judge. For a white girl, Casey was certainly giving me a good evil eye. She none-too-gently steered me down the disinfectant redolent hallway.

She leaned in closely, her breath smelling of the strawberry candy my grandmother used to keep on her vestibule table during the holidays. "Look, I'm friends with the judge's family and he offered to hear you out. I say don't look a gift horse in the mouth. It's not our job to worry about his ethics. *Capice?*"

I may not have been Italian, but I understood. Casey didn't need to tell me twice. I pulled out my compact, fixed my lipstick, smoothed my hair, adjusted my collar, and got ready to meet the judge—solo.

Despite being licensed to practice all of these years, I'd never set foot in a courtroom, unless I counted the short time I clerked for Judge Grant. I'd been allowed to stand near the bench from time to time, to hand my former boss memos or notes, or to watch the lawyers argue. But this was the first time I'd be walking into a courtroom from the public entrance as a litigant.

The dark paneled room was empty—the sound of our heels thudded dully on the ancient wood floor.

Casey ushered me into a wooden slatted seat with an uncomfortably high armrest. My silk-clad butt slid on the seat worn glass smooth over the years. We waited. And waited. I couldn't imagine what was keeping the judge so damn busy. The hallway outside his courtroom had looked like a ghost town. But after a few months with Judge Grant, I wasn't immune to the power games a moderately paid civil servant could play.

With too much fanfare for my taste, the judge's clerk and bailiff rushed into the room, compelling us to rise. Then the judge swept in, his black judges robes swishing around his skinny legs. Having seen the unpretentious rayon robes judges wear up close during my clerkship—if pressed, I'd have to say this little old white man had his custom tailored. They were just that much shinier, and that much swishier than the federal judges over on Superior Avenue. The white starched collar was the icing on the cake. Throw a powdered wig on him and he could have stepped straight from a late night PBS English drama.

There wasn't any court reporter present and I didn't dare ask anyone why.

"So you're Claire Henshaw? Is that right?"

I looked up, startled that the judge had spoken to me directly. Casey squeezed my hand under the table and nodded almost imperceptibly.

"Yes, Your Honor, I'm Claire Henshaw. Luke's mother."

The judge looked down at his nearly empty bench. The wood gleamed in its bare state. "Obviously the county can't even get me a name plate. I'm Judge Eamon Brody—that's Judge Brody to you." He flipped through a very thin file. "It says here in your petition to the court that you're seeking to curtail or have supervised visits? Which is it?"

I shook my head, confused. Casey had said that supervised visitation was the best I could hope for, but here Judge Brody was dangling cutting off visitation in front of me. Darius had broken my baby's arm. It was time to teach him a lesson. He couldn't be some half-assed father anymore.

"I'd like to suspend visitation, Your Honor." There, I'd said it. I'd gone for broke.

11

"Hey man, c'mon over to the conference room at eleven. We've got a little something brewing," Charles Fitzgerald said as he walked by my desk, a sheaf of papers clutched in his hand.

I pulled my gaze from my computer screen and checked my watch, ten fifty-five. That was short notice. I was in the midst of typing up my response to a defendant's motion for exculpatory evidence. He'd asked for everything and the kitchen sink, and I was giving it to him—burying his lawyer in papers just to be a dick. All the discovery in the world was not going to make the defendant anything but a thousand percent guilty.

"What's going on?" I asked Chas' retreating figure. Fitzgerald was the Deputy Chief of the U.S. Attorney's office's criminal division. The meeting in the conference room wouldn't be about the kind of petty matter I was working on. The kind of cases I handled were discussed in the break room over coffee and donuts.

He didn't answer, just waved me over.

I painstakingly saved my work—because these government computers were ancient, and who knew when the outdated word processing program would blow up in my face.

In my mind, 'conference room,' has always conjured up images of rich wood paneling, thick piled carpet and subtle lighting. Despite the popularity of all manner of television shows featuring prosecutors, cops and criminalists in sumptuous surroundings, reality fell far short. We're still government employees in government digs. Our conference room was a combination of ancient wood furniture, scarred by years of use, and new ugly fiberboard furniture replacing whatever became unusable—a cross between a jumble sale and the clearance aisle at Target.

When I finally made my way in, I was surprised to see much of the senior criminal team already assembled at the table. What role would they want a rookie like me to play? I dreaded the idea that they'd have me doing the legal equivalent of water boy. It sucked being the new guy. It's not like my assignments weren't on actual cases, but much of my work was the civilian equivalent of making copies. Chas gestured for me to sit and got up to close the door—a rare occurrence. We represented the government, not private individuals; nothing much of what went on in the office was confidential, at least among all of us.

Chas noisily cleared his throat and the individual conversations died down.

"I have you all gathered here because we have a hell of a case coming down the pike, and I'm going to need all the help and input I can get." He gestured to an unfamiliar man sitting to his right. "For those of you who haven't worked with him, this is Lou Valdespino. He works in the FBI's Criminal Investigative Division—doing government corruption." Cuyahoga County sometimes reminded me of a Midwestern Boston. Investigating malfeasance on the part of elected and appointed officials could occupy a whole bunch of full-time agents. "I'll let him take over from here," Chas finished.

Valdespino, more wide than tall, rose from the table, adjusted his striped knit tie, and ran a meaty hand over his salt and pepper buzz cut. He spoke without notes.

"A couple of years ago, we got a call about a local probate judge here in Cuyahoga County who was reported to have been molesting some of the litigants who came before him. We thought about taking him down then, but he was smart. He chose only victims who were trying to defeat guardianship. Any person trying to convince a court that they're competent makes a bad witness. The judge has since moved to juvenile court, and again we've heard rumblings that he's trying to take advantage of women with children in the system. We're looking to get the bastard this time."

Rachel Schaefer, an assistant AUSA I hadn't worked with yet, raised her hand and spoke before Valdespino could acknowledge her.

"It sounds like all you've got is idle gossip from people who already have 'issues.'" Rachel made air quotes with her fingers. "What makes you think we should take up the case?"

Valdespino's composure slipped a little. He seemed like the kind of man who didn't like a woman questioning him.

"Attorney General Liam Brody's name isn't on that door out there," Rachel said, pointing toward the front entrance. "What do you think we can do that the state's top cop can't?"

Valdespino ran his hand over his hair again. "The name B-R-O-D-Y," he spelled out as if Rachel were verbally challenged. "That's why we're here talking to you guys."

"What about BCI?" she probed. The Ohio Bureau of Criminal Investigation was the state's equivalent of the FBI.

"They passed."

"Then don't you think you should take this to the county, or to the AG? If it's some kind of conflict they're supposed to call in a special prosecutor."

After 9/11 the office's caseload had almost doubled. The usual drug cases were still our bread and butter, but now we were also prosecuting a bunch of terrorism suspects as well. During my short tenure so far, I'd learned that anything we could pawn off to another agency, we did.

The FBI agent scratched at the black and grey stubble on his chin. "We've hit dead ends there," he said, giving Chas a sidelong glance. Rachel was our office's Miss Know it All. "I don't think you all are getting this, so let me lay it out for you. The target is Judge Eamon Brody. His brother Liam, *the* Attorney General, declined to prosecute. And his temporary successor at the county, Lori Pope, has passed too."

Almost anyone who'd ever read the *Plain Dealer* knew the Brodys were connected in the state. There wasn't a branch of government that family didn't have a hand in. Unelected government bureaucrats didn't bite the hand that fed them. The room descended into unusual silence. The problems with the case were obvious to anyone with two brain synapses firing.

"I still don't see how this is a federal case," Rachel said into the silence. "What we're looking at here is simple sexual assault. *I* could talk to the AG this time and see if they'll bite. If the guy is convicted, he'll be disbarred for a crime of moral turpitude. No more victims." She brushed her palms together in a dismissive gesture.

"Look, we're used to handling public corruption, RICO, or VAWA stuff—but this case isn't easy to put in one class or another. But one thing's for sure—it's beyond the local level," Valdespino said.

Chas spoke up again, probably regretting the flat reporting structure he'd established. "With all due respect, Rachel, that's not the path we're going to take. I've brought Lou in because this is something *our* office should handle." Though our office meetings were usually democratic, Chas spoke with the finality of a decision already made.

Ready to move on past arguing, he looked my way. "Miles, I seem to recall that there was a federal judge somewhere in Texas prosecuted for something similar. Can you make some calls to our AUSAs out there—maybe do a Westlaw search? There's got to be something we can do to get this guy. Just because we're not the county or the state," he paused, looking meaningfully at Rachel, "doesn't mean connected bad guys should be able walk with impunity."

In the realm of heavy lifting, the assignment wasn't so bad. I'm sure Chas picked me because of my law enforcement background. I'd been a cop longer than I'd been a lawyer and could still connect—at least on the phone—with the guys in blue at any agency. In person, my brown skin and Jewfro didn't always go over so well.

Chas disbanded the troops, but motioned for Valdespino and me to stay. We shook hands, warily. His grip was hard, but mine was harder. Though we were ostensibly on the same team, the natural antagonism between cop and prosecutor, black and white, local cop and fed still divided us.

"Lou, Miles Siegel was on the force in Philadelphia for a number of years. I think you guys would make an excellent team—figuring out how we can put this guy behind bars. I'll give you guys the room for another half hour or so."

He'd left us there because I was a man without an office. Naturally, as professionals, the AUSAs had their own offices. While the federal government was in the process of constructing a spanking new building on West Superior, there wasn't anything left in the budget to get me an office, even temporarily. Embarrassingly, I was stuck at an intern's desk near the entrance to the library.

"Lou will brief you on the investigation, Miles. Thanks." Chas ducked out of the room before we could object to his directive. We would see how well a 'working' relationship would go. I was used the Feebs treating us local law enforcement like the Keystone Cops. As an AUSA, though, I'd be calling the shots. It was a nice change of pace.

"So you were on the force?" Valdespino asked. He seemed up for a game of *quien es mas macho*. I'd play.

"Yeah, I did five in Philadelphia."

"You make detective?"

I nodded. "After a year on patrol," I said. Because I'd had a degree from Swarthmore before I joined the force, I'd breezed through the academy training and gotten my gold shield after passing the promotional exam. Despite my parents' insistence that I had disavowed their peacenik tendencies and thrown away my expensive education, I had never had any desire to die at the wrong end of a gun.

What attracted me to the force was that I liked puzzles, and working as a police detective gave me the chance to challenge myself in ways that my fellow alumni stuck in banking and marketing were not.

Valdespino gave me an assessing look. Having made up his mind about me, he sat down at the table and opened a manila file in front of him that I hadn't noticed at first. I took that as an invitation to pull up a chair next to him.

The first thing he slipped out was the official photo of the suspect. At first glance, he looked like every other American elected official garbed in a dark blue suit, red power tie, with the requisite, slightly out of focus American flag behind him. I silently scrutinized the photo, letting Valdespino lay out the evidence at his own pace. "Guy looks squeaky clean here," Valdespino finally said. Then he pulled out a few more pictures—the victims. The two he handed me were both young, dark-skinned black women in their late teens or early twenties.

"Who are they?"

He propped up the top picture. The smiling girl, standing in front of a ramshackle wood framed house, looked no older than fifteen.

"How old is she?"

"This is Tashonda Williams. She's barely eighteen in this picture. She and her grandmother had come to the Probate court about guardianship of Tashonda's minor child. The child had been hurt in an accident at a public pool. The city paid a huge settlement and the mom and grandma were arguing over the mother taking over the accounts. They each met with the judge separately, and Tashonda got control of the money."

"How did she come to you?" I asked. Victims were the unstable third leg in the balance of justice.

"The girl was still living with her grandmother, but she started acting strange. She was getting weird phone calls in the middle of the night, disappearing, getting into unknown cars."

"Sounds like normal teenage behavior."

"That's what the police said when the grandmother called. She was one persistent lady, though. Evidently, the girl got religion after the baby and had been devout ever since.

"O-o-kay," I said, holding back the obvious comment about devout girls not always being so devout.

"Eventually, the police ran the plates—just to shut her up, I think—then when they came back belonging to various members of the Brody family—they dropped it like a hot potato."

"How did you guys pick it up? Last time I checked, you were all on twenty-four-seven counterterrorism patrol."

"Some of us want to do *anything* other than round up and harass innocent Muslims based on their neighbors' paranoia—so when this call came in from the grandmother, I took it."

"Okay," I said again, drawing out each of the two syllables. Maybe this Valdespino guy was on the up and up. I'd too had my fill of counterterrorism training while I was in Philly. The way the federal government threw money at us, you would have thought southwest Philly was Osama's next target. Of course, the chief of police willingly took the money. Only a moron turned down federal funds. But the downside is that we spent several weekends a year playacting elaborate disaster and civil emergency scenarios.

"Once we brought the girl down to the bureau, she folded like a cheap suit. The judge, according to her, blackmailed her into a sexual relationship by threatening to take away both her kid and the kid's money."

"But he stopped?"

"Once the grandmother found out, she put a stop to it. She took the girl's phone, and locked her and the baby down."

"Wow," I said in awe. When money was involved, it was often difficult for families to put aside their differences for the greater good. Plus, I had to admire any grandmother who was able to control a willful teenage girl.

"I think the dispute wasn't really about the money, but about the grandmother's worry over the girl's level of maturity."

"What happened between Tashonda—that was her name, right?—and the judge?" When I'd been a detective in serious crimes, I always tried to keep the name of the victim at the forefront of the investigation. It was too easy to allow them to become statistical open cases that needed to be closed.

"It was a weird combination of seduction and coercion. I don't know how to categorize it. First of all, he owns this broken down house on the near west side. We haven't had a warrant to get in, but from what I can see—it's bare bones, mattresses on the floor, thrift store furniture and the like. He takes the vic there—like it's a date—gives her alcohol, has sex with her and brings her home. But he also calls her on the phone—talks about his day, demands phone sex, mixes in threats—it's an odd set of behaviors."

"And the girl was naïve enough to think that the judge could take her child *and* money away at the drop of a hat?"

"I know she sounds unsophisticated, but you haven't been in this county long, have you? It's probably a stretch that he could ruin her life in one fell swoop—but a judge's word is rarely challenged in common pleas court—he could have found any number of reasons in his *discretion* to make her and her kid's life a living hell. Plus, you have to remember, she didn't think she had the grandmother on her side."

I was starting to catch on. "Basically, he's like any other predator—get your prey, vulnerable and alone—strike."

Valdespino nodded in common understanding.

"You talked about other victims who made bad witnesses. Who are those women? They are all women, right?" I had to ask. Predators were often equal opportunity harassers.

Valdespino nodded in grudging admiration. Being a lawyer and being a cop are very different—but I hadn't yet forgotten that difference. Lawyers were worried about what they could prove in court. That was less important to cops. Sure, we wanted our cases to stand up before judge and jury. But a mountain of evidence, though inadmissible, could cow a defendant—especially if they hadn't lawyered up. A confession and a guilty plea beat trying to prove something beyond a reasonable doubt, any day.

He walked to a briefcase he must have stashed in the corner and pulled out some other manila files. He thrust them at me. I brought them to my chest. "I'll look at these tonight. Is it okay if I talk to these victims?" I asked.

"Yeah. Their contact info is in there. Just don't get their hopes up," he said impassively. "I've already told them that prosecution was a long shot."

"Not to rain on your parade here, but Rachel did have a point. What federal law do you think Brody violated? Just because he's guilty, and we're the big bad feds doesn't amount to much without a statute behind us."

Valdespino threw up his hands in mock surrender—something I don't imagine he did often. "You're the lawyer. There are thousands of federal crimes. Pick one."

12

Claire
November 1, 2003

Luke was tucked away in his room, with Nick Junior blaring as loud as I could stand it. I'd already told him that his dad wasn't coming around anymore. He'd cried a little, maybe a lot, but I knew a clean break was best. It was time to get Darius out of Luke's life—and mine—once and for all.

Someone like Miles would make a much better father for my son. Miles was the kind of guy I should have brought home the first time. His parents were liberal, east coast, and educated. They probably had more money than mine, especially with his dad being white, Jewish, and all. But more than that, I thought we made a good couple. A Cosby show kind of couple.

I was ready to be a stay-at-home mom. I wouldn't even be averse to giving Luke a little brother or sister, or both.

My man was an AUSA. He could work anywhere in the country. And since neither of us was from Cleveland, I was sure we wouldn't miss it. Maybe after we got married, we could move to Chicago or Philadelphia so the little ones could be around their grandparents. Or maybe we'd blaze our own trail in a smaller city like Boston. San Diego or Houston would be better. I was tired of the cold. November had just arrived and I was already shivering in my little townhouse.

I knew that Miles would eventually fall in love with Luke. They already got along well. Then he could adopt my little one and we could all be one big happy family.

The door chimed its classical tune, snapping me from my daydream. Ignoring the dread pooling in my belly, I rose from the dining room chair, papers in hand.

Darius hadn't even made it up the walkway when I pulled open the door. He lifted a single finger toward me, while talking to an invisible person.

I extended my hand, pushing the papers toward his chest, "You need—"

Neon blue light winked at me from his ear. A whole hand came up to my face, replacing his single digit. He was *not* on the phone ignoring me. I could not believe this sorry excuse for a man. I snatched the Bluetooth piece from his ear and threw it to the ground.

"What in the hell?" Darius' handsome face turned thunderous.

"You ought to be glad I didn't stomp on it," I said, half raising my foot from the threshold. If his son was so damned important, he needed to be present. "Who are you talking to anyway?"

"None of your damn business." So, a girl, probably a different one than last time. He went through them like tissues. I should know. I'd been discarded four years ago.

Thrusting the papers at him, I said, "Maybe you'll want to read this first before you get back on the phone." I turned and made for the front steps. Hopefully he would read it, or get someone to read it to him and that would be that. We could fight it out in court five or six months from now when our case finally came up for hearing. Never was I so glad that bureaucracy gummed up the work of the justice system.

"You better be going to get my son."

"We are not on the plantation, massa." I pushed the door nearly closed. "Why don't you read those papers?" I opened the door a crack more, not able to resist one last dig, "You will not be seeing Luke today or anytime soon."

I don't know if he responded, because after the rattle of the chain on the slamming door, I was again engulfed in near silence. I sat at the dining room table. Once the roaring of blood in my ears ceased, I could hear the too loud commercials from Nickelodeon. I wanted to run upstairs and pull my son from the ceaseless marketing, but resisted. Glow in the dark cereal had to be better for you than seeing your mom on one side of the door, your dad on the other.

The doorbell rang, one peal after another.

"Mama? Who's—"

"No one, honey. You can watch whatever's next." I knew Luke would never come down now. Recipient of his mama's unusual largesse, I wouldn't see him again unless the power went out. And even then, he might wait out the IllCo repair trucks. The child settled, I jerked the door open to stop the noise. Wisely, I'd left the chain on. My mama didn't raise no fool.

Darius wasn't on the phone anymore. His former family had finally commanded his attention. "I read your *papers*. I always knew I'd regret that you were a damned lawyer. Am I reading this correc'?" His voice had gone from belligerent to deadly calm. I could feel the blood pounding in my head, pulse throbbing in my neck. This stony faced Darius was scaring the shit out of me. I'd only seen him like this one other time: when I'd holed up in my parents apartment and threatened to keep the baby in Chicago. Getting between him and his child was the equivalent of throwing down.

I took three deep breaths, marshaling my reserves. This was only his 'concerned father' act. He wouldn't dare hurt me or the baby. "I don't know if you're reading them *correct*. I'm not sure a diploma from MLK High School can make it understandable. But I'll explain it to you. You can't see Darius without supervision as long as this court order stands."

"Why are you doing this?"

"Did you forget that broken arm? You let my son fall out of a window while some woman I don't know *watched* him, and you hung out with your boys."

"It was an accident, dream girl." Darius had more voices than Rich Little. This one sounded more the smooth brotha on the bus who turned my head, and not a thug who could take me out. "Coulda happened to anyone. C'mon, you're not seriously going to cut off visitation."

I looked up, thanking God for Judge Brody. "I already did."

"You're raising a little black boy in there. Don't cut him off from his father. I didn't have a father. It ain't right."

"Neither was breaking my little boy's arm."

"I didn't do it on purpose. Accidents happen. Little boys are curious. My brothers, cousins, everyone ended up in the ER when I was coming up."

"With a mother like you had, it's no wonder." I knew when I thought it, well before I said it, that I'd made a mistake. My good sense couldn't close my mouth fast enough. Darius would take a lot of shit, but between denying him his son and talking about his drug dealing absentee father and his not-so-great mother, I'd pushed all his hot buttons today.

That became abundantly clear when he kicked the door. "I'm done with you for today. Get. My. Son."

I stepped back and pushed at the door, ready to close him out of my day and hopefully out of my life once and for all. But his size ten Timberland had another idea.

"Get your damn foot out of my door."

"Not until you get my son."

"You read the papers. *I* decide when you can see him. And that's not right now."

"Mama," Luke called again. Any minute he'd be down here. I never wanted him to see his parents fighting again.

"Just go, Darius. My son doesn't need to see you like this." I pushed the door one last time, thankful he was giving up. Maybe once the reality set in for him, that he was out of his depth, the cost of hiring a—

Splinters flew everywhere when the chain flew away from the wood frame. Darius pushed me aside, striding up the stairs, gunning for Luke.

"Shit," I heard myself say. Then I grabbed for the phone, dialing nine-one-one. The dispatcher was dispassionate. She repeated back phrases at me like visitation, violation of court order, custody issue. She was taking too long, asking too many questions. She wasn't listening. "I think he has a gun," I cut in.

"The police are on their way," she said with urgency. Finally.

I hung up, running upstairs. Darius was in Luke's room, pulling open drawers and tossing clothes into a large cotton bag I'd used to store the hundred packs of disposable diapers I used to buy.

"You have to leave here, Darius."

Luke had turned away from the engagingly bright animation and was looking between us like a spectator at a ping-pong match.

"You can't make me."

"This is my house, my son. You need to get out now."

"Why should I leave? We agreed to weekend visitation. It's my weekend. You can't change the rules just because you feel like it."

"The police are coming. If I were you—"

Darius dropped the oversized bag and the out of season clothes in his hand. He grabbed my arm, shaking me like a rag doll. "You did what?"

I didn't have to respond. The sound of boots clomping up the steps was his answer.

"Claire Henshaw? Cleveland Police. Are you okay?" a woman's voice called from the hall.

"Help!" I shouted, trying to twist from Darius' grasp.

Luke's door flew open and police, guns at the ready, ran into the room. Before I could figure out what in the hell was going on, Darius' hand left my upper arm. Faster than Rodney King could protest, my baby daddy's face was pressed against the multicolor balloons etched in Luke's carpet. Handcuffs were snapped on his wrists and a foot was at his back. Another officer was searching his pockets. A money clip, loose change, and one fat blunt hit the rug.

"Mama, Mama, Mama, what are they doing to Daddy? Mama!" Luke's screams pierced the fog that had clouded my brain while the officers were subduing my baby's father.

"Ma'am," the woman said to me. "You need to take your son out of this room. We'll talk to you downstairs."

I pulled Luke's sturdy body from his bed, lifting him over his prone father and took the steps two at a time. Anything to shield my baby from that.

Later, Darius sat in the backseat of a police car, its lights casting a blue then red then blue glow through our house and the street. I watched the officers discourage my neighbors' gawking stares.

I held Luke on my lap, my arms wrapped tightly around his shaking little body. I knew this had to have been scary for him, but I hoped he would one day forgive me. Maybe when he was seventeen, and Miles and I were sending him on to college instead of visiting him in jail.

In as calm a voice as I could muster, I answered the police officers' questions and explained what had happened with Darius. When they'd heard their fill, I ushered the police out of there. They were going to take him to the county jail. The police would charge him with felonious assault and misdemeanor drug possession. Though I was horrified that I'd put another black man into the system, I was ready to move on.

13

I plotted the way from my apartment to Tracy Price's. Valdespino had passed her name along without much comment. So I was taking some time out of my Saturday morning to see if there was anything to this case. I didn't quite have Rachel's urge to kick this case, but I didn't know if there was much to it. From that first meeting with Valdespino it felt like the FBI was gunning for Brody because the family was connected.

Chas was a fan of the brick by brick theory. He didn't believe that cases were prosecuted with airtight confessions or flashy courtroom presentations. He thought it was about building an immovable wall of evidence that neither a defendant nor his counsel could break through. So I was on my way to find out if this case would be built on bricks or was merely on stilts in shifting sands. If it were the latter, we'd wait for a flood of disinterest to take the case away.

Putting down the map, I dropped my car keys, and buttoned my coat when I realized the victim was only around the corner. The walk from Euclid Heights Boulevard to Lancashire Road took only a minute.

"I'm Mrs. Perkins," an older black woman said letting me into the warm second floor apartment. It smelled of coffee and grits, eggs, and sausage. My stomach rumbled.

"Can I get you some breakfast?"

"No thank you," I said. As a cop, I'd rarely said yes to offers of free food and drink. Even though I was hungry and missed my mother's Sunday breakfasts and home cooking, I pushed aside my craving and asked for Tracy.

"She's in bed. I'll get her up for you." As she walked toward the back of the apartment, I heard her soft voice. "Make yourself comfortable."

Comfortable did not make for a good interrogation, so I chose a place at the dining room table. Like a good witness, Tracy, rumpled bathrobe covering her pajamas, sat across from me at the table.

"Miles Siegel," I extended my hand across the table in introduction.

There was a long delay while Tracy considered my outstretched hand.

"Shake his hand, Tracy," Mrs. Perkins said. Then to me, "She's had a very hard time since the accident."

"What happened?" I asked the older woman. For some reason I'd thought Tracy had been born with a mental deficiency.

"A private ambulance hit the side of the number seven bus. She was the only one seriously injured."

"Head trauma," I said turning toward Mrs. Perkins.

She nodded. "Happened when she was seventeen on her way to school. Before that she was on a good path. She was on honor roll at Central Catholic. Took the bus there religiously because we didn't have a car back then."

"How long was she—" I glanced back at Tracy mortified that we were talking about the woman like she wasn't there. "Were you in the hospital?"

Tracy looked from me to Mrs. Perkins.

"About four months between Cleveland Clinic and rehab. Took that long for her to walk and talk again."

Mrs. Perkins excused herself and brought a plate of food and a glass of orange juice to the table. Tracy ignored us and tackled the plate like she hadn't eaten in a year.

I asked a question to drown out the rumble of my stomach. "Why were you in Probate court?"

"Because I wanted to move out. With all that money we should have a nicer place," Tracy said in her first full sentence.

My forehead pinched into a frown, as I struggled to cover my confusion.

Mrs. Perkins knowing expression let me know I'd failed to hide anything.

"Sounded totally normal, right?"

Uncomfortable, I looked back and forth between the older and younger woman.

"It's okay. It takes a long time for Tracy to put those kinds of thoughts together," Mrs. Perkins said matter-of-factly. "Ask her a direct question."

I looked at Tracy. "What was your favorite subject in high school?"

Tracy looked back at me for a long minute or two. She blinked a few times, but no response was forthcoming. She picked up her fork and resumed eating.

"I—"

"Doctors could never much explain what happened to Tracy's brain. Something wrong with her speech center, some said. She can understand everything like she used to. But her speech is compromised."

My hopes deflated. Without good recall or an undamaged speech center, Tracy would fail miserably as a witness.

"Can I have coffee?" Tracey asked.

Mrs. Perkins came back with three mugs on a tray along with cream. I violated my own rule and helped myself. "What happened with Judge Brody?"

"After the accident, we got three settlements," she started. "One from the driver's insurance company, one from the ambulance company, and one from RTA."

"Two million dollars," Tracy interjected.

That was chump change for what had happened to her. I held my tongue. Mrs. Perkins seemed like the kind of lady who'd make it last Tracy's whole life. "After the lawyers got paid," Mrs. Perkins started. Tracy wanted to move out of this Section Eight apartment and into a house. She thought we should get a new car. She wanted to—how do the kids say it?—live large. I thought we were doing just fine. This apartment may not be perfect, but it's nice."

I had to agree with her there. It was the first place I'd seen that looked like it had a true mix of higher and lower income tenants. The outside didn't look any different than my apartment building around the corner. Graffiti and junked cars hadn't marred the landscape.

"One of the people at Tracy's outpatient clinic got a hold of her debit card. She lost nearly twelve thousand dollars before I found out. So I paid a lawyer to give me control of her money and medical needs, now that she'd turned eighteen."

"I'm a grown woman," Tracy said.

"You are grown," Mrs. Perkins said. "I gave the lawyer all the information and he took our case to court."

"Judge Brody," I prompted.

Mrs. Perkins was beating around the bush, I thought, because she felt guilty. She'd probably been doing the best she could, and still the girl had been victimized not once, but twice.

Her sigh was long. She took a sip of coffee and set her mug on the table carefully. "I work nights," she started. "From what I can piece together, the judge started calling her. Told her that if she did what he said, she could have her money."

"How'd you find out?"

"I came home early one night and Tracy wasn't here. I'd called the police and was waiting outside, when an old Lincoln pulled up. Tracy got out only after that man was done feeling up her titties. They were hanging out for anyone to see. When I looked to see who was in the car, an old white man started right back at me."

"Judge Brody said he'll take care of me," Tracy said.

"I didn't recognize him right away, but when the police showed up, they took the license plate. Things changed right then. They'd been helpful up and until they ran those tags. Then they couldn't get out of here fast enough talking some mess about Tracy being an adult. I asked a friend on the force to poke a little. He gave me the judge's name and told me I'd walked into a big fat mess."

"How did you—"

"Changed the phone number," Mrs. Perkins interjected. "Went to court without her. Told him he'd gotten her pregnant and the DNA would tell all. Dared that man to try it again. My ma always said bullies were cowards. When he found out I'd pull him down to the gutter with right along with me, he left her alone."

"How long—"

"Probably two or three months is what I can figure from looking back at the caller ID."

"What happened to the baby?"

"There weren't no baby. But nothing scares a guilty man more than proof."

I had to hand it to Mrs. Perkins. She was one savvy woman. But the visual of Judge Brody fondling this girl out in public like he owned her made my blood boil. Every movie I'd ever seen where a slave master took what he wanted from an unwilling woman came to mind. It was too damn bad hearsay rules prevented Mrs. Perkins from testifying. I was sure a jury would want to lock Judge Brody up and throw away the key after they heard what he did to Tracy. But I knew her short view of some fondling in the dark night wouldn't be enough to indict much less convict the man. I stood up ready to put this judge, this violator of the public trust behind bars, not matter how many bricks it took.

The minute I closed their door, the phone rang in my pocket.

Claire. Another emergency. I jogged to my apartment, retrieved my keys and gunned the car through the throngs of leisure shoppers to Claire's house. When I got past the traffic, my mind shifted back to what Claire had said during this call. It wasn't Luke this time. It was Darius and the police were there.

Domestic violence. As I wound my car through a hodge-podge of urban blight and renewal, I thought I must have heard wrong. Darius had been arrested, Claire had said. He was an ass, sure. An irresponsible ass, absolutely. But a wife beater hadn't ever crossed my mind. My cop nose wouldn't have made that call. Either I was losing my touch or something wasn't quite right.

Another car pulled up to the driveway of Claire's town-house the same time as mine. I nearly collided with the erratic driver. One look at her car and I figured she didn't care much what happened to it. Her car ground to a halt, and she turned in her seat to make eye contact with me through the back window. She shrugged with a little grin. Yeah, she knew she was a crazy driver. Frizzy blond hair and a cute smile wasn't going to make me forgive the fact that she could've slammed right into me if I weren't being careful. The woman, mute mouth and gesturing hands appeared to apologize profusely, got out of the car and walked to Claire's door.

Who was that? Claire didn't have many friends. I was sure I'd met them all. Maybe she was some kind of domestic violence counselor the police had sent out. I'd seen it in Philly. You had to pin these women down or else they'd be back with their abuser before the ink was dry on the charging papers.

I parked across the street, safely away from the blond woman's car, and got out. Claire opened the door, swept the woman in, glanced right, then left and swiftly closed it again. What in the hell? Ever since that day in the emergency room, I'd been thinking about taking a time out from Claire. All signs pointed to her desire to get serious. And maybe a mom with a kid should get serious about her relationships.

But I was finally starting my career up right. Got a case with some legs, and needed to focus on that. I'd thought about getting married someday. That day, though, was far in the future. And if I didn't see one with Claire, I knew better than to stick with her, or get any more involved with that kid.

I sighed. I needed to see what had happened, what kind of state she was in before I suggested a time out. Pulling my phone from the passenger seat, I had a quick look at my e-mail. Damn, something from Valdespino. I turned off the screen before I read it. It was the weekend. Work would have to wait the couple of hours it took to sort out this whole Claire thing. I tossed my Blackberry into the glove compartment.

Taking a deep breath, I made my way to the door. I got the same open door, glance, glance, that the woman had got, and then I was ushered into Claire's home.

Claire's kiss was too intimate. Grateful when the other woman made a shuffling noise with her chair, I pulled away. Despite the visitor, Claire used her fingers to wipe away lipstick from my mouth.

"Thank goodness you could both come," Claire said, looking from me in the vestibule through the arched opening toward the woman at the table.

Walking through the opening, I stuck out my hand, "Miles Siegel." The woman stood, scattering papers on the floor, and shook my hand firmly.

"Casey Cort."

"Miles," Claire started, retreating to her place at the dark wood table. A shredded pile of tissue told me she'd been there for some time before either one of us got there. "I told you about Casey. She's the one who represented Judge Grant."

This wasn't putting two and two together. It was more like algebra—moving my mind from Darius and jail to Claire's former employer. "Sure," I said, still uncomprehending. I'd figure it out later. The one lesson I'd learned from watching my parents interact was that men were better off saying little. Less chance of inserting a foot into the wrong orifice.

"I hired her to handle Luke's custody case." Since when did she even *have* a custody case? "I talked to my parents," she continued. "We all agreed that Darius was too irresponsible to take care of my boy." Images of quadratic equations unspooled in my mind. If Darius and Claire were coefficients…. "Casey filed an emergency petition. Judge Brody did an *ex parte* hearing, suspending unsupervised visitation."

I looked at Casey more closely. She was better in the courtroom than the open road, I guess.

"How long until the full hearing?" I couldn't imagine any court that dealt with children was a fan of cutting off one parent's access for long—axe murders and serial killers notwithstanding.

Claire interjected before Casey could answer. "Doesn't matter much now. Darius has the criminal court to face."

I unbuttoned the top of my flannel shirt, trying to free my body of its sudden stricture. I'd have loosened my belt, if I could. My heart knocked around my chest a little.

Arrows were pointing to Claire having got Darius arrested on purpose. I knew this was a bad, bad time, but I needed to get this off my chest, lay the groundwork now.

"Claire, I need to talk to you for a minute."

"I'll, uh, make some coffee," Casey said before she disappeared into the adjoining kitchen. Water splashed, glassware rattled. The message was loud and clear. She wasn't listening.

Claire's face was expectant. I got the sense that with Darius firmly out of the way, she was waiting for me to step in.

"Work is really heating up right now," I said, pulling at my collar.

"What are you working on?"

"It's kind of top secret." I didn't want to get into it with her. I knew she worked only on the periphery of the juvenile system with the moms she advised. But sharing details of a case in progress wouldn't be cool.

"You can tell me," she said.

But I couldn't, or didn't want to, at least. "Actually, Claire, I can't."

"So if you can't tell me what you're working on, then what do you want to talk to me about? Not five seconds ago, you told me your job was *heating up*."

"Us, is what I wanted to talk to you about," I said, resisting the urge to cross my arms in front of my chest. "I think we need a break."

A myriad of expressions crossed her face, ending in disbelief. "What do you mean by a break?"

"I think I want to break up."

"You think or you know?"

"I know."

"Why are you doing this?" Her voice was plaintive. "Why now? What about the future we'd always talked about?"

Claire had done all the talking about a mythical future. I'd done a lot of listening and nodding. But now probably wasn't the time to draw those fine lines of distinction.

"I know that you need stability right now. A dad for your kid. I can't provide that. I've only been with the U.S. Attorney for a bit. I'm only getting my legs under me."

"I thought you liked Luke …"

"I do like him. He's an awesome little boy. But he has a father."

"Darius?" Claire's voice was entering screech range. Was it Neil Sedaka who'd sang about breaking up? That man couldn't have been more right. Damn for leaving the Blackberry in the car. If that had beeped again, I'd have an excuse for getting out of here. For a long moment, we looked at each other. Then the tears started, streaking their way down Claire's cheeks.

Casey materialized right then, grasping Claire's shoulders, leading her toward the kitchen.

"Maybe you should go," she whispered at me urgently.

I took my cue and showed myself out.

I started my car, unsure of where I was going to go on a late Saturday morning. Maybe I could stop in at the office, get some research done while it was quiet. I wasn't a weekend worker, normally. My parents really discouraged that sort of thing. They believed in a very European lifestyle of family and leisure first, work a distant second. Which was fine if you had a family and friends and fun, but I didn't have any of that in Cleveland. Breaking up with Claire cut down on my social circle enormously. Her friends were the only people I'd met outside of work since I'd come here. And I gathered those women wouldn't be inviting me to any neighborhood barbecues after today.

14

"What do you want?" Tom asked, putting the tall, skinny menu down between us.

I picked it up from the shiny wood table. If wine intimidated me, this wine bar nearly killed me. There had to be thirty white *and* thirty reds on the menu. Before I'd met my neighbors, Jason and Greg, I'd only played at drinking wine. They'd taught me a little, but not enough to tackle this. How I'd ever thought I could be the perfect Brody wife, I'll never know.

"Why don't you choose?" I said. It's what he wanted anyway. Someone must have told him, probably the beautiful Lizzy Cofrancesco, that women wanted to be consulted. Because this asking what I wanted, first at Charley's Crab and now at the bar, was brand new. The Tom I'd dated before had never consulted me.

He picked a wine. I acquiesced. "I'll get a charcuterie plate as well," he said, walking away. I was looking around the bar, when Tom came back and gave me an unexpected full mouth kiss. No casual brush of the lips here. He'd used all of the tools at his disposal to seduce me, just a little, in a public bar. Dazed, I watched him go to place our order. The little devil of doubt was losing its battle. I needed to stop wondering what Tom wanted from me after all these years and instead, bask in the glow of a new relationship.

I put a hand to my tingling lips. I'd obviously never gotten over Tom. Sure, I'd been able to banish him from my mind for all those years. But clearly the man had seen the error of his ways and was ready to come around. He hadn't made any rules, set any time limits. If I wanted a relationship with him, maybe marriage, kids, the whole nine yards, all I needed to do was open myself up like all the magazines suggested.

A few people patted me on the shoulder in greeting. Tonight was happy hour for the bar association's young lawyers group. I'd been nervous all day. It was the first time Tom and I were out as a couple with our colleagues. It's not that I was so self involved to think that we'd be the talk of the town. Though our breakup was legendary in my mind and that of a few friends, I was sure no one remembered my lost job or law school humiliation. It was the idea of being a couple. Putting that out there. Facing the humiliation if it didn't work out, again.

Mentally batting away the negative self-talk, I looked around expectantly. I hoped my best friend Lulu showed. She and Tom didn't exactly get along, but I could have used the buffer. Someone to stand between me and either the best or worst decision of my life.

When the door opened, my head snapped up hopeful. No Technicolor patchwork billowing coat wrapped friend. Instead it was the guy who'd broken up with Claire last weekend.

When I discovered that my client wasn't in legal trouble herself, I'd tried to steer clear of the problems that had nothing to do with the custody of her son. And that tall, tan-skinned guy was one of the complications I'd avoided.

His eyes scanned the crowd. I wasn't sure who he was looking for, but he looked relieved not to have found him or her. When they locked with mine, I tried to look away, but they met and held. Next thing I knew, he was pulling a seat out from my table.

"Mind if I join you?" Since we'd gotten there, the bar stools and tables had filled with the young Cleveland lawyer crowd.

"Um, no," I said, looking around for Tom. He was nowhere to be found. Maybe he'd run into someone he knew or had gone to the bathroom.

"Wait, are you the woman who almost hit me the other day?" he asked, squinting at me in the dim light.

"Hit you? You were driving like you were Batman in the Batmobile coming to save the day."

"Seriously. That scrap metal Honda was going the wrong way up Chester."

"Did you call my car scrap metal?"

"That's what it is. Do you hold it together with shoe string and a clothes hangar?" I should have been insulted, but I felt mirth bubble in my stomach, instead.

"Can't afford that. More like postage stamps and spit," I retorted.

I gave him my sternest face. He did the same. His serious face was seriously funny. Before I knew what hit me, I was laughing. He'd done the same. Thrown back his head of big curly hair and guffawed.

When Tom came to the table followed by a waitress with two glasses of wine and a platter of food, my boyfriend wasn't laughing.

Coolly, he appraised Claire's friend. "Can I help you?" Surprise snapped my spine straight. Tom was usually way more suave. He came from a political family that never alienated anyone with the right to vote.

"Miles Siegel," he said and extended his hand.

"Tom Brody," Tom said, pulling Siegel's hand into a tight grip. "How do you know Casey?"

My mind raced. 'Client's friend' was not a good answer. Tom would not be happy if my clients were acquaintances, given the nature of my practice. While I looked back and forth between the men, Siegel stepped in.

"I'm a AUSA. We met through a former clerk of Judge Grant's." He pulled his hand back and helped himself to a slice of prosciutto.

"I'm in major crimes in the prosecutor's office. Haven't seen you at any joint task force meetings." Tom said, eyeing the tray then Miles.

"Started in September, after I quit the force."

"Cleveland police?"

"Philadelphia."

"Go to night school?"

"No. Penn after I left the force. Needed to see law enforcement from the streets before I went to law school and joined the AUSA."

Tom's eyes narrowed. In the high stakes game of legal rock, paper, scissors, Siegel had just smashed Tom's scissor with a rock.

Bacon wrapped dates congealed on the plate. Tom grabbed my shoulders in what I assume was supposed to be a hug. "Casey and I started dating while we were at Cleveland Marshall. We were on law review together." The fact that Tom made it seem like we'd been dating for the better part of the last decade didn't slip by me.

Siegel flagged down the waitress and ordered a pizza and beer. Why didn't I think of that? I'd have been way more comfortable if I could have ordered an old standby instead of staring at this plate of meat, cheese, and bread like a room full of strangers. I pulled away from Tom's arm, grabbed the little spatula shaped knife and tried to cut myself a wedge of cheese. Of course, it scooted off the small wooded cutting board. It would have landed on the floor, but for Siegel's hand eye coordination.

"Whoa, there. You cut nearly as well as you drive. Let me help you." He neatly sliced bread, and plopped a slice of salami and a thick wedge of cheese on it.

I took a big sip of wine and accepted the offering. Dainty bites weren't possible without getting crumbs all over my clothes, so I had my mouth full when Siegel addressed Tom.

"Are you related to Judge Eamon Brody?" he asked.

"He's my uncle." Tom shifted in his seat uncomfortably. That was weird. He usually loved to talk about his family and their influence in Ohio. "You have occasion to be in probate or juvenile court?"

Siegel sat back, looking like he was trying to hide something. "Nope. I think I must have read about his move from one court to another. Doesn't happen often, huh?"

"It's happened. My dad is presiding over in the county courts, and he's mentioned it a time or two. Judges are always looking to move up."

"Your dad?"

"Patrick Brody." Tom was back on sure footing.

"So your other uncle is the Attorney General, right?" Siegel seemed neither fascinated nor impressed.

"Yep. Used to be *the* county prosecutor before Lori Pope stepped in. But he didn't show me any favoritism, that's for sure." I almost sighed aloud. Tom's 'I'm one of the people,' speech wasn't convincing.

"You said you were in major crimes?" Siegel probed.

Tom nodded. "Serious felonies, murders, death penalty. Been working my way up for the last seven years."

Antagonism between the two men underlaid the outwardly friendly tone. I was happy when Lulu arrived at the same time as Siegel's order.

"Lulu Mueller," she said, taking the hand that Siegel was going to use to pick up his pizza and roping him into a soul brother handshake. "Tom," she said, making no similar move for my boyfriend's hand. "Good to see you after all these years." My best friend held a grudge.

"Lulu went to school with us, too," I said by way of introduction.

Miles looked her up and down, raising a single eyebrow. My best friend's ample hips were covered in a black skirt that shimmered with silver thread. Her cat-eye glasses sparkled with rhinestones. On the whole, I thought she was pretty subdued, but I could see how Siegel never having seen her before in her less subtle outfits might disagree. He went for his pizza again.

Lulu helped herself to one of the four slices of the foot wide pie. "Hope you don't mind, but that fussy stuff ain't for me," she said, pointing to Tom's contribution to the table.

I sat silent as Lulu and Miles exchanged resume information. She worked at one of the top firms in town but was oddly modest about this accomplishment.

"Are you investigating anything interesting?" Lulu asked.

"I'm working on that Christianson case, where the father murdered—" Tom started.

"I wasn't talking to you, Tom. No doubt your uncle paved the way for you to work on whatever's on the front page of the *Plain Dealer*. I was talking to our new guest, Miles."

"A lot of anti-terrorism. A little anti-corruption," Siegel answered, a small smile playing around his lips.

"You should investigate the Brodys here. They're as corrupt as they come."

Miles choked a little on his pizza.

"Hey, that's not fair, Lulu," Tom protested.

"I think family legal dynasties are anti-democratic, that's all."

"Everyone in my family was elected fair and square by the fine folks of Cuyahoga County and Ohio."

"Blind little old ladies pulling the party lever is as fair—"

Siegel watched them like it was a game of tennis. I caught the ball and took it out of play. "Guys. Let's just have a drink and play nice."

Tom and Lulu gave each other quelling looks, but stopped the bickering. I wanted Lulu to support our newly budding relationship. Accusing Tom's family of cronyism didn't seem the smoothest way to do that.

Listening to Siegel didn't seem high on Tom's list. While Lulu laughed at a story he told about being on the police force, Tom downed his wine and came behind my chair.

"I'm going to mingle a little bit. There's a couple of defense attorneys I'd like to talk to. You'll be okay here?" I nodded. "Okay," he whispered near my ear, before giving me a kiss.

I didn't remember Tom being big on public displays of affection. It felt really good that he was willing to acknowledge our relationship in public. It made it much easier to believe he was in it for the long haul this time.

When I turned back to the table, there was a long moment of silence.

"So, how long have you been dating?" Siegel asked, his face impassive. That 'since law school' speech hadn't worked on him.

Nervous laughter escaped my lips. Lulu looked at me like I'd lost my mind. "A few weeks." Siegel looked confused. There were a lot of mixed signals being sent and received. "We dated in law school."

"Then he dumped her like toxic waste." Lulu lacked subtlety.

"Lulu!" I protested.

Siegel look infinitely more interested, if his sudden lean toward the table was any indication.

"I was persona non grata for a while there. But I understand it better now. Someone with a political family, with aspirations, couldn't be associated with me."

"What in the heck had you done to make you radioactive?" Siegel asked. He sat back, arms and legs crossed, waiting for an answer. For some reason I wanted to give him that answer. To have him understand that I wasn't some horrible person, but the victim of too much honesty. I leaned toward him, pulling together an acceptable explanation that wouldn't vilify Tom.

"She ratted out the scion of the Strohmeyer family," Lulu answered for me.

Siegel started to sing. *"You'll be a high flier—"*

"The very same," Lulu said cutting him off. That jingle had been long banned from our conversations.

"What did he do? What did you do?"

I finally spoke. "Strohmeyer plagiarized his law review submission. I reported him. The school sided with him. End of story."

"End of story, my ass." Lulu said, waving a waitress over and ordering a second drink. "She lost her job offer, and Tom turned his back."

"It wasn't that bad," I said for Siegel's sake even though it *was* that bad.

He put his hand over mine, fisted against the table. Jesus, Mary, and Joseph, blood seemed to leave my heart and rush both up and down. I knew that my face had turned bright red from the tightness in my cheeks and forehead.

"You—" I gave Lulu a glance and she stopped talking.

"I really admire honesty," he said. "A willingness to swim upstream has made many a case for me."

Tom came back to the table right then. Snatching my hand from Siegel's grasp, I tried not to look guilty, but my facial muscles were failing miserably. When Tom asked if I was ready to head home, I had my coat on and purse in hand faster than a teenager at the end of a church service.

Walking down West St. Clair, I made my excuses. "You don't have to drive me home. It's so out of your way." He lived only a couple miles west of where we were standing, while I was a good six miles and fifteen minutes away.

When Tom looked indecisive, I scoured my pocket for my RTA pass. I held up September's monthly for his inspection.

"Would you be okay on the train?"

"Of course, this is Cleveland, not the Bronx," I said.

"If you think—"

"Besides, if I get too cold, I can get a ride from Lulu. Maybe I should go back in there before she closes the place."

"Nope. It's late. I'd be happy to drive you," he said, suddenly grabbing my free hand. It wasn't warm like Siegel's had been. I shook my head, wondering why I was comparing Tom Brody to some guy who for all I knew was still involved with my client. And even if he wasn't...

Tom was silent in the car. And not for the first time, I wondered what I should say to him about Eamon. Maybe he could explain his uncle's behavior. I shook my head. Maybe there wasn't much to explain. People had affairs. Clearly Judge Eamon couldn't cavort with the young ladies in the house he shared with his wife. I kept my mouth shut as the shadows of brick buildings played across Tom's face. What happened between consenting adults was none of my business.

15

"Why did you report a gun?" Miles asked me.

It had been nothing but endless questions since we'd sat down to breakfast at the Inn on Coventry. I hadn't paid for babysitting and driven all the way over here to be chastised.

"I told them he had a gun so the cops would come," I whispered over banana French toast. I didn't know a lot of people in Cleveland, but it was a lot smaller than Chicago, and I treasured both my privacy and my job.

"Where is he now?"

"In county lockup as far as I know." I took a long pull of orange juice then changed the subject. "Do you want to come Christmas shopping with me today?"

Miles looked around as if excuses were as prevalent as sugar packets in this diner. "Isn't it a little early," he finally settled on.

I gestured out the window. Cleveland had latched onto the holiday season like a drowning man would grab a lifeline. Twinkling lights, faux trees, and heaps of shopping opportunities were everywhere. "Not really. I want to get something nice for Luke this year. To make up for his dad not being around."

"I don't think this is a good idea, Claire." Miles was looking everywhere but at me. And he hadn't made a dent in his lox. He'd always loved that salty fish.

"What isn't a good idea?"

"Us getting together like this."

"How? If we're going to eventually move in together, maybe get married, a little shopping will make us closer. Come on," I cajoled. "It'll be fun."

He cleared his throat. "We broke up."

"You mean that little talk we had a couple of weeks ago? Oh Miles, I didn't take you seriously. We're good together, good for each other. Couples have bumps in the road." Sometimes he was a little immature. With Darius I'd had more relationship experience than most women got in several lifetimes. The only thing my ex and I hadn't done was get married and divorced. Everything else, though, we'd done.

Miles shifted in his seat, patted his hair, pulled his phone from his pocket and shoved it back in. "I've been thinking about this for a while. I think we need a break."

"How long of a break, Miles?" All the girly-girl was gone from my voice; all business Claire had replaced her.

"If you're not going to spend the rest of your life with someone, I think it's best to break up as soon as you realize that."

I heard my back hit the wood of the chair before I felt the hardness digging into my shoulder blades. "So you don't see any future for us."

"I'm law enforcement Claire. I was a cop and now I'm a prosecutor. I can't be with someone who plays fast and loose with the law for her own gain."

"I needed him out. I didn't want escalation to domestic violence."

"I don't want to talk about this. You made your choice." He paused a long time pushing the now limp fish around the plate. "We can be friends," he offered.

"Friends?"

"We're both from somewhere else. You've been here a little longer than me, but we've talked about how insular Cleveland is. If you haven't been here your whole life, people don't welcome you. So I was hoping we could, you know, be friends."

I blinked away the sting behind my eyes trying to keep the tears at bay. He didn't want me. He wanted anyone but me. He wanted a future that didn't include me. "Sure," I said pulling sunny, cute Claire back out. If he wanted to be friends, the door wasn't closed.

He picked up his Blackberry. "You can call me anytime, you know. If you need something, I'd be glad to help."

Miles paid for breakfast, kissed the top of my head, and then begged off to work. On a freaking Saturday. He must have wanted to get out of there. I walked down Coventry, looking at the toys in a shop window. I was pretty sure I

was suddenly single. And Luke was without a father figure—again.

16

I hadn't been planning on going to work until I'd given that excuse to Claire. As I drove toward downtown, I replayed brunch in my mind. I knew I'd done the right thing, breaking up with her. She needed a lot of things I couldn't give her. I rolled down the windows to let in the crisp air hoping it would scrub away the tiny bit of guilt that played around the pit of my belly.

While I was stopped at Chester and Fifty Fifth trying to figure out why a sole high-rise blotted the otherwise flat landscape, my glove compartment buzzed. Almost downtown, I ignored the device until I'd pulled into the deserted parking lot. After I parked and got some papers from my trunk, it buzzed again. This time it was in my hand.

"Miles Siegel."

"Valdespino here. Where have you been?"

No way was I going to get into Claire or the anatomy of a break up. "Girl trouble," I summarized.

"Where are you now?"

"Coming up to the office."

"Good, I'll see you in two."

Valdespino was twirling in my chair when I got to the empty office. The FBI was in a different building. With no one else here, I kind of wondered how he'd made his way in here with no US Attorney badge, access card, or key. Nah, didn't need to know. "They moved him around like a Catholic priest," Valdespino said without preamble.

"You tried talking to the prosecutor?" I was treading old ground, but the head of steam I'd built up after the visit to Tracy Price had dissipated. Claire's problems with Darius, with playing fast and loose with the law, with her fatherless black boy were in my head crowding out work. I'd caught Rachel's attitude. I wanted the whole Brody thing to disappear. My win rate was one hundred percent. I didn't need my first significant case to turn into a big loser.

"Look, even I can tell the issue would ruffle a few feathers." Valdespino said. "After our first little conference I put bugs in a few more ears and asked around discretely. State prosecution is an absolute no go."

"If this guy was prosecuted under Ohio law, what would he be guilty of?" I needed to bang my head against this wall one more time. Maybe I could shake something loose and kick this to state court.

"That's your department."

"I know that. I know Pennsylvania, and your garden variety federal drug and RICO statutes. Give me a minute."

Or ten. I'd been working on so many cases, and this one kept slipping down the priority ladder. Chas hadn't bothered me much. Not to mention Valdespino's occasional disappearing act on super top secret counterterrorism shit well above my security level and pay grade. I kept hoping Valdespino would pull a few women out of the woodwork and make this a sure thing. Tracy's story was compelling, but it wasn't even the mortar between the bricks.

I pulled up Westlaw and did a few searches, starting with Ohio's sex offense statute. Looking back at Valdespino over my shoulder, I asked, "If we could prove what happened to Tracy, he could be convicted under the Ohio rape statute. Mental incapacity eliminates the need to prove lack of consent."

"Haven't been able to get that one up the flagpole."

Of course, it wasn't going to be that easy. Mental impairment eliminated consent problems, but we needed corroboration for an incompetent witness. This case was going to be full of sad stories that didn't mount to evidence in court, I could tell. I wondered if Judge Brody outright promised them results for sex, or if the bastard's approach was more subtle.

I swiveled on my chair. "How'd you hear about these other women anyway? I don't see any victims exactly wailing on the courthouse steps."

"When a single family controls the biggest county's prosecutors and the BCI, and a few hundred litigants, there are always whispers. First it was the sore losers from the elections, claiming corruption. Nothing there. A few others complaining about cronyism. Had to remind them that they doled out jobs and favors to their friends and family when they were in power. It was a time waster, until we got a genuine whistle-blower." Valdespino stretched out the syllables of the last two words with a twang.

"Who?"

"Clerk to one of the probate judges. She claims to have seen the judge having sex with the slow girl. Figured there was no way it was consensual. When my buddies were poking around, she came forward."

I pushed away from the glowing blue screen. "Why am I here? Call the cops, have them arrest the guy. Under twenty-nine oh seven, subpart C, he'll be in jail day after tomorrow."

Valdespino blew out a breath. "Did you think I fell off the turnip truck yesterday?"

"Sorry, I—"

"Would you have arrested the prosecutor's brother without at least running it up the chain of command when you were on the force?"

"Not if I valued my career," I conceded.

"Got a few guys I know to do just that. I'll say it again. It's a no go. Can't find anyone to be the sacrificial lamb."

"But Liam Brody isn't prosecutor anymore."

"The new gal isn't willing to cross the family."

"Prosecutorial discretion, right?"

Valdespino nodded. Of course, prosecutors didn't go after every defendant that crossed their path. Some weren't worth the time, or the money, or the aggravation. Some were better off being chased by the feds, or being deported by immigration. A good prosecutor saved their time and resources for the worst of the worst, and whomever else would bolster their reputation.

Whether it was low level drug dealers to prove they were tough on crime, or taking down a major kingpin and posing for the camera with stacks of money and tons of weapons, each did what they needed to prolong their political career. They all came up for reelection or were gunning for higher office, and public opinion was important.

I rolled back to the computer and closed the Ohio Revised Statutes page, and started researching federal laws. Valdespino went to get lunch and was back while I was still typing away.

"So?"

"I'm in Title Eighteen," I said, referring to the section of the U.S. code that covered crimes.

Valdespino's meaty thumb wiped mustard from the corner of his mouth. "If you were anywhere else I'd be worried."

I clicked the mouse and chewed at the tasteless sandwich he'd brought. "Two forty-two."

Abandoning his lunch, Valdespino rolled his chair forward. "Never heard of that."

I turned toward him, away from the monitor. "Under the color of law."

"What?"

"Says here that if any person deprives someone of their rights, under the color of law, they're guilty of a federal crime. There's a Texas case from nineteen eighty-three. A couple of border patrol guards required two women to have sex with them to get into the country." I wondered if this was the case Chas had been talking about. Damn Claire and everything else from distracting me from this. Getting Judge Eamon Brody was moving to the top of my priority list, fast.

"And if they hadn't done it—"

"They'd have been turned away. They were Mexicans with no legal right to enter the U.S."

"So you think—"

"It plays the same. If the vic hadn't had sex with the judge, she'd have lost custody of her kid."

"Would she have lost custody anyway? Sounds like the drug-dealing boyfriend is still in the picture."

"We'll never know, will we? Once Judge Eamon got involved, she was never going to get a fair hearing. He deprived her of due process of law. That's another violation."

"Doesn't sound like due process would have gone in her favor."

"We can't be judge, jury and executioner. You wanted a crime," I said, thrusting my hands toward Valdespino. "Here's one on a silver platter."

"Has anyone in this office done something like this?"

"Don't know. Doubt it. I'll bring it up at the next meeting, and run this up the flagpole before we go anywhere." I valued this new career.

"Your own prosecutorial discretion?"

"I just got here. I'm not taking the dive for any single case, no matter how much of a shit this guy is. I want to be employed next week."

"I hate bullies. I want to see this guy go down," Valdespino said, his voice guttural.

"I met his nephew a few weeks ago." My tone was conversational.

"Tom Brody?"

"He claimed he was some hotshot prosecutor in the DA's office. Is he one of the cronies people complained about?"

"Nepotism at its finest. He skipped over the shitty assignments and moved right downtown to felonies. Doing death penalty after only seven years on the job. Most guys wait ten, fifteen years for that to happen." He looked around, probably realizing his voice had gotten high. "Where'd you meet him?"

"Young lawyer thing."

"You're considered young?" Was Valdespino ribbing me? It was the nicest thing he'd said to me in the few months I'd known him.

"Funny. Thanks for lunch. I'll talk to Chas and let you know."

17

"Meet me in your office when you get back." Valdespino had barked the message into the voice me. "I'll be waiting."

True to his word, Valdespino was waiting for me at the elevator bay. Before I could step out, he shoved me and my bag back in.

"What the—"

"Got a victim interview. Was going to go without you. But it'll be better with you there," he said, jabbing heartily at the 'P' button in the elevator.

Why better with me? Was the girl going to be poor and black? Somehow I was supposed to relate to her, no doubt even though I'd grown up only half of one and none of the other.

Twenty five minutes later, Valdespino pulled up to a older wood frame house that looked like a million others in Cleveland, with a slightly sagging porch and peeling blue paint. The festive Christmas lights did little to brighten the pall that poverty cast.

We walked up a rocky path that had once been concrete in between patches of lawn. Part of me wanted to know what in the hell I was walking into. But my experience of interviewing witnesses over the last years kept me mute. I knew bringing fresh eyes to a situation was best. Preconceived notions got you into trouble. Knowing less, though not an asset in most areas of life, was better in this one.

Valdespino badged our way into the house. The two women, one older, the other younger, didn't look happy to let us in. But I'm sure the consequences of ignoring the FBI weighed heavily in our favor. The local police could be abused and ignored up to a point. But nobody messed with the Feds.

"Are you Kyanna Oliver?" Valdespino asked. The younger woman nodded. "We need to talk to you. Jayden here?"

There was a long pause before either woman answered. "He's with family," the older woman said, her eyes darting from mine.

Valdespino cut me a look. We weren't partners. I had no idea what to read into it. All I could tell is that he wasn't thrilled with the answer.

"We're here to ask you a few questions about Judge Eamon Brody and your custody case," he said.

We all sat. The mother sighed, the weight of dealing with 'the man' sitting heavily on her shoulders. Kyanna shifted on the couch cushions so many times, I wanted to pronounce her guilty right out of the gate. My former partner and I would have gotten a confession out of her in five seconds flat.

I looked at Valdespino, trying to transmit just that thing. He didn't look at me, but he stood and paced for a moment. Classic cop move. He got it. This was a one and done interview.

"Miss Oliver, can I call you Kyanna?" Valdespino asked.

"Sure. Why you here? I ain't never been involved in Deonte's business."

I didn't need an answer key to figure out that Deonte's business was probably drugs.

Valdespino looked at the women with a hard-eyed stare. "We're not here for that." He finally picked up a dining chair and sat close to Kyanna. "When did the county take Jayden?"

"I didn't know Deonte was slinging. But when he got arrested, they came for Jayden." Half lie, half truth. We could work with her.

"Why?"

"Why you think? They said that living in our house was neglect. We got thrown out from the apartment."

She was probably in section eight or the projects. In the zero tolerance drug war era, dealing led to eviction for everyone in the apartment, whether or not they were involved in the illegal activity.

"How long did the county have Jayden?"

"Three months. They kept sayin' that I could get him back as soon as I found a new place. I moved in here, but that wasn't enough. They kept breaking they promises."

Valdespino's eyes shifted left to right. One day I'd have to let him know he had a tell before going in for the kill. "So, how did you eventually get Jayden back?"

"The social worker brought him back. They must've realized that I wasn't the problem."

"Where is Jayden now?" I asked. The women looked at each other. The older one closed her eyes, looking down. Her lips were moving as if in silent prayer. "Where is he?" I asked again, putting a little more badass cop and less nice guy in my voice.

"Don't take him."

My head spun. Was I a mandatory reporter? If her child was in the basement eating slugs, would I have to call the county? The FBI agent answered.

"We're not here for that. We don't have any intentions of calling the county on you, if you cooperate with us."

"What do you mean, cooperate? I told you, I ain't involved in Deonte's business. Don't know nothing about it. He paid the bills, had us living nice. I didn't ask too many questions about who was comin' over or what they needed. As long as he took care of us. It's not like it's easy gettin' a job with a record." Kyanna looked pointedly at me. "I'm sure you ain't never been to jail. That's why you sittin' pretty with your government job." Neither one of us said anything, letting her rant until she was out of breath.

"So he's with his father," I concluded.

"Yeah, and what of it? He don't take the boy around his work. Little boys 'round here don't have enough fathers as it is. And Deonte's a good one."

There was our leverage. Leaving her kid in the care of a known felon. That had to be a statutory offense of some sort.

Valdespino pulled out a folder and flipped through some papers. From where I sat, I couldn't tell what he was looking at, or if it was a prop.

"Says here," he jabbed with his finger, "that Judge Eamon presided over your case."

"Thank God for the judge," the older woman said, finally speaking aloud. "Until he got on the case, we weren't getting anything from juvey. He cleaned up that other guy's courtroom right quick."

"Have you ever seen the judge alone?"

Kyanna's eyes went wild. Valdespino had hit the right question. I'd wondered how he was going to do it. I might have flat out asked if she'd had to perform sexual favors. But then I was used to having guilty men finger guiltier ones, glad to be relieved of the burden of the truth. This case required a more delicate touch. I had to admire the meaty fingered agent. He was playing her like a fiddle.

"Yeah, I had to come to court alone, right," she said. Ex parte had no meaning for her. "He wanted to talk to me, get the real story, make sure my baby would be okay."

"Neither your lawyer, nor the prosecutor were there?"

"I called my lawyer, told her the judge wanted me to come in. You know what I got from her. The same nothin' I been gettin' all along. That Uama lady, Claire kept telling us to trust our lawyers. But that lawyer ain't lost her child. They were probably tucked away safe in their nice beds in the Heights somewhere, while my Jayden was sleeping on some bug infested sofa bed. So yeah, I went there by myself. And you know what? I did a better job. We had a short conversation and Jayden came home. End of story."

"Conversations between a litigant and a judge without all sides present is illegal," I lied.

"What you sayin'?"

"If a court looks at this," I said, leaning in, "they could reverse Judge Eamon's decision. Give Jayden back to the county. Have a new judge hear the case."

"Who's gonna tell? From what I saw, the county has too many cases to count. Unless you got me on videotape, I ain't talkin'. I bet that judge ain't either."

"Why wouldn't he talk, Kyanna?" Valdespino asked. "Why wouldn't he say you propositioned him?"

"Did he say it was my fault?" Kyanna's voice was getting louder with each word. "He told me that one time would be enough. I'm going to kill that motherfucker if he's going back on his word." Her eyes were mother-bear murderous.

"What he did was illegal," Valdespino said, his voice a balm. "We're trying to put him behind bars so he doesn't do to anyone else what he did to you."

"What did he make you do, Kyanna?" the older woman asked. "You told me that he wanted to cut through the red tape. You told him your story, and he sent Jayden home. What that man make you do?"

Kyanna's sigh could have been that of any of the billions of victimized women in the world's history. "I only had to have sex with him that one time. He's an old white man. It was quick. No worse than what dozens of men have tried to take from me." She looked at the older woman, some shared understanding passing between them. "I made sure he signed the papers before I pulled down my pants."

I'd heard bad, worse, and despicable during my years on the force, but I couldn't help shifting in my chair. There appeared to be no end to human depravity. I wanted to get this guy more than I'd ever wanted anything. Valdespino and I locked eyes. This time his unspoken message was one hundred percent clear. He'd laid out the evidence. The rest was up to me.

18

"Miles, it's Claire." I said into the telephone. I hadn't quite resisted the urge to light up Miles' phone. My other hand gripped a glass of orange juice.

"What time is it?" he croaked.

I glanced up at the kitchen clock and cringed a little. "Six thirty," I whispered.

Silence proceeded a long, drawn out sigh. "What's up?"

"Can you sit with Luke today? Just for a little bit? I have to go to my Uama meeting."

"What about that granny down the street? Was her name Lorraine, Luanne—"

"Carletta."

"I thought Carletta was going to watch him with Darius out of the picture."

"Are you saying you're not coming over?"

"Claire. This has to stop. I know that I said you could call me if you needed me, but I was wrong to do that. Maybe you should stop calling me."

"But—" I know a few weeks ago, he'd said that he didn't love me and I should be with someone who did. He'd said that someone like him in law enforcement couldn't be involved with me who was involved in a domestic violence incident. Trifling nigger. I'd thought he was different, but he wasn't.

"There's no chance that we're going to get back together, Claire," he continued, intruding on my thoughts. "I don't think we can be friends right now. We come from two different worlds, and it just isn't going to work out."

"So, that's it?"

"I probably shouldn't have sprung this on you the day Darius was arrested, but I'd been thinking about it for a while. It's been nearly a month since we had that long talk."

"Have you met someone else?" That must be it. There couldn't be any other reason. We'd gotten on well. We were both well educated, committed to our careers. We were practically the poster for Jack and Jill.

His hesitation was one beat too long. I wouldn't chalk it up to sleepiness, either. "I'm not seeing anyone—"

"But you have someone in mind, don't you?"

"I don't think we should talk about this." His voice was faint, as if he were putting physical distance between himself and the phone.

"We just broke up, Miles."

"Claire, I have to go. I have a busy day ahead. Good luck with your meeting."

Then he hung up on me. I couldn't believe it. I'd been dismissed. When he said I could call him anytime, that we could be friends, I'd taken him at his word. We were both from out of town, and needed people to lean on. I thought he could still be one of those friends. And maybe I'd even thought we could get back together eventually. With Darius out of my life....

"Mama!" Luke called from his bedroom. "It's morning time!" I cleared my head. Time to put on my mama hat. I downed my orange juice and turned on the toaster oven. I'd give him a couple of frozen waffles and some milk before I took him over to Carletta's house. I was hoping I would have been able to call to cancel.

I hated that old lady shaking her head and wagging her finger, going on about little black boys with no fathers. Good thing I hadn't given in to the urge to cancel last night. After the two wine coolers I'd drank to help me fall asleep, I had been feeling very confident about my future with Miles. I walked upstairs mentally going through Luke's drawer thinking about what he'd wear today. Like all of the ladies I counseled in jail and out, I was on my own.

Walking into Uama, I shook my head clear of all the expectations I'd had this year. Like the women I was going to spend the next two hours with, I needed to focus on how to make the future the best I could for my little man.

When I got the group assembled and quiet, I silently counted heads.

"Where's Rhonda?" It was worse than herding cats. Sometimes I got a sense of what it must be like being their lawyers. I'd have to ask Casey about this. Maybe she had some advice after dealing with these kinds of clients for years. I wanted to help these women, but they had to help themselves first.

"I'm here," Rhonda said, bustling in the door. I was surprised to see Kyanna who'd called to say she'd gotten her son back, coming up right behind her.

"This is little Jayden," Kyanna said, taking off his coat and putting a Game Boy in his hands.

Jayden put up with the hugs, kisses, and pats from mothers who were desperately missing their own children. One of the women had brought her teenage daughter.

I caught the teen's attention. "I tell you what. Can you keep an eye on the kids in that little room over there?" I pointed to a little side room that held a few toys.

"I been watching kids since I was six. What you gonna give me?"

"Twenty bucks."

Money was a great motivator. She was turning on the lights and shuttling Jayden and the others to the room before I could say another word. That done, I called the meeting to order.

"Before we start today, I think we need to clear up some rumors. You have all been teenage girls and have to know better than anyone that rumors and lies can hurt other people. No one wants to be known as that girl in the hood who gives it away. It can be dangerous." The women nodded, silent. I continued, "Last month there was some talk about moms here giving sexual favors to get their kids returned. I want you to know that's not true. No judge would abuse their power in that way. I know that it's hard not having your own kids home, but jealousy has no place here. Am I understood?"

Everyone but Rhonda nodded.

"Rhonda?" I asked, a note of warning in my voice. I didn't want to have to throw someone out of the group, but I wouldn't put up with ghetto girl sniping around here. The last thing I needed was some kind of knock down, hair pulling fight. My bosses would quash this weekend group faster than a June bug.

"But I heard it straight from your girl, Kyanna." She looked directly at the alleged offender. "Ain't that right?"

"Rhonda!" That teacher voice again. My dad would be proud. "That's enough. Let's get on with the progress reports."

"All right, I won't say nothing else." Before I could say anymore, she cut her eyes at Kyanna. The other woman looked away, toward the room Jayden was in. He and the other kids were happily laughing and squealing at something the teen girl had said.

The meeting was no different from the last and would probably be no different from the next. They reported their frustrations with the social workers, bureaucrats, and lawyers who were supposed to be serving them.

"It's like they work for themselves," Min-ji said. "Every single person acts like it's a big deal to answer a question or schedule an appointment." She took a deep breath. Rhonda got up and got the Kleenex. "This is my kid we're talking about," Min-ji said, tears streaming down her cheeks. "I know they don't think much of us. But how would they like it, if they had to be on hold for an hour to get information on their children? They see their kids every night and don't have an ounce of compassion for us."

Rhonda scooted the metal chair over and patted Min-ji on the shoulder.

I wasn't a Scared Straight counselor, nor was I in jail with my usual suspects. So I wouldn't tell them that their own actions had gotten them into this mess. Instead, I steered them toward the positive. Made them stand up and take command of their situations. They needed to be the squeaky wheels. Leave the worst to the apathetic parents out there, the ones not ready to work the system.

Two hours later, with everyone bundled in their coats, I'd achieved what I came here for. They were again fired up and ready to go. Ready to make calls, knock on doors, do whatever it took to get their kids back.

I was jiggling the keys in the door when Kyanna approached me.

"Where's Jayden?"

She jerked her thumb toward the car, smoke curling from the tailpipe in short puffs.

"What do you need, Kyanna?" I wasn't able to keep the exasperation from my voice. If this had been summer and she'd left that kid in the car, I didn't want to think about the consequences. So much work, these women were. Totally sounded like Miles there. He had the funniest way of talking. I zoned back in on the woman standing in front of me.

"You was right."

"About what?" I thought I was right about a lot. I was glad she'd done what was necessary and gotten her son back.

"The rumors. Maybe you can tell the other women about this next month 'cause I won't be back."

"But you'd be an inspiration to...."

"The FBI came to see me."

In no way was I expecting that. I leaned against the cold steel of the security door, ignoring the little shiver that shimmied up my spine.

"What? Why?" My curiosity overcame my bosses' admonition not to in any way act as a personal lawyer for these women

"They're investigating Judge Brody, and they'd heard the same rumors as Rhonda."

"Shit, what did you tell them?"

"They want me to come in and testify. I can't do that. I could lose Jayden all over again."

"Are you saying the judge molested you?"

"I ain't saying shit." She thrust a couple of cards into my hand. "Can you please call them and tell them to stay away from me?"

The overhead security light shone on my hand. The FBI seal was on one side of the card, and Louis Valdespino was on the other. In addition to a printed phone number, another was scrawled across the card. The second card was from Miles Siegel. I nearly dropped it like a lit match in my hand. I had one of these in my wallet. The eagle in the big ol' Department of Justice symbol gave me the eye. I schooled my face.

"Kyanna, I can't do any individual representation. I've told you guys that from the beginning."

Hurt screwed up her face. "I just thought.... Forget it. I'll handle this like I've handled everything else. My way."

I went home before picking up Luke. I wanted to call Miles so bad. To see what in the heck was going on. Was there something to the rumors? Did they affect some women, but not Kyanna? Or had Kyanna needed to do something more than provide a clean home to get her little boy back? Mentally, I flipped through the lawyers I knew. Maybe I should refer her to someone. That drug-dealing boyfriend of hers could spare a little something on a retained lawyer.

After changing into my sweats, I threw on my coat. Smoothing my hair back into a ponytail, I steeled myself for the long nighttime routine: bath, books, and bed. I tucked three twenties into my pocket along with my keys. My hand was on the knob when the phone rang. My heart beat faster in my chest and I hoped it was Miles.

"Claire Henshaw," I answered. I didn't want him to think I was sitting by the phone, waiting for him to apologize.

"Just the woman I wanted to speak with." The old man's voice sounded both familiar and out of context at the same time. "Judge Eamon Brody here," he said. In one instant I knew Rhonda hadn't been lying. "I believe we have something in common."

19

"Where's he taking you tonight?" Jason asked. I was standing in my neighbors' apartment while they gave my outfit the once-over. I hated the scrutiny, but knew that my view of myself was sometimes dysmorphic. Either I went for clothes that were too tight, imagining the thin self I used to inhabit. Or they were tents, as I tried to hide what my body had become. Not even a ringmaster looked good in a tent.

"I think you've lost weight," Greg said.

I breathed a little easier. An adjustable belt could be deceptive, but I was feeling pretty good these last few weeks. More like myself.

"Who can eat? I'm getting cases referred to me right and left. And not the crappy paying juvenile cases. Divorce and custody cases in domestic relations."

"No more juvenile?" Jason sounded hopeful. For a long moment, my staunchly Democratic self wallowed in guilt over my lack of dedication to serving the poor. Had I made it sound so dreadful? Who was I kidding? It was dreadful. A nearly two-week absence and I was already downright nostalgic.

"Not done there, yet. But I can see a light at the end of the tunnel." It was shining brightly, beckoning like an end of life white light.

"What's making it click now?"

"The Brody family," I said matter-of-factly. With Greg and Jason there was no reason to pretend that I'd suddenly become one of the cool kids. "Maybe Tom feels guilty for what happened all those years ago. Maybe they do as well. Don't know. But I'm not going to look a gift horse in the mouth. No siree."

"So that's a new dress?"

"Got the money, and the bigger ones wouldn't fit." I took a twirl in my pointy shoes, thankful I wouldn't have to walk too far. "What do you think?" With the boyfriend diet, I could now seriously consider myself a size smaller.

"A wrap dress works for you."

What he didn't say is that the peplum built into this dress hid a world of flaws. He was at least diplomatic that way.

"Have you guys done it yet?"

"Jason!" I squealed like a teenager.

"What? It's a legitimate question." He threw up his hands in mock outrage.

A heat cloud of embarrassment surrounded my head. "Not since the fall of nineteen ninety-two."

"What's his problem?" Greg asked, his voice sober.

"God, I hope you've gotten laid since then," Jason interjected.

What was his problem, indeed? I mean, I know I was seven years older, and I wasn't as cute as I'd probably been in my twenties. I wanted to both kiss and kick Greg; kiss him for looking out for me, kick him for making me feel like inadequacy central.

"We're feeling each other out," I improvised.

"Not literally, though," Greg said.

My land line rang, the bells filtering under the doors. He was here.

"Gotta go," I said, very happy to be leaving. They were making me think about things I'd shuttled aside for the past three months.

"Think about what you're doing," Jason advised.

Riding in Tom's car through the darkened and deserted streets of Cleveland from my side of town to the Brodys', I could do nothing but think about how he had contacted me out of the blue. I didn't even know if we were having a relationship. We'd had a few dinners, that one kiss in the car, the one in the bar, and not much more after that.

I must have sighed in exasperation, because Tom turned to look at me. The stop light overhead bathed his smile in a red glow. I did my best to raise my lips to my cheeks then turned my head toward the window.

The family was in full force in the formal living room when we arrived. It was like an Ethan Allen showroom threw up in here. Though I suspected this furniture predated elegance gone mainstream. Each of the Brody men had a woman on their arm. I shook hands with Liam's wife, Mary. Eleanor hugged and kissed me. I'd always liked Tom's mother. She'd treated me like one of the family, even when it was clear I'd never become a Brody. To this day, she sent me Christmas and birthday cards. She was the classiest of the Brodys. I could only hope to have a tenth of her class one day.

After Eleanor made sure that Patrick had gotten me a drink, Tom took me over to meet Eamon's wife. I don't know what I'd expected, but she was small and fragile. Pearl barrettes clipped her carefully arranged wisps of blond hair flat to the sides of her head. The cream cashmere pantsuit she wore draped beautifully.

I don't know what I thought a cheater's wife would look like, but this wasn't it. I took her limp hand in mine when offered. "Nice to meet you, Mrs. Brody."

"There are too many Mrs. Brodys in this crowd," her thin voice mocked slightly. "Call me Moira."

"Casey," I said.

"I heard that you helped my dear husband with decorating his office. That was so very nice of you."

Her very mention of that morning brought back the images of that young black woman, heaving breasts and bulging stomach laying over the table. I wanted to forget that. Forever.

"Have you seen it? Did it turn out well?"

"Oh, my. You haven't been back?" She turned to her husband. "Eamon, you have to give this young woman a tour."

"I'll be sure to," Judge Eamon said half-heartedly. He didn't want to see me any more than I wanted to see him, I expect.

We made eye contact. I tried to assure him his secret was safe with me. Who was I to say anything? For all I knew, he and Moira had an open marriage.

When the housekeeper announced dinner was served, I was relieved. Though I'd vowed to keep what I'd seen to myself, the urge to blurt out something was overwhelming. I hated secrets.

Turning to put my drink on the tray the housekeeper offered, I was surprised to find Eamon rolling over a wheelchair. Tenderly, he helped his wife in, steering her through the open pocket doors to the table.

The weight had started coming off when I stopped eating. Since starvation wasn't my thing, I'd compromised at finishing only half of what was on my plate. I was never hungry, and I was wearing a size ten. Pushing away half the creamy potato soup was hard on that resolution.

"Was the soup okay, Casey?" Moira said from my left side.

"It was very good, thank you," I replied. Her blue eyes never left mine. I felt...probed. What was it about this family that made every encounter slightly uncomfortable? "I'm trying to keep my weight down," I ended up blurting.

"Young people and worries about appearance." Moira Brody turned away with a sigh.

I tuned back into the bigger conversation when voices rose over the roast beef and vegetables that had appeared as if by magic.

"What's Antonio Cofrancesco up to? He still building?" Patrick Brody asked.

"I hear he's putting together a big project on St. Clair," Liam Brody responded.

"That townhome thing he tried to get us in on?"

Liam nodded. "Yep. Didn't need us after he got redevelopment money for doing an enterprise zone."

"What Lizzy's father did to Simon needs to be rectified."

Tom's brother Simon set down his heavy silverware. "You don't need to fight my battles. I lost."

"That mook played dirty."

"I don't think that St. Clair subdivision is going to get out of zoning review in two thousand four," Patrick said.

The men all nodded. Their wives sipped wine. I blinked several times, trying to process what had just happened. I was about ninety eight percent sure the beautiful Lizzy Cofrancesco and her family were going down. It would probably be a tough two to seven years for them. If her family had been squashed like a bug in less than ten minutes, stalling my career had only taken a second.

Patrick turned on the charm and beamed it all in my direction. "So how's your practice doing?"

"Better, thanks. With Judge Brody's help, it's off life support."

Patrick patted Eamon on the back. "Are you interested in doing criminal again?"

I felt my eyelids close then open. Everyone stared back expectantly. "Sure," I said. "Only felonies, though. I don't have the time to travel from city court to city court on misdemeanors."

"Who does? I'm next up on arraignments. If you stop by in the mornings, I can kick a few F-1s your way."

I could practically feel my bank account fattening. At a thousand dollars a pop, felonies didn't pay much compared to retained cases. Unlike the two hundred fifty dollar juvenile cases, though, these defendants didn't fight back. Nine out of ten would take a plea to a lesser charge. The Brodys had put another ten thousand dollars in my pocket, and all before the dessert course.

"How's juvenile, you ready to be out of there?" Patrick asked.

"There's Ellingwood, of course and I have a few other retained cases."

"Do you want to do any more of those appointed abuse cases?"

"I like the clients, and the work," I equivocated. "But the money...."

"The money ain't shit." Patrick spat.

"At the dinner table, honey?" Eleanor admonished.

"No need to mince words here," he said, ignoring his wife's reprimand.

The dinner plates disappeared and cassata cake materialized. Damn, the Italian dessert was one of my favorites. Suddenly, I was ravenous. Every bite quashed the fear, slowed the beating in my heart.

"I'll talk to the judges. If you give me a list of your cases, I can have you out of all those assigned cases tomorrow." Judge Eamon added. "Write up an affidavit talking about the 'press of business' and I'll circulate it."

Another strawberry heavily laden with cream slid down my throat.

Patrick recited my work number. "That you?"

I nodded, proud of the triple zero I'd talked the phone company into giving me.

"A few people should be giving you a call. Some divorce referrals."

I looked around the table at the happily married couples. The women weren't smiling. Maybe not happily, but at least long married. "How—"

"Club dinner last night. The divorce rate's near fifty percent. So there's always business."

I declined brandy in the study. I didn't need to add second hand cigar smoke to the possible list of carcinogens I was exposed to in Cleveland.

"Want to go outside," Tom said.

It wasn't a question. I pulled on my new wool coat, gathering the attached hood close around my face and followed him to the guesthouse.

"Did you ever want to live here?" I asked. We were in the living room, which easily dwarfed mine.

"I did, maybe a few months after law school." He pulled my coat off and draped it over the back of the couch. "But after I got back from my bar trip, I needed to do my own thing."

Of course he'd taken a bar trip, a tradition of the well-heeled. Graduate law school, study for and take the bar, then gallivant to places far and expensive. I'd spent the four months living in my childhood bedroom biting my nails, hoping I'd passed, and perfecting my latte art while a barista at Arabica.

I sucked down my jealousy. "Where did you go?" I knew very well where he'd gone. Our monthly alumni newsletter made stalking easy.

"Simon and I volunteered for Habitat for Humanity. We worked on a house in Macedonia for a few weeks. Then kicked around Greece, Italy, Morocco." Tom almost stepped in it, asking what I'd done after the bar. I could see him think better of it. "Come here," he said, laying an arm across my shoulders. He pulled me closer. Two adults, alone, on a couch. I knew what should be coming next, but my enthusiasm was flagging.

He lifted a remote from a table. The lights dimmed. Another button depressed, and classical music came up. I guess we'd come to the sex part of the evening. Hours ago, I'd felt slighted. Now, I shifted in my seat, a little uncomfortable.

"Hey," Tom said, taking my chin in his hand. He kissed me. Time slipped away. I couldn't tell the difference between this minute and minutes like this seven years ago. We'd sat on the same couch, and made out before or after his family dinners. Five more minutes of kissing, and we'd be in one of the guest rooms, taking off our clothes and putting on a condom.

Lulu had often said that every woman was a prostitute. I wondered. What was I trading sex for?

20

Maybe I should have stayed with my parents. But after two days of my mother's sighing and silent recriminations, I'd paid the fifty bucks and had taken the long train ride back to Cleveland. I'd pick up Luke a few days before my parents had to go back to work. My little boy loved his grandparents and they loved him. Luke hadn't grown old enough to disappoint them yet.

Orange juice and coffee churned together, eroding the lining of my stomach. Judge Brody had commanded my appearance and I was going. I'd paced out the small square of my living room. No other choices presented themselves.

I'd thought of calling Casey. But what could she do? I didn't even know what the judge wanted. Some supposition based on rumors from women with axes to grind was not how I wanted to burn through my retainer money. Last thing I needed was my lawyer losing faith in me.

The wind from the lake stung my face as I walked from the parking lot to the courthouse. Little more than a skeleton security crew manned the front door.

"You're here to see...?" the guard asked his leading question.

I'd pulled out my bar card over my driver's license. He'd have no way to tell what my business was. "Appointment with Judge Brody."

He eyed the card then looked me up and down. I'd worn jeans, Timberlands, thick wool sweater, and a parka. I was dressed for the weather, not to impress.

"Go on back."

The march through the stone corridors was slow going. I had no idea what to expect. I'd added a baseball sized raisin scone to the acid mix while driving over. Dread pooled in my belly, morphing the masticated dough into something akin to lead.

I didn't bother knocking on any of the closed doors. No one was there anyway. What was usually bustling with humming computers, clacking copiers, and busy women was silent. The air chilly, I hugged my jacket around me as I pushed my way into the judge's office.

A single lamp lit the room. Judge Brody sat behind his desk, reading the latest Ohio Lawyer. My own copy had arrived in the mail yesterday. But I doubt he wanted to discuss the legal aid funding crisis or bar passage rates.

"Glad you could make it, Miss Henshaw. Have a seat." I sat in one of the chairs, placing my purse on the other. I didn't say a word. This was his show. He opened a manila folder. Even upside down, I could read my son's name. "How is young Darius?"

"Luke. Everyone calls him Luke," I said. Then wondered why I'd shared even this intimacy.

"Did he enjoy Christmas?" When I didn't answer, he cleared his throat. "Kwanzaa?"

"His grandparents gave him a nice holiday."

"Toy trucks and trains? My kids loved that kind of thing at that age."

I looked at the watery blue eyes, thinning gray hair, jowls. His kids probably hadn't been four since the Nixon administration. "Mmm."

"I think we could be friends," he said.

Seriously? I didn't have any old white friends. What would we talk about? I almost laughed out loud trying to picture us in a bar together. I'd get a Cosmo. He'd get a sherry. We'd talk about shoes, shopping, dating and waiting lists at assisted living centers. Yeah, that would work.

"What do you think?" he asked, leaning forward.

I didn't have an answer. There was no outright proposition. He hadn't asked for sex. Maybe those other women had misread the situation. Lonely may be his only crime. "I guess we could be friends," I said, finally. My voice was swallowed by the still, cold Midwestern air. The usual hiss of steam heaters was absent.

"Then we should go out to celebrate," he said.

Unbidden, the image materialized of us in a bar. Did old people even go to bars? "I can't really do anything over the holidays."

"Where's Dar—Luke?"

"He's with his grandparents." Damn, I needed to stop that truth train from running out my mouth.

"It seems you have some free time, then. I have a little place not far from here. We could have a drink. Talk. That's what friends do."

God answered my prayer. My phone rang. Fishing in my purse, I pressed talk like it was a lifeline. It was my mother. I was never so happy to hear from that woman. She could call me the devil if she wanted. Turning away from the judge, I cupped my hand over the receiver.

"Everything okay with Luke, Mom?"

"Why are you whispering?"

"I'm in a work meeting. But if this is an emergency—"

"Nothing like that, Claire. I just wanted to know which he'd prefer for dinner, fried chicken or spaghetti."

I tried not to sigh in frustration. They treated him like a prince. A prince with no opinions. They were forever asking me what he wanted, when my little man was perfectly capable of telling them that very thing.

"He likes both. Either would be fine."

"Biscuits," my mother said, her voice getting fainter. I knew she was pulling open the cupboard, ticking off ingredients in her mind. She never fried chicken unless she could serve biscuits alongside. Corn on the cob was her favorite, but creamed corn would probably have to make do with the dormant cornfields covered in snow.

"Do you need me to come right away?" I said, injecting a note of panic into my voice.

"What?" My mother's distracted voice came back to the phone. "Of course not honey, dinner is not an emergency."

"I'll be there..." I made the look at my watch obvious. "...in about twenty minutes. Let me wrap things up here."

"There's really no need to drive that far in this weather. They're predicting a snowstorm for tonight."

"Gotcha," I said, ending the call. "Issue with the kid. I've gotta go."

Judge Brody's look was not exactly sympathetic. I probably wouldn't win an Oscar, not even an Emmy. My performance had been somewhat lacking. But I'd started down the road and was going the whole way.

"What's your schedule like tomorrow?" Judge Brody asked, looking down at his oversized desk calendar.

"I don't know," I said. "I have a kid, parents, holiday stuff."

"Are you trying to brush me off?"

"No, no," I said. "This is a bad time, is all."

"You'd be best served, not ignoring me. Understand?"

I nodded then hustled my way out of there. Once on the street, I called my mother back, explaining that I'd needed an excuse from work. Her lecture about me not taking work seriously was worth the escape hatch. I wasn't exactly sure what in the hell had happened in there. Was it a date he wanted? Sex? My imagination was working overtime. I couldn't believe I was taking Rhonda or Kyanna seriously.

He never said my case would go south if I didn't become more friendly. I'm not even sure that was implied. Maybe he was just a lonely guy. There was some rumor about his wife being an invalid. His kids were probably busy.

When I'd worked for Judge Grant, there were plenty of old judges who would talk your ear off, given half the chance. It had happened to me when I'd made the mistake of asking for a signature or something else from the other judges, instead of their secretaries. Once, Magistrate Conlin had insisted I share his sandwich. By the time I'd left, the sun had set and the courthouse had emptied.

Work was slow the rest of the holiday week, but it made it easy to ignore all the calls to my house. A single call, a single message every day reminding me of my agreement to be friends. By Friday, the message had taken on a different tone.

When I got home, I acknowledged the insistent blink of the tiny red light, dialing the number to access my voice mail. Setting the phone on speaker, I started poking around, choosing among the frozen dinners I'd stacked in the freezer.

"Miss Claire, I'm disappointed in you. I thought we'd come to an understanding, but you seem to be ignoring me. A little reminder of my determination may be calling on you shortly."

Instead of deleting, I saved the cryptic message. What reminder? I jumped nearly a mile high when the doorbell rang. Judge Brody wouldn't come here, would he?

I was so flustered, I ignored lifelong instructions from my mother and opened the door without looking through the peephole first.

"Darius…" I faltered. "Did you…did you make bail?" I looked to the heavens, praying silently that his family had relented on their anti-bail stance.

"I didn't even waste my phone call on those trifling niggers. They ain't changed." He paused, his smile practically beatific. "Nope. I'm out free and clear. Everything has been dropped. I'm one hundred percent out of the system as of two hours ago. So when can I see my boy?"

21

"Did you sleep with him?"

"No 'hello, how are you, Casey? Can I take your coat? Would you like something to warm you on this cold night?'" I said while pirouetting in my new coat. I still loved the faux fur lining and decorative buttons. Felt much more like an adult in this rather than the parka I'd been wearing for three years running.

Lulu reluctantly took my coat, hanging it on a hook by the door. "There you go."

"Maybe a hanger?" The last thing I wanted was a tiny dowager hump rising above my back. Wet wool, a wood peg, it could happen.

She pulled a metal hanger from the back of the coat rack and shoved the pointy ends into the shoulders. "There. Happy?"

"Happier," I said, emphasis falling on the third syllable.

"So, did you do it?" Her cat eyeglasses slipped down her nose with her emphatic hand gestures and head movements. She shoved them up with no thought to the prints she'd left on her lenses.

"I thought about *you*," I demurred.

"I'm cute, but probably not the face anyone wants to see when they're in the midst of it. Unless they're gay. Are you gay?"

"No, not gay, and not that other thing you're thinking."

"What you talking about?" Lulu asked, her 'you' sounding like 'chew.' When she put an accompanying pout on her face, I expected her to morph into Gary Coleman at any moment.

I ignored her foray into popular culture and got back to the conversation at hand. "Your belief that every women is making a trade off when she sleeps with a man."

"Did you make the trade?"

"There's a lot of appeal there. The Brodys have money and political influence," I said. Unfortunately, that's exactly what I'd been thinking when Tom asked if I had any condoms. Not the sexiest moment of my life.

Lulu got up and bustled around the kitchen. The ding of the microwave sounded. Five minutes later, she was back with two thick ceramic mugs of hot chocolate. I took a sip. The sharp tang of rum stung my throat and numbed my lips. The generous dollop of whip cream soothed. Perfect. This was exactly how I liked it.

"That sounds great," Lulu said, like great was the same as a hanging at the public square. She eased herself down on the floor, leaning against her favorite easy chair. "Sounded great when we were in law school and you were planning your wedding in the backyard of that acre they have in Lakewood." She flipped her hand palm up then down. "I find your enthusiasm lacking."

I set my half-finished toddy on the coffee table. Putting the best spin on it I could, I explained the Brodys' plans for the Cofrancesco clan.

"What did that family do to them?" Lulu's brow pulled together, deepening the groove between her eyes. Clearly, spinning was not my forte. I'd leave prettying up the dirty to Ari Fleisher.

"I have no idea," I admitted. "Didn't seem polite to ask. What do you think? Should I have paused in between the salad and the soup? 'Hi, you're declaring war. Might I ask the motivation?' I kept my mouth shut. I've already been on the business end of the Brody gun."

"So...." She wasn't asking about sex anymore.

"I'm almost out of juvenile court," I said. I didn't want to talk about the aborted act that had almost occurred at the guest house. It was embarrassing to go from thinking he didn't want me to having to fend him off.

"What do you mean? You have about a thousand cases there, give or take." Lulu brought me back to the present.

"Maybe a little over a hundred."

"Holy shit! That many, really?"

"The ones that go to permanent custody are closed. It's the other ones. They keep the guardian in at fifty dollars a year. But to get that first two fifty upfront, you've got to commit to the family."

"How did you get out of a hundred cases?"

I shrugged. "Tom's dad asked me if I wanted out. I said yes and signed a few affidavits. Before the week was out, my mail was flooded with postcards full of judgment entries letting me out of the cases."

"I know those cases are like anchors, but they've kept the Casey boat afloat for years. Can that Ellingwood case you landed a few months ago pay all the bills?"

"The Brodys, they giveth and taketh," I said. Lulu stayed quiet, letting me talk it out. "I have new cases coming out of my ears. Not all big money like the first, but my name's getting around town. I signed ten new domestic relations cases this week. Plus there are all the cases I got when Tom's dad was on arraignment. And even with him off, I'm still getting felony assignments."

"Holy fucking shit. No wonder you were mad."

I didn't follow. "Angry about what?"

"Tom dumping you," she said plainly. "Not only did you lose your boyfriend, you lost the gravy train. If you'd kept your Morrell Gates firm job, no doubt there'd be a stream of business coming your way in that arena." Lulu paused then pointed at me and my half-filled mug. "So you've got a boyfriend whose family influence could keep you in brand new faux fur trimmed winter coats. If the sex was good, then you've got it made. Send me a wedding invitation. I'll buy you something from your Tiffany's registry."

I looked out her window onto the street. She lived on Overlook, but I could never figure out if there was supposed to be something to look at. With a carbon copy six-story brick apartment building across the street, her view was the same as mine, albeit with a prettier moniker. In a single gulp, I downed the rest of the drink.

"I didn't sleep with him," I said, bracing myself for the snappy comeback. There wasn't one. Silence from a woman who couldn't keep her mouth shut was disturbing.

"You should ask Miles Siegel out," she said with surgical precision.

"Left field, that came from," I said. Damn Lulu. It had taken me a couple of weeks to banish that man from my dreams. When Tom was kissing me and groping for my bra clasp, I was working myself into the mood by pretending he was Miles. Damn, damn Lulu.

"Okay, Yoda." She rolled her eyes, then more silence.

"He was nice," I said.

"Why is your face red?"

"Is he Jewish?" I deflected.

"Did he look Jewish?" I waited her out. I knew that once Tom and I had left, she wouldn't have been able to help herself. Lulu had probably scribbled his family genealogy on the back of a napkin. "His mom is black. His dad is Jewish. He's from Philadelphia. Graduated from Swarthmore. Worked as a cop. Went to Penn. He's been at the AUSA's office for nearly a year." Since she'd gotten to the present, I knew she was done and not just out of breath.

"Did you finish that background check before or after you ate all his pizza?"

"Wine bars are for douche bags. Who likes that small plates crap? Those bacon wrapped dates have been giving me nightmares for weeks. Salty greasy bacon, sickly sweet gooey dates. They looked like little turds."

"Maybe you're predisposed to hate bacon."

"That *trayf* crap is bullshit. I'm a cultural Jew, not a religious one. No way am I going back to the days where I'd have to hide my hair and ankles. Chauvinistic crap." She was off. For a good ten minutes, Lulu went on a Judeo-Christian religions versus feminism tirade while I tried to stop my head from swimming. I looked up when I realized she was no longer talking. "Fucking A. You did that shit on purpose. Why didn't you sleep with him? I kind of recall you not being able to get enough of him that first time around."

I'm not sure if it was embarrassment or humiliation that sped up my heart and gave me that fizzy feeling in my veins. I'd never told her about Tom's low sex drive, and what I'd tried to do to get him interested. It'd been easy to pretend he'd asked for the lingerie and toys, when in truth he claimed the stress from law school had killed his sex drive.

Last night he'd been a whole different Tom. I didn't know what to make of this new, aggressive guy. He knew what he wanted and seemed eager to get it.

My head was still spinning from the turnaround. But as I had to keep reminding myself, it had been more than a handful of years. Maybe working major felonies from the winning side of the courtroom was stress-free.

"I'm not sure I'm in love with him anymore." There was some honesty for her.

"What do love and sex have to do with each other?"

"When we were dating the first time around, I was really in love. It wasn't like high school or college when dating was mostly drinking and sloppy make-out sessions. This time, I don't know. Back then, I could see us walking down the aisle, having some kids, discussing the law over coffee in the morning." I could still sort of see it in my mind, but Tom was no longer the man in that picture. My breakfast companion was much more nebulous and looked kind of like Miles.

Lulu wiped away a fake tear. I made a mental note to get less irreverent friends. "So, dump him. Would serve him right."

"I'm not one hundred percent sure I'm ready to give up on my dream to marry into the Brody clan."

"Sounds like you're not ready to give up the money."

Hammer, meet nail. I shook my head vehemently, though there was more than a grain of truth to what she said. But I deserved this. It was little enough recompense for what they'd done all those years ago.

"I really have to think about it this time. Something tells me I will not get a third bite at this apple."

"Look what happened to Eve after a single bite. Don't get greedy."

22

Miles
December 31, 2003

The apartment building seemed unusually quiet when I stepped in. Didn't anybody lock the door around here? New Year's Eve wasn't an excuse for playing fast and loose with safety. I pushed the door shut, giving it a shove for good measure.

The noise got louder and I got hotter as I made my way up the four flights of stairs to Casey's apartment. I gripped the cold bottle, and pushed my way through the crowd. Not a social butterfly by nature, I looked around, wondering what in the heck I was doing here.

"You made it!" Lulu cried, prying the bottle from my hand, the coat from my back, and disappearing with them both. Casey stood between the dining room and kitchen, handing out small plates of something and plastic forks.

When she looked up at me, I think a small smile peeked out. She took off some black hat with sparkly things, patted her head, and then put it back on. Odd duck behavior.

I looked around, not knowing a soul, so made a beeline for her despite the head pat. "Can I help you?"

"Sure." She handed me a triangular spatula with a serrated side. "I'm dessert." That was not a proposition, I instructed my overactive imagination. When my head cleared, she was making a square with her hands. "Cut pieces about yea big and give them to Greg." She pointed to a man fully outfitted in a vintage tuxedo.

I waved the tarnished silver implement toward him. "I'd shake your hand, but…."

"She put you to work. Greg Salazar. I live across the hall."

I looked for Casey, but she'd disappeared. The line for her dessert hadn't though, so I got to cutting. "Miles Siegel," I said to Greg as we played pass the plate.

"You a friend of Casey's?" he asked after the final person in line claimed their dessert.

"Acquaintance," I said, passing the last piece of pastry his way.

"That's yours. Taste it. It's good."

My mother had spoiled me for good food. I took the tiniest bite a man could get away with. It was fucking sensational. "Damn, did she make this?"

"Casey? God, no. Her mom's recipe is straight from the old country. She makes it every year around the holidays."

"I met Casey in a bar," I said, answering the earlier question.

Greg's face hardened like a father whose daughter was about to go out on her first date—with a mass murderer. "Casey doesn't bar hop."

"Whoa, there. It was a Cleveland Bar young lawyer's function."

His hard face was replaced by inscrutable. "So you met Tom."

"Her boyfriend. Sure."

"I wouldn't go that far. Tom's got a lot to make up for."

For lack of something better to do with my body, I sat at the small breakfast table in the deserted kitchen. Greg squeezed in, pretending to sweep crumbs. It was a draw. We both wanted information. I wanted to know why Tom was doing the macho possessive thing at the bar, why if Lulu said they'd only been dating for a few weeks, how the man could have a lot to make up for.

"What's the Tom story? Whatever happened wasn't bad enough to end their relationship." Greg looked like I'd put him on the spot. I held up my palm. "Hey man, no worries—"

Lulu thumped us on the shoulders. "You can't trust guys to do anything. You all are sitting down like union workers on a construction job. Help me pour the champagne, it'll be midnight in three minutes."

Pressed into service again, I pulled plastic flutes from a box under the table, while Greg poured. Lulu passed them out. I had two flutes in my hand when Casey reappeared, noisemakers in hand. I traded wine for a whistle covered in streamers and clasped her hand, pulling her with me to join the others in the living room.

Dick Clark was narrating while a bunch of people, who must have originated from the cold-blooded branch of the evolutionary family tree, stood in Times Square. "Five, four, three, two, one," I counted down along with the others.

"Happy two thousand and four," Dick Clark shouted from New York City. He kissed some blonde co-host dressed in pink. Everyone was doing the same. Somehow I'd abandoned my noise maker, and was pulling Casey into a celebratory kiss. Damn, this was the second surprise of the night. I really liked kissing her. Probably would have continued on, but her silence backed me off.

The partygoers around me drowned out the ones from TV. I hoped my cheeks weren't flaming when the hoots started up. The kids used to call me Peachy when I was pre-pubescent. Perpetual embarrassment had been my constant companion until I was out of my teens and could control my flushing face.

"We're the last stop of the night," Greg said, corralling folks out Casey's open door from her apartment into theirs. When they didn't move fast enough, still looking back at us, Greg upped the ante. "I have port we brought back from Villa Nova de Gaia." The promise of alcohol more substantial than a thimble full of bubbles got the crowd moving. Less than a minute later, I was standing alone with Casey in her apartment.

"I'll be back," Lulu said, slamming the door behind her.

"I'm sorry," she said.

"I don't know why…I know you have a boyfriend."

"Oh, right. Tom."

I sat down on the couch when I should have gotten up to go. I didn't need port. Maybe a good night's sleep. Casey started picking up plates and forks when my phone rang.

"Happy New Year!" my parents chorused.

"Hey guys," I said, pressing mute. To Casey, "My parents," I explained.

She nodded and moved to the kitchen.

"Where are you?" This is what I hated about untethered cell phones. Every damn conversation was about location.

"I'm at a party, Mom. I have to go."

"Kind of quiet for a party," my dad said.

"Have you found a new girl?" my mother probed.

I have no idea about earlier, but I was one hundred percent sure my cheeks were warming. I had to get off this phone and figure out why in the hell some girl from Cleveland with a shady boyfriend was getting under my skin.

"It's a progressive, and they've moved on to the next—"

"What's a progressive?" my mother asked. She was insatiably curious. If I let her go on, she'd be at her computer researching the history of dinner parties and wanting to talk about it for hours. I wouldn't put some late night discussions about cross cultural comparisons beyond her. I wasn't going to do it tonight.

"Going, Mom," I said. I slid the plastic in the back pocket of my jeans.

"You didn't have to get off on my account," Casey said.

I stood and started putting empty plates and flutes in the black trash bag. "It was rude. I'm sorry. My parents could have talked another hour."

"You get along with them?"

"They're the best parents I could have had," I said truthfully. "That looks nice on you." She was wearing some kind of sparkly black top that dipped off one shoulder.

"Thanks." She paused, like she wanted to say more but stopped herself.

Lulu opened the door, slamming it against a plastic stop. That girl probably never did anything quietly. "Gotta get my coat," she said, running down the hall toward the bedroom.

When she came back fully wrapped, I glanced at my watch. "Maybe I should be going too. It's getting—"

Lulu shoved me toward the kitchen. "You have to stay and help her clean up. She'll never ask, and I don't want Casey waking up to a mess."

"I'm right here." Casey waved her free hand in the air.

Lulu squeezed my biceps. Her strong fingers pressed through the material of my sweater, gripping like a vice. "You're a strong guy. Help her with those pans. She needs to bring them back to Mama Cort spanking clean."

After Lulu slammed her way out a second and final time, Casey dropped the bag and looked up at me. "You don't have to stay. I'm more than capable of washing dishes and tossing out trash."

I took off my watch and rolled up my sleeves. "Point me toward the sink."

While she finished cleaning up, I slipped my hands deep into the soapy suds, suddenly grateful my mom had made me work in the kitchen alongside her as soon as I could climb up on a stool. I applied a lot of elbow grease, and the pans were washed, dried and stacked on the small counter in about twenty minutes.

Casey was on the couch having strudel from a real plate with actual silverware.

"It was good, your mom's pie."

"Strudel," she said in perfectly accented German.

"Your mom's from Germany?"

"Grandma. But my mother learned her strudel at the foot of the master."

Casey's eyes were some odd combination that could only be described as hazel. My throat was as dry as sandpaper. "Do you have water?"

She looked at me strangely. "The pitcher's in the fridge."

I pulled a glass from the shelf above the stove, filled it, downed it. Then tipped the pitcher into the glass again. "About earlier," I said, making my way back to the couch. The half-full glass in my hand gave me purpose.

"Heat of the moment. It happens."

"That doesn't happen for me. I like you, though I know I shouldn't."

"Why shouldn't you? Because of Claire?"

"You were there the day Claire and I broke up," I said emphatically. "Because you're dating Tom Brody. He made that one thousand percent clear at the bar."

"I'm not..." she paused a very long time. The faint sounds I'd heard from next door were gone. The building was eerily quiet once again. "It's complicated."

I put my hand near her knee. The shimmery fabric of the pants she wore slid under my fingers. "Tell me," I said, wondering when I'd become her confessor.

Her reluctance only lasted a second; then a long tale of treachery emerged. First the Strohmeyers, then the Brodys. Like Philly, and probably like every city worthy of calling itself that, rich families did what they wanted with impunity. Everyone else either fell in line or got trampled.

I took a deep breath and did two things I knew were dead wrong.

First, I kissed her again. There was no mistletoe or flaming ball to blame it on this time. I did it because I wanted to. I did it because she needed it. I leaned forward and gently touched her pursed mouth. Casey melted into me. My hand came up, sifted through her unruly hair, smoothing out first one curl then another. Smooth bare shoulder and soft skin along her back enticed me next.

I wanted more than I was getting. There was no resistance when I deepened the kiss. She tasted like wine and apples. I toyed with the hem of her shirt. Mentally stopping myself, I pulled back before I went too far. I could too easily see us rolling around in that four- poster bed of hers. Tom wasn't the right guy for her. But maybe I wasn't either.

She looked as confused as I knew I was.

Then I knowingly made a second mistake. I told her the truth about the Brodys. "I'm working on this case," I started. She needed to know her boyfriend's family hadn't changed, probably couldn't change. Nostalgia wasn't a good reason for a relationship. By two-thirty in the morning on the first day of January, the only sounds were those of a few revelers walking from Shaker Square to wherever they were going to lay their heads.

When I stopped talking, Casey got up and paced the room. She walked back and forth toward the fireplace, back and forth between the five windows spanning the front of her living room to the archway to the dining room and back again.

"He's done this to others?" she asked, her voice a whisper.

I brought my hands together mimicking prayer. Others? Did she know something? I rubbed the spot between my eyebrows. Jesus, this judge had tentacles like an octopus. I nodded. "We think so. I talked to one girl myself. Another is mentally challenged and her family's rallied around her, afraid they'll lose the rights to her injury settlement."

"Is that why he moved from probate to juvenile?" Despite the late hour, I could see her mind agile and working through something.

"That's one working theory. Either he crossed the wrong person, or maybe someone threatened to talk. Or someone stupidly thought the litigants on Twenty Second would be less vulnerable."

"You don't think the women are doing it voluntarily?" Casey was rubbing her own head, temples to be exact. Apparently I was one headache inducing man.

"Not a single one." I shook my head at each word for emphasis.

"Shit," she said, stopping her pacing suddenly and plopped down near the candle filled fireplace, several feet from where I was sitting. I could tell that if she could rewind the clock seven hours or seven years, she'd do it in a heartbeat.

"Do you know something about Judge Brody?" I'd thought when I told her this, it would put an impenetrable barrier between her and Tom Brody. That she'd think twice about getting back together with him. Now this conversation had taken a turn I hadn't expected. She'd seen something she thought was consensual sex, that probably wasn't. I'd brought two thousand four in with a bang.

"I'm not doing this again." Casey held up both hands, pushing away some imaginary person.

"Doing what?"

"Going up against a big family. I lost big last time."

"But—"

"Do you see this?" she asked, gesturing toward the ceilings, walls, carpeted floors. "I can finally pay for this. My loans are out of deferment. I bought this outfit new and didn't have worry that my card was going to explode while I was at the department store check out."

"I don't follow."

"I'm almost done with my penance. I crossed the Strohmeyers. I paid the price. I have no idea what god answered my prayers. But there's been a reprieve. I have paying clients. Interesting cases. I can breathe. If I play my cards right, at the end of this year or next, I could be married. Be a Brody." I started to speak. A Brody? Casey could not be serious. She didn't want that. I didn't want that for her, for me. My mouth opened then closed when she pointed hard, silencing me. "Don't ask me to give it up a second time. I couldn't survive it."

23

Claire
January 2, 2001

I stood outside the juvenile court building, my back to the wind. If the first ex parte hearing had borne fruit, this one would be all thorns. Every call from Judge Brody that I'd ignored had put a little chink in my case. I knew that as well as I knew that my middle name should have been my first. Even if he'd never threatened me outright, every time the phone quieted, my chances of keeping Luke from Darius were growing slimmer.

My eye caught Casey's trimmed down figure exiting an old Honda from the parking lot across the street. She looked nice today, assured, professional. The debate that'd kept me up most of the night started replaying in my mind. If I told Casey what the judge had demanded, however obliquely, would the lawyer believe me? Could she get a new judge, or somehow figure a way to protect me and Luke from this man? Resolved not to brave this alone any longer, I squared my shoulders and watched her approach. I'd tell her, and we'd go from there.

Casey locked the car door then started the walk to the court. The lawyer stumbled, nearly twisting her ankle on a pothole. Just like that, my resolve crumbled. If she couldn't get out of her car and across the street without killing herself, she probably couldn't handle Judge Brody.

"Happy New Year," Casey said, shaking my hand.

"You too." I hated this small talk. Could we get to court already so I could hear the other shoe drop? There was no polite way to say that, so I returned a superficial smile instead.

"Did you have a good holiday?" she asked.

No, I had a shitty holiday without my little boy, ignoring my judgmental parents and avoiding judge Brody. I didn't say that. I tried to hide my nervousness by answering her small talk. "Spent some time with my parents," I said truthfully. "Cozied up with my boyfriend on New Year's Eve," I lied.

She cocked her head, looked at me like she knew I was lying. I raised my chin. "That guy Miles, I met at your house?"

"Yup. I'm thinking we'll be engaged come spring. Hopefully this," I gestured generally toward the brick building, "will be resolved by then. It would be great if he could adopt Luke." I turned away from her probing eyes, of no discernable color I could see, and started moving toward the building. "Did you spend your holiday with someone special?" I threw at her. No offense, but I couldn't imagine a bunch of guys lining up at her door. She'd probably been better off when she was younger and hopefully thinner.

Her face went from being as pale as the cold concrete beneath her feet to as red as the old brick of the courthouse.

"I spent some time with my boyfriend Tom." She handed her bag over to the security guard, fishing her keys from her pocket. I followed her and did the same. "In fact, he's Tom Brody," she said. "Judge Brody's his uncle."

I tried to smile like she'd bestowed the best news ever, even though I felt like one of those anvils from Luke's cartoons had fallen on my head. She'd never believe what I had to tell her about Brody. No doubt she was in tight with that family. I cursed my bad luck. If this were any other case, having a lawyer who was practically married into a judge's family would be a godsend.

Even if judges were supposed to be impartial, they weren't. I'd seen it with Judge Grant. If she'd gone to law school or even dinner with someone a few times, she smiled a little more, listened to their argument more closely, gave them the benefit of the doubt. I picked up my stuff from the second security guard and gathered my resolve.

"I'll admit, I'm a little nervous about this," Casey said.

"Why?"

"I'm not comfortable with ex parte justice," she said, pulling me into an alcove. "The first time I'd filed an emergency motion, so that kind of hearing was warranted. I probably should have notified the other side, but I wanted you to get some space from Darius. Sometimes when the dads realize we're serious, they straighten up and fly right."

"Instead he came to my house and threatened me," I said, laying blame at her feet. "Now that he's out I'm terrified he'll keep coming back like he did that first night."

"Do you need a restraining order?"

Restraining orders were paper tigers in Cleveland. "No, I need custody."

"How did he get out anyway? When I'd checked, he'd been booked on a felony."

"All Darius told me were that the charges were dropped. Once he realized that Luke was with my parents in Chicago, he left my house. So I didn't call you or the police—this time."

Casey shook the keys in the pocket of her wool coat. "It's weird. He was arrested and booked. But then he never went to arraignment or had a preliminary hearing. There was no grand jury indictment for him. It's like someone waved a magic wand and made it all disappear."

I knew that Judge Brody or one of his kin had waved that wand and let Darius out of his cage. If I wanted that wand waved again, I knew what I'd have to do.

"So what are you going to do about today's summons?" Maybe she could pull a rabbit out of a hat.

"I'm going to call Vernon Dinwiddie."

"That civil rights lawyer?" I'd seen that old man with his cowboy hats and bolo ties in and out of the federal courthouse. I think he'd even been in Judge Grant's courtroom on a discrimination case once.

"Yup. Him. Darius retained him."

"I have to go to the ladies room," I said. I stalked down the hall. The only sound was the echo of my heels on the stone floor. The bathroom was close and hot. I shut the ancient, scarred wood door and sat down on the black plastic toilet seat.

If I'd stayed at home that cold day, instead of rushing to the last lecture. Or if I'd eaten breakfast and had taken another bus. I shook my head vehemently. But then I wouldn't have Luke. He was the light of my life. Without Darius, I wouldn't have a little boy who loved SpongeBob, the color orange, and Apple Cinnamon Cheerios all in equal measure.

I took a deep breath of the moist, fetid air and prepared myself for what would come next. Dinwiddie and his dim-witted client would show up. The judge would do whatever he was going to do, and I'd be left to fight harder than ever. Maybe I'd take Luke to Chicago. At least I'd be on my home turf. Darius would never have the wherewithal to fight it out there. Or maybe he'd die behind some foolishness. Not that I wished harm on him. I only wanted him to grow up, be the kind of father a little black boy needed.

Casey flipped her phone closed and slipped it in her pocket as I approached. "Darius and his lawyer will be here in half an hour. I'll go let the bailiff know."

Thirty minutes later, we were in the judge's chamber.

"Glad to have you all here. Didn't need to go in the court-room or on the record for this. You all look like reasonable folks. I thought we could talk," Judge Brody said after eve-ryone had introduced themselves.

I looked down at my hands, folded in silent prayer, re-fusing to meet Judge Brody's eyes. Casey nudged me, but I didn't raise my head.

"Thank you, Your Honor," Casey said. "We were here back in December on an emergency ex parte because the child's arm was broken while in the respondent's custody."

"How did it get broken?" Judge Brody asked, his sooth-ing voice full of equanimity.

"My girl said he fell out the window," Darius answered.

"So he was in the care of a competent adult?" Judge Brody asked.

"Yes, he was Your Honor." Dinwiddie spoke for that tri-fling nigg—Darius, senior. I needed to censor my own thoughts for the sake of my son. "He kept going near the window. The young woman kept pulling him back. But she went to get water from the kitchen, and out he went. It could have happened to anyone, Your Honor."

"Why wasn't there a screen?"

"My client was replacing the storm windows that week-end. He'd done almost all of them. But stopped working to visit with his son," the lawyer finished.

"Ms. Cort?"

"Since this was Darius' time, my client wasn't there, your honor. From what she heard, the respondent wasn't visiting with his son. Instead, he was playing basketball with some friends."

Judge Brody ruffled through some papers. If I hadn't worked for Judge Grant, I'd have thought he was seriously weighing matters. But I knew that move. He'd already de-cided how this hearing was going to go. The rest was for show. "From what I see here," Brody said, "Sunday wasn't actually on the official visitation schedule."

"They've made special arrangements for the third Sun-day of the month when my client works, Your Honor," Ca-sey argued on my behalf.

"What we seem to have here is a caring father who is going above and beyond the call of duty. That, and an un-fortunate accident. Mm, hm." I could hear the judge's chair creak on ancient springs. I imagined he was leaning back, looking self important, while deciding the fate of a child he'd never met. "I think I may have been hasty in my earlier judgment. The defendant has been released from jail with all charges dropped. No restraining order has been filed in the meantime. So, I'm vacating my earlier order. Darius Gaines, Senior, your previous visitation schedule is reinstated. And you can have this weekend as well to make up for lost time."

"He has a felony conviction, Your Honor," Casey added.

"We're working to get that expunged right now. As a matter of fact, Your Honor, we're before the other Judge Brody in Common Pleas," Dinwiddie said with a lot of bluster.

"Sounds like he's moving in the right direction," Judge Brody said ticking off something on the court's file. "This weekend," the judge said again. I knew if I lifted my head, his eyes would be boring into mine, daring me to defy him again.

"Your Honor—" I heard Casey protest. Maybe I should have told her outside that she was wasting her time.

"So ordered, counselor." Judge Brody cut her off mid sentence.

I looked up then, meeting the judge's eyes I'd felt grazing my body. They held no guile. A little bit of triumph maybe. Brody got up and left the room without ceremony. Taking our cues, everyone stood to leave.

"I'm sorry," Casey said when we got to the hallway. "I don't understand the judge's complete reversal back there." I didn't blame her. I *did* understand, one hundred percent.

"Darius is capable of a complete about-face when necessary," I said to placate the attorney's ruffled feathers. She'd just been handed her ass. I didn't want her to lose total confidence when she wasn't aware of all the facts.

"Let's meet at my office next week, and make a plan of attack for the next hearing, okay?" She pulled a leather planner from her briefcase, when something fell out.

I picked up a TAG Heuer watch. It looked just like the one Miles' parents had given him for law school graduation. He'd loved that thing. It and that Blackberry never left his side. Before I could read the engraving on the back, Casey snatched it from my hand. "My friend left that by mistake. I need to return it." She shoved the watch into the deepest recesses of her bag.

As sure as I knew Judge Brody was after me, I knew that was Miles' watch. Was she seeing my ex? Wasn't one boyfriend enough for her? She'd handed me a business card with an appointment scribbled on the back before she hustled out of the door.

Duplicitous bitch. I'd brought her to my house to help me with Darius and she'd walked out with my boyfriend. She'd been the someone else. No wonder he'd been in such a hurry to run out of there that day.

"Claire Henshaw?" I turned around to see the judge's assistant. "The judge will see you now."

I looked up and down the hall. Not a witness in sight. Clever. I don't know how he did it. I followed her lead and stood in front of his desk. He came out from his little bathroom, rubbing his liver spotted hands together like a cartoon villain.

"Looks like you're going to have some free time, with your little boy off your hands. Why don't you come see me this weekend?" The judge pressed another card in my hand. Out of habit, I flipped over the card and read the tiny spidery words. This one had a west side address on the back. I snatched my hand away and ran out of the courthouse. I didn't give a shit who saw me or what they thought.

I took a deep breath when I got to my car. Resisting the urge to chuck the little card on the ground, I tucked it into my purse instead. What would this man do to my little boy if I didn't do what he wanted?

24

"I think we have an eyeball witness." I'd made a big leap to say that. But my gut told me it was true.

Valdespino put down the coffees he'd volunteered to get. "You shit me not?"

I shook my head. "No kidding. Kind of backed into it over the holidays."

"What's the reason we're not in the car right now nailing down this statement?" He readjusted his holster under his sport coat, and looked ready to scout out keys for a pool car.

"She won't talk."

"Why?"

"She's in thick with the Brodys."

"If she says anything—"

I cut him off. There was no witness protection that was bulletproof. "They'll ruin her career."

"Sounds like an exaggerated sense of self." He sat hard in a chair and pulled the lid off his coffee, taking a huge gulp.

I could tell he wasn't buying it. I half regretted bringing it up. But I wanted Casey to do the right thing. Maybe this guy could help me figure out a way to get her to do that.

"They did it once before. And it wasn't even them that she'd crossed."

Valdespino leaned back hard in the chair. "Is there nowhere this family doesn't have its tentacles?"

"The U.S. Attorney's office and the FBI."

"Ha, ha. Funny."

"What do you have?" I asked the investigator.

He took a long ass time to put down his half-empty coffee cup. "Got Tashonda Williams on paper."

It was my turn to be surprised. "The girl from probate court? How'd you swing that? I thought that family's door was closed to you. And why wasn't I there?"

"You didn't answer your phone. Turned off while you nursed a hangover, I expect. Heard that churches did sermons on New Year's resolutions. Caught them on their way back from service. Threw a little Jesus guilt at them."

"Damn," I said. I was impressed. We'd made no headway for weeks, and suddenly we were rolling. I looked at the watch Casey had returned to me via the office receptionist. "Let's see what we can come up with at the meeting." Maybe they'd have some way to pull this together. This case was all over the place for me. Don't know how I'd ever get enough information to indict Judge Brody much less convict him. Coercion was a slippery thing. Until I'd said something even Casey'd thought what she'd seen had been between consenting adults.

In the conference room, Chas sat at the head of the table. Rachel was to his right. The rest of the criminal unit filled in around the oval. Valdespino and I stood at the end.

"It's been three months, what do you have?"

"Other cases to work on," I half-joked.

"I want to go to grand jury in April, or let it go." Chas was all business in today's meeting. I cleared my throat nervously.

It hadn't been a never ending investigation, like counter-terrorism, I knew that. But this was a deadline certain. I looked at Valdespino. He'd lived with the case much longer than I. He could take the lead. He shrugged, sat, opened a paper bag from Arabica and took a hefty bite of a baseball-sized muffin and patted crumbs from his belly. Fine. I was the lawyer in a room of lawyers. It was my show.

I pulled a marker from a tray and started writing on the white board.

"We have three victims on record: Tashonda Williams, Kyanna Oliver, and Shanice Watson. Tashonda was in probate court because of a fight over money. The other two are fresher. Oliver and Watson were in juvenile because the county had taken their kids."

Rachel put her hand up halfway. That was modest for her. "And would they—"

"Hold up in court? Maybe. Brody is careful. His first victims were women whose families were seeking guardianship. They'd be incompetent witnesses. Tashonda's the most solid one, but she's the youngest. Eighteen at the time."

Chas looked down at his pad. "The other two?"

"Family services took Watson's kids because she's..." I hesitated. This wasn't a room full of jaded cops. Sexual harassment was a real thing. Damn.

"A hooker," Valdespino spoke up from his chair. "She was doing her johns in the same apartment where her kids slept."

"She has the shortest history with Brody. He laid out what he wanted, she did it, got her kids back in a few weeks."

"And Oliver?"

"Her boyfriend's a dealer who got caught. Oliver was in public housing."

The room was silent. Everyone got that. In our zero tolerance society, it didn't matter that the mom and kids would be homeless. If there was drug activity in subsidized housing, everyone was out.

"To get her kids back, she needed a place to live. Housing wasn't easy for her because there's a lot of friction between Oliver, her mom, and the baby daddy drug dealer who was in jail all of a few minutes. Once she did what Brody wanted, she got the kid back. Oliver was a harder nut to crack but we've got her statement."

"How did you find out about her?"

"Victim's mother. The one time tit-for-tat was okay. But when Brody didn't stop calling, the mother got pissed."

"A lot of mother of the year awards going around," Rachel said.

I took a deep breath and let it pass. Rachel obviously had never had to make a hard choice in her life. Judgment was so easy for others.

"I think one or two others would be helpful. Any press conference we do, we're going to need a few victims behind us for optics. The human equivalent of guns, money, drugs."

"Tell them about the eyeball witness," Lou said.

If I could have put a fist in Valdespino's face and gotten away with it, I would have. For a brief minute, I missed the cop shop. A little fisticuffs between partners would have been overlooked. Chas leaned forward expectantly. No way I could avoid this one. Valdespino knew that.

"I didn't mention this because I'm not one hundred percent sure of what she saw. It came up at a New Year's party after a few drinks."

"Were you discussing cases outside the office?" Papers shifted, chairs rolled back as everyone waited for Chas to take me down.

"It's nothing like that," I said. Almost every investigation was confidential. But we had to give a little to get a little. Civilians didn't get it. What they didn't know wouldn't hurt them.

"Will she testify or not?" Rachel asked, for once diffusing tension instead of amping it up.

"The conversation never got that far." I felt like I was betraying Casey. We'd never specifically talked about this. I was assuming a lot. Damn Valdespino. Damn him.

"She's Tom Brody's girlfriend," I said. Though I wished she wasn't that either.

"Oh, shit," Rachel said then covered her mouth.

"Judge Brody's been giving her cases. I think she walked into something, assumed it was consensual, and walked out. Brody's wife's disabled. A nice lady apparently, but probably not—you know—so this wit assumed he was merely unfaithful."

"Would it corroborate one of the vics?" Valdespino asked.

I turned on him. "Don't know, Lou. Why don't you go out and investigate something?"

Chas stood, ready to smooth over any ruffled feathers. "Guys. Let's talk this out." He came over to the dry erase board and made a new column next to target and victims, labeling it eyewitnesses.

"What's her name?"

"She didn't volun—"

Chas gave everyone the hard stare. "Nothing goes outside this room. Nothing."

I paused a long time then reluctantly gave her up. "Casey Cort."

"Why does that name sound familiar?" Rachel asked.

"Because it is," Valdespino said.

"Wait? Is that the girl who lost the Judge Grant case?" *Oh My God,* she mouthed to the woman next to her.

"That's the one," I confirmed.

"She's dating Tom Brody. He's a catch," she said like Casey was lucky to land him. I'd met Tom. He was the lucky one.

"She's a very nice woman," I said defensively. Why did everyone act like Casey had cooties? That kiss was pretty good. I'd bet that she looked damned fine without…. It took me a minute to clue back into the conversation.

"Rachel," Chas was admonishing, "we're not voting her on or off an island. We need to know if she could be a witness. Whether she could solidify a case that has some easily discredited witnesses."

"I think she'd make a solid witness. But she's not going to do it," I said.

"We have the power of the subpoena," one of the AUSAs said.

Yeah. I'd thought a subpoena was powerful the first year I was a detective. Get 'em in court, I'd thought. They'll tell the truth, and the bad guys would go to jail. "If used wrong, witnesses get quiet, lose their memory, get a lawyer, plead the Fifth. This is premature. We don't even have a statement. And even if we did, why should she cross the Brodys?"

Chas flattened his palms on the table. "Anything else?"

"I'll get you a witness list, and draft a grand jury indictment," I promised.

"Can you expand on your two-forty-two memo? The big guy wants another look at that. He doesn't want the judge poking a big hole in our theory."

Everyone filed out. I looked at Valdespino.

"What?" he asked, all wide-eyed and wide-armed innocence.

"I'm not sure she saw anything."

"We should go after her, hard. A family friend will go over great with a jury. Better than four poor black women."

"So what, black women can't be victims?" I asked, my dander fully up. "Black women have been the most victimized in this country's history."

Valdespino's hands made a valiant effort to push my words away. "Whoa. Not saying that. I'm talking about a suburban Northern District jury. You haven't been here long. They're mostly white, not from Cleveland. Solid citizens."

I hadn't pegged this guy for a racist. "So these women who the judge targeted and victimized aren't solid citizens?"

"That's not what I meant. Are you mad about Casey?"

"What she and I discussed was in confidence. It was at a New Year's party for Pete's sake."

"Where was this party?" Valdespino looked suspicious.

"At her place?"

"Jumping Jesus on a pogo stick! You've got a thing for her. I can't believe I didn't see this before. Gonna have to get my eyes checked." He balled up his fists and rubbed his eyes dramatically.

"She's got a boyfriend."

"Who's from a family of colossal, corrupt assholes. That won't last long."

"She might marry him. Said so herself."

"Nah. I wouldn't bet on it. That was the last defense of someone who knows it's over.".

25

"It's looking good. I don't think we'll even have to go to court," I said.

Marisa's face looked the most relieved I'd ever seen. "Really?"

"Once you gave up claim to his future earnings, he lost all interest in custody."

"I don't want his money. As long as I have my kids and we can travel back and forth to *España*, sorry, Spain, without hassle, that's enough. I don't have this American obsession with money, and I don't want my kids to have it either. Family is more important," she said.

Easy to say if you have money. "Family" and "leisure" were for those who didn't have "loans" and "bills." I stood, trying to steal a glance at the small clock on my bookshelf.

Upside to the Brodys' generosity with referrals was that I was as busy as ever. Downside was that I'd had to learn to shuffle clients in and out more efficiently. No longer could I hand Kleenex over one at a time as clients told me how a boyfriend/cop/social worker had done them wrong.

Now I collected money, asked the important questions, and then tried to get them out before they saw the next one coming in. People with a little bit of money and an exaggerated sense of social prominence didn't want to meet each other at the lawyer's office.

Unfortunately, Marisa didn't take the hint. Her butt remained firmly planted in the second hand chairs I'd recently had reupholstered. I tried not to let my sigh emerge. Her face said she wanted to share a secret.

This is where it always happened. I learned about the hidden love child, torrid affair, or embezzlement. I sat back down, hoping whatever she was going to say wouldn't demolish the carefully laid plans we'd worked on for the past few months. Victory—or a settlement she could live with—was in sight.

"Do you know Lizzy Cofrancesco?"

My stomach clenched with envy. Tom's ex-girlfriend came up at every turn. There wasn't an inkling that she was back in the picture, but jealousy stabbed at me nevertheless. Beautiful Lizzy had merited an engagement ring. "I've never met her," I said, trying to make my face as expressionless as possible.

Marisa's sigh was long and drawn out. "How serious are you and Tom?"

She was going to be one of those. I leaned forward, putting on my earnest face and started the talk. "While I appreciate having you as a client, I like to keep my work and personal—"

She waved her hands, cutting me off. "I know the difference. We're not friends. But as one woman to another, I want to say this. No one is going to tell you what you're getting into. They all have too much to lose."

"No offense, but I dated him years ago. I know all there is to know about my boyfriend."

"Do you know why he broke up with Lizzy? They were engaged. Newspaper announcement, big party in Lakewood. All of it. Suddenly one day, they're apart and you're back in the picture a minute later. Did you not wonder?"

Of course I'd wondered. I was a typical woman, with big insecure moments, who didn't trust what was going on around her. But that insecurity hadn't done me any favors in my teens or twenties. Now I took what came my way at face value. Tom liked me, wanted to marry me, maybe. I'd take it. "What did you want to tell me?"

"Have you heard about the prostitution stings on the west side?"

Free-floating pieces in my brain started to fit together like a game of Tetris. No. I shook my head. I didn't want to know this. "No, I—"

"Tom nearly got arrested."

I shook my head more vigorously for a time. But my curiosity and self-preservation got the better of me. I asked the next question. "For what?"

"You weren't born on the moon. You can guess."

"Maybe he was there for work. I mean prostitution isn't a felony, but maybe there was a trafficking sting."

I didn't want to hear anymore. Marisa kept on going. "Lizzy had caught him once. She found pictures of skinny dark-skinned girls. At first maybe she'd thought they'd fallen from a file. But when the cops did the courtesy of dropping him off at home, he couldn't deny it."

All that time I'd spent trying to make myself sexier, all that money I'd spent on uncomfortable lingerie. I'd thought I was lucky because I didn't have one of those boyfriends who'd pestered me for sex, and it had never been me he'd wanted.

This time when I stood up, she followed suit. Just like that, it was as if the last ten minutes of conversation had never happened. She was the cool European actress done wrong, and I was the attorney who was going to help her save her children from the domineering American mogul.

Another crime, another cover up. I was supposed to meet Lulu for a drink, but I was too tired for this. Seven years ago, all I'd wanted was to be a Brody. Right now, I was wishing I'd never met any of them. Maybe I could get a job in Dayton or Cincinnati. It would probably be cheaper. I could start a whole new life without any of this shit following me. And my parents would only be hours away. I'd miss them and Lulu, a lot. But federal loans weren't dischargeable in bankruptcy so I needed to find a way to use my only marketable skill outside of the Brody sphere of influence.

I feinted, dodged and left messages with Tom's and Lulu's secretaries. I wasn't ready to see either of them. Like Sophia Loren, I wanted to be alone.

Miles was at the front of my apartment building when I trudged up. Was there no relief? I needed to be by myself. I didn't want to hear what I should do or could do. I wanted to make a decision without the influence of someone who'd say they had my best interest at heart, but was really thinking of themselves.

"How can I help you?" I asked. Even I could hear the edginess in my voice.

"I thought we were friends."

"What do you want?" I asked. I wasn't feeling friendly.

"Can I come up and talk to you?"

"Whatever," I said. If he followed, fine. If he didn't, that was fine too. I hadn't forgotten about that kiss. As a matter of fact, I was reminded of it at the most inopportune times. The last thing I needed was a relationship. Not that I knew if he was even offering. I mean, I know he wasn't with Claire on New Years. Poor thing had thought it was important to lie about that. But I wasn't dying to pick up my client's sloppy seconds.

When I dropped my bags in the hall of my apartment, Miles was still there outside the door, looking expectant.

I relented, letting him in and closing the door behind us. "Do you want a glass of wine?"

He nodded and took a place at the dining room table. I pulled pinot grigio from the fridge and unapologetically filled my glass more than the customary half. I poured a smaller glass for Miles.

"I want you to testify," was his opening gambit.

I took a long drink then said, "I guess no one's ever accused you of beating around the bush."

"What did you see?"

"What I assumed was consensual sex between Judge Eamon and a girl."

"How old?"

"A young woman," I paused, the long banished images floating before me. "A young black woman. She was bent over the desk. He was naked except for his robe. Sex. There was what looked like sex."

He was quiet. "That was out of character. He usually uses his apartment." He caught my raised eyebrows. "The Brody brothers own a rundown building in Lakewood, near the railroad. He uses the empty manager's apartment to meet women. Why'd you think it was consensual?"

"Who am I to judge? I've met his wife. She's got Parkinson's, really advanced. She's in a wheelchair. They probably don't have sex anymore. I figured he was getting it elsewhere. Maybe his wife turns a blind eye. Maybe she even condones it. But I didn't expect it to be in his house."

"Who was the vic?"

"Don't know more than I told you," I said, draining the glass and rising to refill it.

"What was the date?"

"Sometime in September. I don't know." Something rose up from my belly. It was laughter. Deep rumbling laughter. I tried to hold it down. First I clamped my mouth shut. Slapped first my right hand, then my left over my mouth. But I couldn't stop it. The giggling and laughing didn't stop. Even to my own ears, I sounded like a hyena, or what I imagined a hyena sounded like. I'd never seen one. Not at the zoo or in the Emerald Necklace. "What marketing team came up with the Emerald Necklace?" I asked.

Miles looked like he'd rather be anywhere but here in a place full up with crazy, hysterical female. "Are you okay?"

"Okay? That's rich. Wait, that's one thing I'll never be." When the laughter gave over to crying, I really tried to hold back. But I couldn't seem to control anything. One minute this was the funniest thing ever. Then it was the most tragic. "I totally see how it happened," I said, shaking my head.

"How what happened?"

"They probably knew about the prostitution thing all along."

"Prostitute?"

"So Lizzy dumps him. Because why would someone beautiful and rich put up with that shit?"

"Lizzy?"

"Lizzy Cofrancesco. You should look her up. You must have access to all the FBI agents and databases in the world. Her driver's license picture is probably spectacular."

I watched his handsome face screw up in confusion. "So this girl dumped who?"

"Tom. Tom Brody. You're after the Brodys right? Lizzy finds out Tom likes prostitutes more than pretty rich girls and dumped his ass. I can see what happened next. I was there when they planned to silence the Cofrancescos. Tom needed to cover up his little proclivity. What better than a quick marriage to a willing woman? They stood at the top of the Key Bank building and looked around. I was probably shooting loser beacons from Shaker Square."

"Then what?"

"What? Tom calls me out of the blue. 'Come on over. Meet my uncle. You'll get cases.' My poor ass drives right over to Lakewood, hoping the whole time my transmission doesn't seize up on the highway. Because a fat girl in a tight dress waving down a good Samaritan in holiday traffic is too sad for words. I get there. The judge feels me up a little. I ignore it because—well—money. And I get a big case. You heard of the Ellingwoods non-common law marriage?"

He nodded because he'd have to have been under a rock not to have heard about the most salacious thing to hit the Cleveland legal community since Judge Grant.

"I'm on it, courtesy of Judge Eamon Brody."

"And then?"

"And then Tom takes me to Charley's Crab and proposes we get back together. Turns out, I can be bought for eighty dollars of farmed seafood plus a molten chocolate dessert. I hear wedding bells and have paying clients coming out of my ears. I got my 'get out of jail free' card."

"Mm hm."

"Don't nod your head. I can see it now. Tom, why don't you use Casey as your beard? It's believable. You dated her before. She's got blonde hair, hazel eyes. Not like the women you prefer. Your kids will be lovely Aryan specimens. How do we know? Did you see those childbearing hips? Plus, her mom makes great strudel."

"And now?"

"What? My boyfriend likes his girls young, black and available." I suddenly realized he of the beautiful caramel skin might not like that phraseology. "No offense."

"None taken."

"Now that I've witnessed the crime of the century, my ego is crushed. Why don't I singlehandedly end my career in Cleveland by going up against another influential family? Why not? Sign me up." My hands grew more frantic with each nail in my coffin.

He pulled my hands down to the warm wood table, covering them with his. "Shhh."

"Why? There's no way this is going to end well."

"You're wound up. Let's figure this out, one step at a time."

"Seriously, how do you—"

He took my chin, pulled me toward him and kissed me. I was the sweetest balm. I had not a single idea what in the hell I was doing with this guy, but I went with the flow. One minute, we were straining to reach each other across the dining room table. The next minute or ten, we were pulling each other's clothes off in my dark bedroom. Its two windows faced an airshaft between buildings, leaving us in late afternoon darkness. Neither of us reached to turn on the light.

The only words he spoke were, "Do you have a condom?"

"Yes," I answered because I did. I'd been saving them for what I thought was inevitable with Tom. I wanted both to get it over with and make the obliteration of the present last forever. It was like a shooting star, impossibly bright and hopeful; then it was gone. We came crashing down to the present. He untangled his sweaty limbs from mine. I lay naked in my bed while Miles washed up in the bathroom. Shamelessly nude, he came back and slid under the covers.

"What just happened here?" Maybe he knew, because I certainly didn't.

"I made love to a woman I'm very attracted to." My blood fizzed. That wasn't at all the answer I was expecting. I'd assumed he'd kissed me instead of slapping me to stop my hysteria. One thing led to another because hormones take over when brains stop. "Don't overanalyze it, Casey. I didn't kiss you on New Year's Eve by mistake."

"But you apologized." I'd assumed champagne and Dick Clark had pushed him over the edge.

"No buts. I didn't call you because you had a boyfriend. I respected that. But I think that's safely off the table, right?" When I didn't answer, he rose on his right arm, and rested his left hand on my shoulder. He brushed my hair back from my face, ran a finger down my neck and around my shoulder. I trembled involuntarily. He made me feel all shivery, and wanton, and sexy in a way Tom never had—now, or even while we were in law school. "Help me out," he said, not waiting for the obvious reply. "Lou Valdespino, the FBI agent on this will show you some pictures. Figure out who this victim of Judge Brody's was. Help us put this guy away by testifying. It's the right thing to do."

I wanted to nod. Every fiber of my physical being wanted to say that I was done with Tom and his family. But I hesitated. And when I looked into his brown eyes, I knew the hesitation had been a beat too long.

"You're not going to be with a guy who—"

Miles stopped speaking when I got up and pulled my robe from inside the closed door. With my back to the bed, I tied first the inside loops, then the belt—tight. Socks spilled from the dresser drawer I jerked open. I put on the first pair I found. Chunky wool rainbow, hand-knitted ones from my grandmother warmed my feet. When I got to the kitchen, I shielded my eyes from the glaring fluorescent light then checked the time. Only seven o'clock. I sat down at one end of the dining room table and refilled my wine glass, this time up to the lip, relying on surface tension to keep the table dry.

When Miles made it out to the front of the apartment, he was mostly dressed in his work pants and a sleeveless undershirt. His button down shirt hung open and untucked.

"I represent Claire."

He sat at the other end of the long table. The extra leaf was still in from the holidays. I wondered when Rosebud would make an appearance. "I know," he said.

"She told me she'd rung in the new year with you."

"I was here kissing you. Claire and I broke up back in November. The day you nearly totaled my car." The last he said with a half smile playing around his lips. I looked away before I did something stupid like jump across the table and kiss him again.

"I don't know if she's on the same page regarding your break up," I said, looking at stippled plaster on the wall. I wondered if there was some grand pattern to the walls or was it completely random?

"Why are we talking about Claire?"

His voice pulled me back. I stared into those deep brown eyes, watching the bob of his Adam's apple. "I don't—" The phone rang in its hall alcove. The clanging of the old style bell echoed off the bare walls of the long hallway.

"Do you need to get that?" Miles said over the noise.

I let it ring, crossing my fingers, hoping it would be my parents, or at worst, Lulu. We were quiet when the answering machine picked up. The sound of my voice filled the hall, then a pause, then the long beep. Next came Tom's voice.

"I really wanted to talk to you tonight." I tipped my chair running to the hall. My robe got caught in the leg of the chair. I lost precious seconds unhooking the baggy cotton. When I got to the hall, I was too late to pick up the receiver. After setting the chair to rights, Miles was beside me in an instant. If I lifted the phone, I risked Tom hearing. We glanced at each other, then stared at the machine. The disembodied voice continued.

"Casey, I wanted to make sure your schedule was clear for The Soiree on Valentine's Day. I was hoping…this is weird to say to a machine, but here goes. I wanted to announce our engagement that night. What do you say? Call me."

The machine clicked to a stop. I looked up at Miles. "I can't testify before a grand jury."

26

I'd dutifully bathed, groomed and fed my son before sending him into the lion's den. I might not have ever really practiced law, but I knew that defying the judge's court ordered visitation schedule would win me points with no one.

Four rings bleated from the phone then six. After having Luke, I'd increased the number of rings until the machine picked up. I'd learned the hard way that a mommy elbow deep in matchbox cars wasn't quick on reflexes.

After eight long rings, the machine started recording. "Claire Henshaw. I'm at the Lakewood apartment now. I'd like to see you. Come by at eleven. I know you're free." Click. Done. The blinking red light stared at me from the kitchen counter. I jabbed a button deleting all messages. Opening my purse, I retrieved the hastily scrawled card the judge's sweaty hand had pressed into mine. I needed to find out where in the hell Plover Street was.

Sighing, I rifled through the junk drawer until I'd pulled out a map of Cleveland. I was running my finger along the street list when the door rattled. Startled, I looked up. Who was knocking on a Sunday morning? The little old ladies who kept eagle eyes on the neighborhood were safely tucked away in church for the moment.

"Coming!" Without looking, I pulled open the door. Miles. Hope came alive in my chest. "Hello, stranger. Nice to see you." I pulled the door open and stepped back. He hesitated a long time on the threshold. "I won't bite unless you want me to." The pale skin of his cheeks turned pink.

"I was driving through the neighborhood. Thought I'd stop by and see how you were."

I could feel my shoulders come down along with my hopes. "I'm fine, Miles. Still counseling women in prison. Still in court over custody."

"Is Darius putting up a fight?"

"Surprisingly, yes. But Casey's keeping it on the court's front burner. You remember Casey, right. Frumpy girl, my attorney?"

Miles struggled with keeping his cool. Guilty. I knew it. How he could prefer her over me, I don't know. Not to toot my own horn, but I knew I had got it going on. I'm the girl rap guys write lyrics about. Probably because she was white. In the end, they all wanted the American standard of beauty right? Blond hair was all it took to hook a man. Didn't matter how else the woman looked.

"She's—"

"Miles, spare me. I know you're seeing her."

"How…" If I'd been in a more humorous mood, his perplexed look would have been priceless. "It had nothing to do with us. It happened after we broke up."

"Are you here to assuage your guilt?" When he didn't say any more, I shook my head. "Look, Luke's not here, and I've got a lot of stuff to do before he comes home. So if you'll excuse me." His mouth opened and closed like a guppy. I pushed him out the door and got back to my map.

I plotted my route then checked myself in the bathroom mirror. With my hair back in a headband, my make-up free face stared back at me. The sweatshirt, jeans, and sneakers I was wearing wouldn't give anyone ideas.

I hit every red light between my house and the highway. My adrenaline-fueled foot jiggled on the brake at every stop. It was smooth sailing after that, thankfully. Any more delays and I would have turned around from this fool mission. I pulled up outside the nondescript apartment building. Its yard was dotted with snow-covered disposable charcoal grills and beaten up cars. I pulled my car into an alley. Zipping my coat to my chin to keep out the severe chill, I quickly located number four and pressed the bell.

"I knew you'd come, eventually," Judge Brody said, backing away from the door. I looked right and left, but didn't see a single soul. He wouldn't kill me and leave my child an orphan, I silently repeated to myself. That wasn't his MO.

This broken down apartment isn't what I'd expected from a judge. The plaid couch in the studio apartment listed to one side. A double bed, with a sheet barely covering the mattress was tucked in a corner of the bare room. I nearly jumped from my boots when a loud sound filled the room.

But it was only a small refrigerator coming on, I realized. I gulped air, trying to slow my heart rate.

"Take off your coat. Get comfortable," he said. I could see his breath in the air. Didn't this place have heat? Despite the cold, he was wearing sweatpants and a matching jacket over an undershirt. Nothing more. The pants did nothing to hide his arousal. But then, he probably wasn't trying to hide it.

"It's cold."

"Oh." He turned and pulled a space heater from its resting spot against the wall. The lights flickered and dimmed as he set it to blow dry hot air. I huddled on a stool. The room was so small that it heated quickly. "It's warmer now. Let me see what you're wearing."

"I think we need to talk, Your Honor."

"Call me Eamon. And take off your jacket."

I pulled off my parka revealing the thick sweater I'd chosen earlier. It hid almost everything. Though I knew that my curvy figure showed through even the biggest tents, I thought I had done a good job of keeping it under wraps. I'd hated my figure as a teen. Loved it as an adult. Hated it right now.

"Judge…Eamon, I'm not sure what you think is going on here."

"You want to keep your son with you?" My nod was automatic. "Then you'll do what I want."

"What's that?" Though we both knew, he'd never spelled it out. I dared him to do it. I should have brought some kind of recorder. Damn, damn, damn. A little blackmail would have worked in my favor. It was as if fingers snapped waking up the thinking side of my brain. That's it! I'd try that next time. I had to string him along this time and get out of here unscathed.

He laughed softly, menacingly. "Think you're a smart one."

"I went to Northwestern Law," I said.

He walked to a small trunk and pulled out something small and red. "Here." He shoved the scratchy fabric into my hands. "You wear that next time you come."

"Why should I come back?"

"I haven't shown you what I can do."

27

I had a bad feeling in the pit of my stomach. Claire had stared at her map with a certain fatalism. While my ex-girlfriend sat in her car waiting for it to warm up, I punched Casey's number into the phone, glad I'd pried at least that information from her.

"Who is the judge on Claire's case?" I asked before I thought to say, 'hello.'

She paused a beat before coming back at me, hard. "You're crossing the line. Juvenile court proceedings are confidential—"

"Casey. Tell me now," I barked. "Claire could be in trouble."

Her sigh was long and drawn out. But in the end, she trusted me. That was something. "Judge Eamon. Judge Brody is her judge."

I didn't bother saying good-bye, Claire was on the move. I tossed the phone on the seat and followed my ex as she eased on down the road. I hadn't done much surveillance during my time on the force, but I'd learned enough to follow someone who wasn't trying to lose me.

Eventually, she pulled up to a squat row of townhouses in Lakewood. Claire looked around before going in, but I was pretty sure she never spotted me. The street was dead quiet. I didn't hear or see much in the time I sat there trying not to turn into a popsicle. Because it was bitterly cold, there wasn't a single soul outside who didn't need to be. Which would mean no witnesses; I cursed. My car shook every time the MTA rattled by, stirring the frigid air.

I palmed the phone, my frozen fingers finding difficulty with the keys. Called Valdespino. Asked him to check on Casey's boy Tom. Was he really soliciting on the side? I don't know which upset me more, the idea that her so-called boyfriend was stepping out on her, or the fact that good ol' Tom was cut from the same cloth as his uncle, flouting the law while sworn to uphold it. The Brodys gave all new meaning to oath of office.

Eventually, I turned on the car to spare my mother the horror of finding out her only son had frozen to death. An hour later, Claire came back out, clutching something in her hands.

Had Judge Brody done something to her? I shook my head vehemently. Not likely. Claire was a pretty together woman. Except for having a case before the judge, she wasn't anything like his usual victims. Claire was educated and had resources. Surely she'd call the police or turn to...me. Damn, maybe that's why she'd called me those weeks before. My ego had assumed it was all about the amazingly wonderful Miles Siegel.

After she backed out, I rubbed my hands together, bringing them back to life, then turned on the ignition again. While the car shuddered to life in the cold, I picked up the phone from the floor on the passenger side, and hit redial.

"I'm coming over."

"Miles, I don't know if this is a good idea."

"It's not about us. It's about Claire."

***

Even the sound of the buzzer letting me in was reluctant, but I pushed my way through the front door and made it to the fourth floor, taking the steps two at a time. I pounded on the door loud enough to rouse the neighbors.

Still in pajamas, Greg peeked from the door across the hall. "Everything okay?" He asked it in such a way that I knew if my answer was the least bit wrong, I'd have to fend off the Cleveland Police. And I was one hundred percent sure they wouldn't be as lenient on me as they'd been on Judge Brody.

"Everything's fine, Greg," Casey said once she opened the door, pulling me in.

"Jason and I are staying in today if you need us." His message was clear. If I put a finger out of line, two grown men would tackle me in an instant. I almost volunteered for a good smack in the head for being so oblivious.

Casey pushed the door closed. Weary would be the best way to describe her. I didn't think of her as thin, but her jeans and sweater were hanging off her frame. "I don't know what we have to say to each other right now. You want me to do something I'm unwilling to do."

"It's Claire."

For a long moment, Casey looked like she was going to cry. Then she pinched her nostrils together, her eyes darting away while she pulled it all under control. "What about Claire?"

I pulled her hands in mine. "We're not back together."

Her shoulders dropped in relief. My hope for us rose in equal measure. "What, then?"

"She's Judge Brody's next target."

She looked at me, equal parts disbelief and resignation on her narrow face. "I need more coffee," Casey said, taking herself to the small kitchen. I took a seat at the small melamine table. She jerked her mug at me. "You?"

I put my hands on my knees to stop them from bobbing. "No, thanks."

Five fortifying sips later, she spoke. "Claire?"

"I saw her go to Brody's hideout."

"You followed her?" Every question was a test.

"I went to see her this morning."

"Did she call you?"

"No...I was worried about her. Rightly so, apparently."

"You're here, in my apartment, and not for the coffee. What do you want me to do?" she asked, plunking her now empty mug on the butcher block counter top.

I leaned forward, pleading with my eyes. "Bring her in. I think she could be the lynchpin."

28

I think Claire and I showed our identification about twenty times before we got to the little FBI waiting room. I shoved my driver's license through the bulletproof glass one more time.

"They'll be with you in a minute, hon," a receptionist said. If receptionists wore holsters.

Ten minutes later, Miles and a short guy with a dusting of colorless hair came through a metal door. The kind without a knob or latch on this side.

"Lou Valdespino. Claire Henshaw and her attorney, Casey Cort," Miles said. Claire shook the guy's hand first. Then I did. "Let's go on back."

Then it got awkward. Miles bent his head and arm as if to kiss me. I backed away into a chair, toppling it.

"Sorry," I said, turning the chair upright.

"Good to see you," Miles said, backing away from the mess I was making of things.

The four of us finally assembled in a windowless conference room. The hum of the fluorescent lights made the room feel like it was vibrating.

"We want you to wear a wire," Lou said. If his badge and gun were anything to go by, I assumed he was the FBI agent on the case.

Claire looked at me, her eyes widening. It was easy to see that this whole thing had morphed out of control. I didn't know what to say to her. I'd made her a sacrificial lamb of sorts. Hoping that if I turned over Claire, I could keep the role of attorney and they'd forget my role as witness.

"I got this in the mail today," I said, passing the green and white postcard over to Miles.

"Motion to Show Cause why respondent Darius Gaines, Senior should not be allocated parental rights," Miles read. "Who filed this?"

"I called Dinwiddie. Wasn't him. He acted like Christmas had come again, though."

"*Sua sponte?*" Miles asked about the judge making the decision on his own.

"I'm guessing." I shrugged.

"He turned the screws tighter when you didn't do what he wanted," Lou said to Claire.

"Can he really take my child on a whim? Where are the so-called checks and balances in this damned justice system?" Claire demanded, tears leaking from the corners of her eyes.

"I could always take his final decision up on appeal," I said, hearing the weakness in my own voice.

"No interlocutory appeals?" Miles was asking if we couldn't appeal now before the end of the case instead of later.

"You haven't been in Cleveland long," I said, shaking my head. "It has to be certified by the judge, and the appeals court has the discretion on whether to hear the matter."

"That's a non starter then," he said.

"Are the two of you done planning out my case?" Claire asked.

I sat back in my chair, chastened. Miles and I had slipped into casual legal banter, while my client's life and child were on the line.

"So if I wore this wire, then what?"

"Our hope would be to arrest him on the spot. You'd probably get a new judge, at least," Lou said.

"Would I have to testify?" Claire didn't sound too keen on the idea. I could understand her feeling on that one. She probably wanted to stay employed in Cleveland long past this case, however it turned out.

Lou and Miles looked at each other. "Yes," Lou said. "We're trying to put this one behind bars for a good long time. This case has been slow going. We're building it brick by brick. But we're close. You're the last brick we're going to mortar into place. I've talked to the victims. Women who felt like they had to trade sex for certain results in their case. But we've never been able to catch him in the act. You can help us do that. I don't want this to happen to anyone else."

29

Superstitions had no hold on me. But I couldn't shake the feeling that something was going to go wrong. Claire had found childcare, taken the day off work and made the call to Brody from her house. We didn't know if he had caller ID. So we brought the equipment along and recorded the conversation.

Judge Brody was weasely, all right. He never mentioned anything illegal. He made it sound like *she* was pursuing *him* for a relationship. Kept asking Claire if she wanted to come over. If she wanted to be his friend. If she was a dedicated mother. But we needed to get her to his place, so we had her play it up. And like any horny twisted fish, he took the bait.

Valdespino and I followed Claire to Plover Street in a white panel surveillance van that made us look more guilty than the judge. We parked near the railroad, keeping the van from sight of Brody's apartment.

After some knob fiddling a technician pointed to the headphones. Valdespino and I each put on a pair.

There was some shuffling as Claire knocked and the door opened.

"I knew you'd come, girl," Brody said.

"Good morning," Claire said formally. I looked at Valdespino and he shrugged. She sounded a little stiff and nervous, but maybe she would be in this type of situation. Hopefully Brody wouldn't get too suspicious.

"Are you wearing it?" he asked.

I could hear a soft gasp. Claire's mind had probably gone the same place as mine—the wire. More rustling as Claire did something. "I couldn't do it at home. Can I change here?"

"Go on ahead."

"Can I use your bathroom?" A grunt of impatience from the judge. Then Claire walked and a door slammed. "I'm putting on the damned nighty," Claire whispered. "This better work," she finished. A door opened again.

"Where'd you get the bathrobe?"

"On the hook on the back of the door," Claire said.

Bed springs squeaked. "Come here," the judge growled.

"Not so fast. My lawyer got a notice that you're thinking of giving Darius custody of my baby. I need some guarantees."

Springs squeaked again. "You're going to have to trust me."

"Nah-uh," Claire said. "I'm not one of your hood rats. I need something more. I told you that on the phone."

More squeaking, and the sound of rustling papers came through the headphones. "Here."

"It's a judgment entry, giving me sole parental rights," Claire said for our benefit.

"That's what you wanted. You got it. Now come here and give me what I want."

"Take off your clothes," Claire said. Damn, the girl was cruel. It was below freezing outside.

With a single 'go,' from Valdespino into a mic, agents poured out of the van behind us wearing zipped up blue windbreakers, FBI in eight-inch high yellow letters on the back. Unarmed, I hung back a bit. In my Philly days, I'd have had my trusty Glock at my side. Not anymore.

This was a no fuss, no muss arrest. The judge wasn't trying to hide a meth lab or flush crack. Valdespino read him his rights, and in five minutes, the judge was outside in handcuffs, a coat thrown over his skivvies. Ten minutes later, Claire fully dressed, came out as well.

"What now?" she asked, weary despite the early hour.

"You'll come back to the office and make a statement. Then you can have the weekend to yourself," I said. "Your lawyer will meet us down at the office."

"What about Darius? All I'd ever wanted was him out of our lives."

"You're going to have to ask Casey when we get there," I said, knowing my answer was ineffectual.

"Are you guys together?" Her question was surprisingly without rancor.

"Not really," I started. Then more emphatically. "No. Not at all. She's a nice girl and I like her. But she has a boyfriend.

I may think he's from a law-breaking family, but I don't get to make a decision about how she lives her life."

"We could have been good together," she said, motioning between us with her index finger.

"Maybe," I gave her. "But you need a committed father for little Luke."

"I hope I pick better the second time around. If it weren't for him, I wouldn't be standing here with tacky lingerie in an evidence bag," she said, thrusting that plastic into the hands of a female agent, blowing on her hands and getting into her car.

30

"Get out of here," I said to Greg, Jason, and Lulu. My bedroom was the smallest room in my apartment, and it was getting hot with the steam heat rising from the beveled radiators and four bodies. All three of them were there helping me get ready for The Soiree. They were happy for me, I suppose. Because of course, Tom was supposed to propose to me. I'd told them that much. The rest that I'd shared with Miles was still our secret. If they knew the truth, I'd be chained to my bedpost.

I'd asked around my limited circle as carefully as I could and got only blank stares when I asked about local prostitution rings, and a lot of head shakes when I asked about prosecutors being involved. I chalked up the rumors to Marisa's hatred of the Ellingwoods, the Brodys—anyone in the Cleveland power structure.

But I wanted love, marriage, children, a secure job, recognition in Cleveland's top legal and social circles. I deserved all of it after the years of drought I'd lived through. So I told them nothing about rumors or suspicions or gut feelings. Because who made rational decisions based on speculation and conjecture. Tom said he wanted to be with me and that had to be enough.

The guys left, but Lulu stayed. Rightly so, because I needed her help with the thing Lulu called Spanx.

"These are hell to get into," I said, breathing heavily. I didn't wipe the perspiration that beaded my brow or lip, fearing a makeup smear.

"But worth it, I promise," Lulu was huffing a little too as she helped me get the legs situated and straps on. My body from shoulders to knees was gripped in spandex that was supposed to make me look sensational in any dress.

My friend perched her glasses in her hair, then helped me slip the gown over my head. The chocolate brown dress was a faux wrap accentuated with a little diamond brooch at the waist. I sat daintily on the trunk that served as my off-season storage, as Lulu pulled shoes from a pale cream box on the floor.

"I can't believe you're lending me these," I said.

"This is the first and last time. But it's a special occasion and I don't need four inch heels just now. They were a gift from my mom, so be gentle."

The beribboned bag and box looked like they weighed more than the sandals themselves. The shoes were a few straps and gold beads on the heels, nothing more.

"How in the hell am I not going to freeze to death?"

"I'm going to drop you off, and you'll check your coat and run inside. The heat's always turned up at these things since half the women show up nearly naked." Lulu, displaying talent I'd never seen, pinned my hair and fixed my makeup. I looked in the full length mirror on the stand in the corner. Damn, I looked nearly beautiful. The form fitting underwear made me look like a size eight and elegant. I might not be as beautiful as Lizzy, but I didn't think anyone would blink and bat their eyes at Tom and me. For once, I thought, we'd fit together.

I thought Greg's jaw would fall off and Jason would hit the floor when I finally emerged from my bedroom. "Look better than a prom date," I said flippantly.

"Wow," Greg said. Jason was silent.

"So, can one of you help me with my coat?"

Jason scrambled to get it from the closet. Carefully, I descended the ninety-six steps to the door. Lulu helped me in the car, and we were off.

Halfway to the Lakewood Country Club, Lulu started in. I knew I should have taken Tom up on his offer of a limo driver. "So are you really going to do it?"

"Do what?" I played dumb.

"Marry Tom."

"Fortunately, I don't have to decide right now."

At a stoplight, Lulu took an exaggerated look the dashboard clock. "Oh, okay. Two hours from now."

"Let's see how it plays out."

"Seriously? You sound freakin' delusional. This is the biggest decision of your life, and you're leaving it to the last minute." She paused while navigating a slick patch on the road. "Is it Miles?"

"No," I answered too quickly even for my own ears. "It was only a kiss," I lied.

"Looked like more to me."

"He just broke up with his girlfriend, who happens to be a client of mine. That water's too complicated to wade in."

"Men have always just broken up with someone. You're sure it's not because he's black?"

That was a kick in the gut. Lulu's family was very liberal. She made my union-loving, staunchly democratic parents seem conservative in comparison. "No," I said truthfully. "I like Miles just the way he is." And I did, too much for my own good. But he wanted me to do things that would make my life a thousand times harder than it already was. He might still believe in the justice system, fairness, and all that. I was a seven-year veteran of unfairness, revenge, and injustice.

Lulu pulled her dad's Buick up to the motor court. A tuxedoed man with white gloves helped me to the door. Handing over my coat and clutching my little rhinestone encrusted bag in my hand, I took a deep breath and went in.

Tom was there to escort me, as if he'd been waiting all along.

"You look beautiful," he said. "More like your old self."

"Thank you," was all I said before accepting his chaste kiss on the cheek. I tried not to think of him kissing other women more intimately. The Soiree wasn't exactly the forum for a public display of affection. More than he'd just done would be in poor taste. This wasn't a high school hallway.

I snagged a glass of wine from a passing waiter and held tight to Tom's arm. We made small talk with lots of different people, many of whom promised referrals. Everyone, it turns out, knew someone on the brink of divorce or in the midst of a custody battle.

After dinner, I danced with his father, Patrick, and his uncle Liam. For the first time in my life, I understood the fairy-tale princess fantasy. When a woman I hadn't seen since law school pulled me aside for refreshment and cross examination, Tom scurried to a corner of the room, putting his head together with his father and uncle. When he looked back at me, the easy smile he'd worn all night was gone.

I disentangled my arm from my former classmate and walked toward them as fast as I could on teetering heels. "What's going on?" I asked when the huddle broke up. Liam and Patrick looked from me to Tom.

"If she's going to be family she should know," Liam said.

"Eamon's been arrested by the FBI."

"For what?" I asked way too loudly, feigning surprise. "Sorry," I whispered in a lowered voice. "What's going on?" I asked innocently.

"They're saying deprivation of someone's civil rights Ransomed," Patrick said, his mouth twisted. That was exactly the way Miles had described it to me the day before.

"Is he in jail?" Tom asked.

"He was for a couple of hours," Patrick said. "Liam called Judge Pittman. He did a bail hearing and sprung him. As a matter of fact...."

Judge Eamon came in then, fully outfitted in formal dress, looking none the worse for wear. Before he could approach, the band changed over from show tunes, and a singer joined them.

The lights dimmed, and the song started. I recognized it in an instant. Bryan Adams' Heaven. Gosh, it had been years since I'd heard that song. Then Tom was on stage with his own microphone.

"Casey Cort," he started. The spotlight settled on his handsome face. I'd never seen him more sincere or earnest. My head swam. It was happening. A force I couldn't name pulled me up to the stage. "You've been with me through good times and bad." He knelt. A second spotlight lit his hand. In it sat a small velvet box. I nearly covered my gasp with my hands, but must have missed because I heard the sound as if from very far away. The box opened, and the single solitaire sparkled as if it were on fire. "Will you do me the honor of becoming my wife?"

I took one deep breath then two and said the one word that would change the rest of my life.

31

"Did you have to go in with guns blazing?" Deputy criminal chief Charles Fitzgerald was dressing me down. Not how I'd hoped to start my Tuesday morning after a long weekend of fretting over the case and Casey's engagement.

"Judge Eamon was going to destroy evidence," I explained.

Both his hands spread out on my small desk, leaving me very little breathing room. "Was that your probable cause?"

"No, the woman wearing the wire was."

"The U.S. attorney's office is not the police force, or even the FBI. After Waco, we're very careful how we do things. Here we build cases piece by piece, brick by brick."

"I understand," I said, but I still wouldn't have done it any other way.

"When are you going to the grand jury?"

"Wednesday and Thursday. I don't think we'll spill over into Friday."

"Let me see what you've got and I'll let you know if I have anything to add."

What Chas meant to say was that he was checking up on me. Making sure that I hadn't totally gone off the rails. He left me to my corner of the room, and disappeared to his office. I ignored the stares from others in the office. Once I booted up the computer, I e-mailed him copies of my subpoenas, witness questions and grand jury schedule.

While I might have found Rachel Schaeffer annoying, judgmental, and condescending, I needed this first big case of mine to go as smoothly as possible. So on Wednesday morning, I put on my best suit fresh from the dry cleaners, buttoned all three buttons, and even had my shoes shined before I entered the grand jury room.

My first brick was Claire. It was easiest starting with a familiar face. She told the eighteen grand jury members about how she'd gone to court looking for full custody of her son. Her story about the repeated phone calls was compelling. Culminating with the cheap lingerie and judgment entry had the grand jury's attention. Most days were filled with simple drug cases and fraud. Telling a story with human interest kept their attention. We had half the usual number of bathroom and coffee breaks.

Next, I had Kyanna Oliver and Shanice Watson tell their similar tales. Now that I had them primed, I called the last witness, Tashonda Williams. Valdespino had pulled out all the stops, and the girl was conservatively dressed and ready to testify.

Though Williams was probably twenty-something, she didn't look a day over fifteen. Sometimes I hated the kinds of people I had to prosecute. They preyed on the weakest among us whether it was hooking troubled kids on drugs, turning girls out, or sex crimes. I vented my frustration within the confines of the criminal justice system, because I wasn't a cretin like them. But in another country or another time, I'd love to have seem them drawn and quartered.

I cleared my throat, and asked the witness her name and age.

"Tashonda Williams," she said. "I'm twenty-three."

"How old is your daughter?"

"Ten," she said.

A few gasps erupted from the jury members. Nearly twelve months into their eighteen-month service, I was glad to know something could still shock them. What had happened to her when she was thirteen was another crime for another prosecutor. I focused on what I needed.

"Did you go to probate court in nineteen ninety-nine?" I asked.

Williams nodded. "My baby girl got her head hurt in a car crash. The insurance company paid three hundred thousand dollars."

"What did you want the court to do with the money?"

"I wanted it to go into the bank so I could pay for her doctors and school and stuff."

"Did the money go into the bank?"

"The judge said no."

"Where did it go?"

"He said we couldn't get it for another eight years."

"Why did you disagree with that?"

"Because I had to pay for doctors and school now. No-body was willing to wait that long for they money."

"Did you explain this to the judge?"

She nodded. "The lawyer did. I did too."

"Did he change his mind?"

She looked away from me. Williams shifted in her seat. I asked the question again.

"Yes," she whispered.

"What did he say?"

Nearly every member of the grand jury leaned forward. "I could have the money if I came to see him," her voice was still dead quiet. Even the court reporter leaned in a little.

"Did you go?"

"Yes."

"What happened?"

"He asked me to take off my clothes. We did the nasty. He promised that I'd get the money for Camille."

"Did you get the money?"

"No. Yes. I don't know what you're asking." Her face was full of confusion.

"After the first time you had sex with Judge Eamon Brody, did you get the money he'd promised?"

"No. That's when my mom and grandma found out."

"What happened?"

"He came to pick me up and dropped me off later. Since Camille was born, they don't like me going out with different mens. They saw who was in the car and wanted to know what I was doing with an old white man."

"Did you tell them?"

"Yeah, but I got the money."

"That was the most important part, right?"

Williams nodded. "Yeah. My baby can go to a good school. I know I'm slow, but she's okay. I want her to get better and go to college."

"Thank you, Tashonda," I said then excused her. I gave my closing statement to the jury, about how this judge did the worst thing in the world, abusing the very people who needed his care and protection. I urged them to indict him for his crimes. Then I left them to their decision.

"Do you think they'll indict?" I asked Rachel while we were waiting in a conference room down the hall.

"Of course. Everyone knows a grand jury would indict a ham sandwich."

I nodded. Hadn't thought about that in years. It was easy to indict in Philly. A lot of less scrupulous prosecutors used it to pressure criminals into turning on each other. Nothing broke the bro code faster than a felony hanging over your head.

"But the Brody family seems to have tentacles everywhere." I was thinking of Casey again, and her unwillingness to testify. I hadn't subpoenaed her and Chas hadn't raised the issue again. I hoped Claire and the others were enough.

"That's state power. They don't have any sway over the federal government." I'd have almost believed her if Brody hadn't gotten out of jail in ten seconds flat, on a weekend no less.

"Maybe I shouldn't have been nervous," I said, trying to be as confident as she was.

"Nervous is good. Keeps you sharp." She looked toward a clerk and nodded. "They're ready for us."

A few minutes later, I had an indictment.

32

"I saw you in the paper," Letty said. Her words were matter-of-fact. But she was looking at me like I was Jennifer Aniston beamed in straight from Hollywood.

"Thanks," I said. I couldn't help but smile. The picture looked amazing. It was a total dream come true. I wasn't on the outside of Cleveland society looking in any longer. I'd watched my mother flip through those newspaper pages so many times knowing her daughter would never be in it.

My mom had looked longingly at the thin beautiful girls, with their dashing fiancés and husbands. Then she would look down at her own ample figure and work roughened hands, and smile almost wistfully. Her parents had never envisioned that kind of future. Neither had my mom. She'd met and fell in love with my dad from another immigrant family. They'd had a modest church wedding, a reception in the basement, then got on with things—having me in the process.

But here I was defying all odds. I'd picked up another copy of that newspaper Letty had exclaimed over, from my mother's doorstep and rang the doorbell of my childhood home just two days ago.

My mama had opened the door then wiped her hands on a flour covered apron tied around her waist.

"Oh, *lieb* did you call?"

"No," I'd said, pushing the paper into her hand. "You should read this."

"Are you in the paper again?" Her tone held disapproval. The last time I'd merited coverage, it had been less than flattering.

"Mom, turn to page two in the last section."

I followed her to the kitchen where she'd obviously been kneading dough. A large ceramic bowl sat on the counter, covered with a worn dishcloth. She put the paper down on the table, carefully flipping through the sections. The shock that registered on her face when my own face stared back at her was palpable.

"Pietrek!" my mother shouted. My dad, who usually went by the more familiar 'Peter' answered right away. Formal names meant business.

"What's all the fuss?" my dad asked, shuffling into the room. Unlike my mother, who had probably risen and dressed hours ago, Dad was still in his pajamas, flannel robe and sheepskin slippers.

"Our daughter has an announcement," my mother said. She was practically breathless. Her bosom rose and fell so fast, I feared a heart attack for a long minute.

Finally, I held out my left hand for inspection. "I'm engaged!"

They looked at each other then me. "To whom, if I may ask?" my father said with formality. "No one asked for my hand."

I ignored the small indignity. "Tom didn't have time, Dad. It was kind of sudden."

My father pulled over the newspaper and scanned the picture. "Is that Tom? Tom Brody you're standing next to?"

"Yes."

"This is no joke?" My father looked at me like I'd lost my ever loving mind.

My mother's smile dimmed a bit. "No, Dad. I'm engaged to Tom Brody."

"Did he put you in a time machine? We didn't know you were dating him again."

"It's a little bit sudden, I know. I didn't want to say anything. He called me out of the blue in September, and we've been seeing each other since. Then he proposed on Saturday night."

"Five months, and you didn't tell us. Not during Thanksgiving, or Christmas, or on New Year's Eve when I loaded those pans of strudel into your car."

"Oh, Daddy," I said, wanting to soothe his ruffled protective feathers. "I'll bring Tom over very soon."

My father grunted then took himself to the living room.

"When do you think the wedding will be?" my mother asked.

"We haven't really talked about it. But maybe fall. His family has offered to pay."

"Oh, *lieb*, the bride's family should pay."

"We can't afford the Lakewood Country club, Mama, and that's where all the family weddings are."

"Let me see this ring," she said, gathering my hand in hers. For long silent seconds, she admired the squared off stone.

"It's a princess cut solitaire," I said. I'd had to look that up. The small stones on the sides glinted in the watery morning sun.

"Tell me about the engagement," she implored.

From my mother's breathless demand, I knew that I'd fulfilled dreams she'd long ago abandoned. That aura of having pleased my mother had lasted for nearly two weeks. She'd fawned over the ring, and then had teared up over the pictures Lulu had taken before I left the apartment. Then the glow started all over with the picture in the newspaper.

Maybe I'd bought ten copies myself. It was possible I'd stalked Kinko's having two laminated, then had driven from there to a framer in Pepper Pike to have one framed. It wasn't like I'd display it anywhere. I was not one of those desperate girls who hung their engagement and wedding pictures over the mantle for all to see. But maybe I could put it in my childhood bedroom, just to peek at from time to time.

"Do you want your messages?" my secretary asked, bringing me back to the present.

"Yeah. Anything worthwhile?" I said, taking the stack of pink slips.

"Just one from a magistrate judge over at the juvenile court about the reassignment of your cases."

Once in my office, I glanced at the big ring on my left hand one last time before paging through the messages. The two cases I was still handling in juvenile, Claire's and

Marisa's, would need attention. The Ellingwood case was nearly settled, but Judge Eamon's arrest had thrown off the momentum. I was dying to get back in court to put that one to bed before Ian Ellingwood woke up and wanted to pry something else out of Marisa, whether for revenge sake or out of a sense of righteous indignation. Then I needed to do something for Claire other than throw her to the lions.

It wasn't like I'd breached my fiduciary duty or anything. But I was extremely conscious that I'd traded her testimony for my own. I'd bitten my nails the entire time I stood outside the grand jury room. She'd never once come out to ask me a question. Instead, she'd no doubt stoically suffered the humiliation of Miles and Rachel probing her about Judge Eamon's improprieties.

33

I hated being a spectator on my own case, but that's how Chas saw it. As much work as I'd put into this case, I wasn't ever going to first chair a trial of this magnitude. Instead I was sitting on the sidelines, behind the bar, while Chas and Rachel who got second chair, sucked up all the glory. Despite the fact that Judge Eamon had a passel of lawyers bigger than a basketball team, Chas thought it better that it didn't look like the government was going after him with guns blazing.

Nine millimeter Heckler and Koch's hidden, Lou and the rest of the FBI agents who'd worked on the case sat with me in the first row behind the prosecutor's table.

After all the preliminary witnesses testified, it was my job to bring in the victims. One by one, I'd led them to slaughter. Because that's what the defense team was doing to them. Making them look like they'd asked for it.

"Your Honor, the United States calls Kyanna Oliver to the stand."

I moved as quickly as I could to the hallway and zeroed in on the woman at the end of the bench. Oliver had done the best she could, following our dress code stricture. Her white dress and white stockings were probably her Sunday best, but made her look like a nurse. I didn't say that, of course. Instead, I laid a hand on her shoulder.

"It's your turn," I said to her.

"Is it gonna be okay?"

No, it wasn't going to be okay. Her life would never be the same. Judge Brody had the smartest and most expensive lawyers money could buy. So I said, "It'll be fine. We've already rehearsed this. All you have to do is tell the truth," I said then walked her to the dock.

Rachel, more soft-spoken than she'd ever been in one of our meetings, led Kyanna through her experience with the judge. She spun a story I'd heard dozens of times by now. Kyanna just wanted her kid out of foster care. So many got lost for no reason and she didn't want her child to fall victim to the system. So when Judge Brody'd offered her a chance to get him out—she'd taken it.

Kyanna had gone to his chambers, lifted her skirt, dropped her panties, and done what was necessary to get custody back.

Judge Brody's lead counsel had left the federal agents, forensics experts, and records custodians to his associates. But today, the day the women were scheduled to testify, Gordon Yarbrough walked to the lectern. He buttoned the jacket of his bespoke suit, and angled his Piaget watch to keep track of the time.

"Kyanna, how many drug dealers have you lived with?"

Rachel had lulled the witness to a sense of complacence. We'd tried to prepare her, but a person who wasn't regularly in court had a hard time believing how brutal defense attorneys could be on a witness. Keeping criminals out of jail was their bread and butter.

"I, um—"

"Objection!" Rachel was out of her seat. "Relevance."

"I'm allowed to impeach the witness' judgment, Your Honor," Yarbrough said.

"Overruled."

"Let me help you, Kyanna." Yarbrough walked to the desk, pulled some paper from a folder, and walked back to the podium. "Do you remember residing on Seventy-Third street the year your child was born?"

She turned toward the judge. His nod of confirmation spurred her to answer. "Yes."

"Was the lease in the name of Felipe Carter?"

"Yes."

"Would you be surprised to learn that Carter was convicted of possession with intent to distribute while you were living there?"

Long silence filled the court. Before the judge could lean down to admonish her, Kyanna spoke. "No."

"Did you live in the Wade apartments last year?"

"Yes," she said, resignation filling her voice. The look she darted my way wasn't friendly. I'd tried to warn her. But she'd been overly confident.

"Who lived there with you in public housing?"

"Me, my son, and my fiancé."

"So you were engaged to Deonte Harris when he was convicted of felony drug trafficking?"

"Yes, but—"

Yarbrough cut her off. "Just answer the questions. Were you evicted from Wade because of Deonte's conviction?"

"Yes."

"After that, your child was removed from your home? Isn't that correct?"

"Yes."

"What did you do to support yourself in the meantime?"

Kyanna's eyes went wild. I knew then there was something she hadn't told us. Something our investigation had overlooked. Something...bad.

"I did what I needed to do," she said.

Yarbrough's walk back to the defendant's table was theatrically slow. Every pair of eyes, from the judge to the jurors to the prosecutors was on him. We were all waiting for what was going to come next.

"On July third of last year, were you arrested?"

Rachel's butt was halfway out of her seat, but Yarbrough hadn't asked a single objectionable question. Not helpful to our side, yes, objectionable, no.

"Yes," Kyanna said.

"What was your arrest for?"

"I'm not sure."

"Your Honor, can I approach?" The judge nodded. Yarbrough took a single sheet of paper to the stand.

"Can you read this?" he asked, passing the page to the witness.

"The whole thing?" Oliver looked intimidated more by the reading than by what the paper said.

"Start at the top."

"East Cleveland Police Report. Oliver, Kyanna. Two nine oh seven—"

Rachel rose to her full height. Chas was only a second behind her. "Objection," they shouted in near unison.

"One at a time."

"Sidebar, your honor," Rachel said.

I got up from behind the bar and followed them to the out-of-jury-earshot conference with the judge.

"Has Mr. Yarbrough never heard of rape shield?" Rachel hissed.

"I'm well familiar with the federal rules of evidence, Ms. Schaeffer. It doesn't apply here."

"What?!" Rachel shouted.

"You requested this sidebar, counselor. You'd do well to keep your voice down."

She gave the evil eye, careful not to direct it toward the judge. But Rachel lowered her voice nevertheless. "He can't just throw out the rules of evidence, Your Honor. And even if four twelve doesn't apply, common law supports the concept of rape shield. We've decided as a country that a woman's past sexual history is not evidence of consent."

"While I maintain FRE four twelve doesn't apply, if your honor were to rule that it did, I'd argue that we're not talking sexual conduct, but rather criminal behavior. My client maintains that Ms. Oliver willingly offered up her, um, services. Judge Brody isn't a saint. His wife's permanently disabled, in a wheelchair. But extra marital sex is not a crime."

"I'll allow it," the judge ruled.

"Your Honor!" Rachel protested.

He tapped the gavel. "Step back, counselors. I've made my ruling. Mr. Yarbrough, you may proceed."

"Kyanna, were you arrested for solicitation?"

"Solici—"Oliver stumbled over the pronunciation.

"Prostitution. Were you arrested for offering sex to men for money?"

"Yes, but—"

"Did you offer sex to Judge Brody?"

"No, he—"

"When Judge Brody was assigned to your case, did you see him in his chambers alone?"

"Yes."

"Did you willingly have sex with Judge Brody?"

"No, I—"

"Did you not come there in lingerie? Did you not take off your clothes willingly? Did you not—?"

"Objection. Compound question."

"Sustained. Counselor, one at a time."

"Did you say no to Judge Brody?"

"No. I wanted my son back. I did what I had to do."

"No further questions."

Rachael tried to rehabilitate Kyanna on redirect, but the damage was done. It looked like Judge Brody was just a lonely old man. Women offered up their companionship, and he took them up on it. The fact that he held the lives of their children in the balance seemed of no consequence in this trial.

After she stepped down from the stand and came into the gallery, I made sure to sit Kyanna next to the other victims in full view of the jury. I wanted to make absolutely sure that those twelve men and women and the alternates could see every single one of the women Judge Brody had taken advantage of.

"Your Honor," Rachel started. "I call Claire Henshaw."

"Is she your last witness for the day?"

"Yes, Your Honor."

That was my cue, I went to the hallway to fetch my former girlfriend. The woman I wanted to be my girlfriend was sitting next to her. They both followed me in. Like every witness who'd preceded her, I directed Claire to take the hot seat. Casey sat in the gallery in the empty chair next to mine.

Rachel had done what any good lawyer should do, she'd saved the best for last. Her questions led Claire through her upbringing in Hyde Park, her undergraduate degree at Spelman, the prestigious historically black women's college, her graduation from Northwestern Law.

In a conservative black suit, white blouse and flat shoes, she was the epitome of presentable. On top of that, all her answers were articulate. She was the most well spoken witness the prosecution had called. I took a look at the jury. They were paying attention now.

Gordon Yarbrough looked like he was ready to play ball. When he gathered up his notes and leaned across the lectern, all I could think was 'that's my girl.' Claire didn't flinch.

"When did you meet Darius Gaines?"

"During the week before finals at Northwestern. It was bitterly cold outside, and we happened to be in the same bus shelter."

"Did you know that he had a string of arrests for theft, drug possession, and loitering?"

"No. He indicated that he was a college student. I didn't run a background check."

"Did you find any of this out before you had a baby with him out of wedlock?"

"No, like your client, he was very good at deception."

"Your Honor," Gordon turned to the judge.

"Ms. Henshaw, as an officer of the court, you know to answer the questions asked. Editorializing is not appropriate," the judge said.

"Ms. Henshaw, why did you bring a case before the juvenile court?" Yarbrough asked.

"My son broke his arm during visitation with Darius. I learned that his father wasn't there. Deeming that inappropriate, I decided to seek full custody."

"Did you make a motion for an *ex parte* hearing?"

"Through my attorney, yes."

"Didn't you go see the judge alone?"

"Yes."

"Did you not think it appropriate to call your attorney or the opposing party?"

"I didn't know I was going to be alone until I got there."

"Was that the first time, or the second time, or the third time?"

"The first time."

"Didn't you offer sexual favors to the judge?"

"I never offered anything to that man. I wanted my son back. If he were willing to flout judicial rules to do that, so be it. My son's safety trumped everything."

"You'd risk your bar card for that? I have a hard time believing that."

"Who's editorializing now?" Rachel objected.

"Sustained."

"You liked the attention from the judge, didn't you?" Yarbrough's voice was full of indignation.

"Oh, please. That man is older than God. I wanted my son safe, that's all."

Yarbrough hammered at her for another half hour, but finally relented. Casey's hand had snuck in mine. I squeezed it hard when Yarbrough sat down. The sharp edges of her big diamond ring cut straight through my heart.

34

Miles' thin fingers were stronger than they looked. His thumb absentmindedly brushed the skin stretched across my knuckles. I didn't want to let go of Miles' hand, but I did the moment the door of the courtroom opened, and my fiancé Tom stepped in. He was the last person I expected, though his appearance should have been no surprise. Blood was thicker than anything else in the Brody family. Tom made eye contact with me and I dropped the AUSA's hand like a kid trying to win a game of hot potato.

I don't know what Tom saw, but the eyes that locked with mine squinted just a bit. I resisted rubbing away the sweat that had broken out my upper lip. I'd never mentioned to Tom that I'd seen Miles again. And he'd never asked, not the least bit suspicious of me. Maybe he hadn't noticed or wouldn't ask about Miles. As Claire's lawyer, I had good reason to be where I was.

Miles looked past my shoulder and watched Tom saunter confidently down the aisle. Yarbrough was done with Claire and the defense attorney leaned in to whisper to Tom before my fiancé took a seat on the other side of the courtroom.

"Anything further from the prosecution?" the judge asked. Miles conferred with Rachel and Chas. Their gazes strayed briefly to me then went back to their huddle.

Rachel stood. "The prosecution rests, Your Honor."

The judge sent the jury back to their conference room. After the twelve citizens and alternates had left, the judge adjusted his robe and pointed to the defense table. "Mr. Yarbrough, would you like to make a motion?"

"Yes, Your Honor." I watched everyone sit back and fiddle with papers on their tables. Every defense attorney worth their salt made this exact same motion. And every single judge worth their salt denied it. I looked at my hands in my lap, wondering what Tom was doing here today. "Pursuant to rule twenty-nine," Yarbrough started, "I move that the court grant defendant's motion for a judgment of acquittal. The prosecution has not met its burden under section two forty-two of title eighteen. The Supreme Court held in McBoyle versus the United States that it's a violation of the defendant's due process when they haven't received fair warning of what the law intends.

"Even assuming all evidence the prosecution presented were true, nowhere in this statute does it give notice to the defendant that said conduct is illegal," Yarbrough concluded.

Chas and Rachel had started paying attention halfway through Yarbrough's argument and were yanking papers from their trial bags, searching frantically for something. Miles did the same, but found what he was looking for. Pulling out a yellow marker, he quickly highlighted a few passages and pushed the paper across the bar to the prosecution's table.

"Does the United States wish to respond?" the judge asked the disarrayed bunch.

Chas, who hadn't spoken much during the trial, took the lead. He picked up the pages Miles had handed to him and argued, "Your Honor, there is no ambiguity in this statute. It clearly states that one cannot deprive a person of their rights by means of subjecting them to aggravated sexual abuse. For that reason alone, the defendant was well on notice that willfully coercing vulnerable women into sexual conduct was a violation of this statute."

The judge paused for a long moment. "Unless the prosecution has anything further, I'm going to let the jury go home for the day and take this under advisement. I'll reconvene the court when I've made my decision."

When the judge had disappeared behind the bench, I turned on Miles. "What does that mean?"

Rachel and Chas had stood. Miles and I did as well. "It means, Ms. Cort, that we could lose this case. It looks like the judge thinks that maybe we were overreaching with this prosecution," Rachel said.

"Do you really think he'd rule in their favor?" Miles asked.

"In all the years I've been here, I've only seen a judge do this once," Chas said. "Usually they deny the defendant then proceed with the case."

"What happened the other time?" Miles asked.

"The court let the defendant go," Chas answered.

As I gathered my briefcase and made to go, I checked to see if Claire was okay. She nodded, and slipped from the courtroom as quickly as she could. Tom was in an animated conversation with his uncle and the defense attorneys.

We'd hook up later, I figured, and got to the hall. Before I could press the elevator down button, trying to get out of there faster than the crush of people behind me escaping courtrooms for the day, Miles and Rachel cornered me.

"Was there something wrong with Claire's testimony?" I asked, feeling a little panicky. After a few dozen felony cases in the county court, I was pretty comfortable with state criminal law. But federal court, with its nearly seven hundred crimes, rigid sentencing guidelines and high stakes was beyond my scope.

"We need to talk to you," Rachel whisper-shouted.

"About what?" My heart sped up. After Judge Grant's case, this place made me nervous. I half suspected the Cleveland police and FBI thought I'd had a hand in her disappearance.

Rachel pushed open a dark wood door that had 'attorney room' in small letters on a brass plate tacked to it. Miles flipped on a light and pulled me in. "I'll wait outside," Rachel said.

"Do you remember New Year's Eve?" Miles asked, searching my face but for what, I couldn't guess.

Heat suffused my cheeks. If he was wondering if I remembered that night or the one that followed, he wouldn't need to look any further than the beet red stain that was no doubt flushing my face, my scalp, my chest. I looked at the scarred wood table, tracing the lines of a pen mark with my index finger.

"Casey?"

"What?" I looked up. This wasn't about us.

"On New Year's Eve, you said something about Judge Brody having done this to others. Who did you see him do this to?"

I was quiet for a long time. Hadn't he heard me that night? I did not want to get in between the Brodys and justice. "Shanice," I finally said.

"How do you know Shanice? Do you have a last name?"

"I don't. I'd blocked out a lot of what happened that morning. But when Rachel asked me about it, I remembered Judge Eamon calling her Shanice."

"Will you—"

Some kind of commotion outside interrupted Miles. I opened the door to get a better look. Any excuse to stop this conversation before it went off the rails like a black and white movie freight train. Tom.

"Have you seen Casey Cort?" he was asking Rachel.

"She—"

"I'm in here, Tom," I said. My fiancé pushed his way in, followed by Rachel. Chas was next, shoving the door closed. Even though it was well below freezing outside, the temperature of the room was inching up by the second. I could feel sweat beading on my upper lip, pooling between my breasts, pricking my scalp.

Miles' glare was thunderous.

"What's going on?" Tom's question was directed at Miles.

"I was talking to a potential witness about her testimony," Miles said.

Tom looked from me to Miles, his face a study in perplexity. "What could she have to testify about?"

"Casey?" Miles questioned, putting me on the spot. Pitted between my fiancé and my soon-to-be family and a man I was insanely attracted to and had slept with, I wanted to click my heels and wake up in my parents' West Boulevard house to the smell of sizzling bacon and an apple covered Dutch pancake. I looked down at my sensible navy heels. Not a red sequin in sight. Disappearing wasn't going to happen. I took a deep breath and dove.

"Tom, the morning I saw your uncle about the Ellingwood case, I lost the gold Cross pen my parents gave me for graduation."

"What does a stupid pen have to do with anything?"

My eyes pleaded with Tom's for understanding. "I, um, debated going back to get it. Like you said, it was just a stupid pen. I don't even like it. But if they ever asked about it, I didn't want my parents to think I'd been careless with something so important to them."

"And then," Miles prompted.

Tom's glance toward Miles wasn't charitable.

"Judge Eamon...Judge Brody, I mean, wasn't alone. He was...he was having sex with this black woman." Once I'd started, I wanted to get the rest out in a rush. I wanted to put the burden of this on everyone else. "She was kind of disheveled, and naked from the waist down. Judge...Brody was in his robe and not much else, standing behind her...well...you know."

For a room full of prosecutors, not one of them had much to say after that.

"You're an officer of the court," Chas said. "Do we need to subpoena you or will you come willingly tomorrow morning?"

"You rested," I protested weakly.

"New evidence. We'll ask to reopen the case," Chas pronounced. "Rachel, Miles, we need to talk," they said and excused themselves.

It was me and Tom, and a hot, empty room.

"Why didn't you tell me?" Tom asked.

"I didn't know what I saw," I said, almost truthfully. The perspiration started again, this time under my arms. I'd have to stop at the dry cleaners tomorrow with a huge bag in hand. "I met Eamon's wife, and men have needs. I assumed...."

"You assumed right," Tom said. He sighed then sat. "Aunt Moira hasn't been well in a long time. Uncle Eamon has...had affairs. A man in his position, a lot of women proposition him. Unfortunately, he takes too many of them up on it. Especially, when he's had a little alcohol, his judgment isn't the best. We've tried to keep this within the family, but with this," he said, waving his hand toward the environs, "well, it's out."

"Do you think he'll be convicted?"

"Fifty-fifty chance, right now."

I felt like a wimp asking, but I wasn't sure enough of Tom to know the answer. "Are we going to be okay? They'll probably call—"

Finally, Tom gave me what I needed. He pulled me into a fierce hug. "I love Uncle Eamon. But you're more important to me. You're my future. You do what you have to do. Know that as far as we're all concerned, you're family."

He grabbed my coat and eased it on my shoulders. He opened the door. The prosecution team still huddled in the hall. Tom grabbed my hand and led me toward the elevator. Jabbing at the down button, he put an arm around my shoulders and pulled me toward him.

"Let's start planning the wedding. Why don't we have all our folks over to your place?"

I relaxed. I hadn't upset the apple cart. All was going to be okay in my little universe. The elevator pinged, and I nodded. When I turned around and put my back against the brass rail inside the car, I looked up, feeling someone's eyes on me.

Miles looked from me to Tom, his expression unreadable. Tom pushed the button for the lobby twice, and the door closer once. Finally, the antique doors slid shut, but not before I saw a little triumphant look pass from Tom to Miles.

35

This is the pit of hell Darius had dragged me to. I sat in a court conference room with the overdressed, over powdered, over perfumed women who were Judge Brody's victims.

The day's testimony that had ended with me was the last time I was in the courthouse. Unlike the other women who wanted to show their solidarity, I could not come back. From what Casey had told me, she'd testified about what she'd seen, and then the trial had come to an unceremonious end. Now we were sitting in a room at the courthouse, no doubt waiting for a pep talk from our illustrious prosecutors about how we'd served the justice system well.

I closed my eyes for a long second when Kyanna took the black vinyl seat next to mine.

"Why didn't you believe us when we told you about Judge Brody?" she asked before saying hello. Why hadn't I believed them, indeed? Didn't she think I'd been asking myself that question over and over since September?

"It seems a little crazy that a judge could use his power like that," I hedged.

"But he did. We tried telling you over and over, and you shut us up like little kids."

"I'm sorry," I said, full of contrition.

"All that schooling you talked about up there, you should know that white men have been taking advantage of black women since we got here on the first slave ship."

Before I had to address nearly four hundred years of America's history, the door opened. Rachel and Chas came in first, with Miles bringing up the rear. Before they could sit, the FBI agent I'd met before pushed his way in.

"Why are we here?" I asked. I needed to be at work, apologizing for not taking our clients' complaints seriously. My boss was asking the same questions Kyanna had. After the full story was summarized in the *Plain Dealer*, all of us who had heard about Judge Brody's proclivities were being held up to some unkind scrutiny as if *we* were the perpetrators.

Rachel looked hard at me. "Jury's come in with a verdict."

My stomach dropped to the floor. I wasn't expecting that. I looked down at my hands. What difference did it make if he were convicted? He'd already ruined the lives of dozens of women, probably. No jury conviction or lifetime in jail would fix that.

Rachel was still talking. "We don't know if he's going to be convicted. For your sake and the sake of the women of

Cuyahoga County, we hope so. But with trials there are no guarantees. No matter what the jury verdict is, we expect you to not shout or cry or clap. After the verdict, the court will probably address a number of other matters and needs quiet and decorum for that."

"So if he gets off, I can't walk up and punch the mo fo in the face?" Shanice asked.

Rachel allowed a small smile. "Yes."

"What?" Every head whipped toward her.

"No," she said and shook her head with vehemence. "No. It's not okay. Any questions before we go to the court-room?"

I swallowed a small smile of admiration. Even that white woman prosecutor had a little bit of ghetto in her.

There was silence. I looked at Miles. His hair was clean cut. His suit pressed. His shoes shined. I missed the normal-ity he had brought to my life. We were new to Cleveland together, new to life with a three year old together. I took a deep breath and said good-bye to the past. I was where I was and not a single thing was going to change it.

The trek to the courtroom was like a walk down the gangplank. No matter how this ended, I was going to be adrift in the ocean.

I trapped my trembling hands between my knees when the jury shuffled into the room. After some preliminaries, the judge got to what everyone—lawyers, victims, media, was waiting for.

"Do you find the defendant guilty or not guilty of aggra-vated sexual abuse, or an attempt to commit aggravated sex-ual abuse in violation of title eighteen of the United States Code, section two forty two? What say you?"

"We find the defendant not guilty."

My body, which a moment ago had been filled with lightness at knowing Judge Brody would no longer be able to victimize another, filled with horror.

Despite the earlier admonition of the judge, Kyanna and the other women dramatically fell from their seats landing on their knees. When they got off the floor, and the 'Oh, Lordy Noes' stopped, the tears started. It looked and sounded like a Baptist revival.

Reporters ran from the room, no longer careful to be quiet. Judge Brody looked as flushed as his red silk tie. His brothers in the gallery behind him, were appropriately stoic. They knew better than to celebrate in public. The judge's gavel hit the sounding block with a loud crack.

The room quieted. Chas Fitzgerald stood. "Pursuant to Rule thirty-one I'd like to poll the jury."

Of each juror, the judge asked the same question. "Did you vote guilty or not guilty on the charges before you?"

Each juror answered in turn. It was split right down the middle. Six had voted to convict, six to acquit.

"I'm satisfied the verdict lacked the unanimity required for guilt. Any other motions, counselor?"

The prosecutor's motion surprised me as did the judge's ruling.

"The defendant is not to contact any of the witnesses who testified against him," he said. "Furthermore, he is prohibited from making contact with any of the litigants who have appeared before him in either juvenile or probate court. Do you understand the conditions?"

"Yes, Your Honor," Yarbrough said.

"I need to hear it from your client."

Yarbrough goosed Judge Brody who came to his feet slowly. "Yes, Your Honor. I understand the restrictions you have placed on my freedom."

36

"Does this look okay?"

Greg inspected my dining room table closely. I tried to see it through his eyes, with its discount store table settings and candles lit instead of the overhead light to hide the aforementioned settings.

"It looks beautiful."

I took a deep breath, trying to slow my heart. "Are you sure?"

"Casey, it looks fine. The food smells wonderful. And you look great. Are you eating anything these days?"

The stress of the trial, worrying about Miles, about Claire, about the possibility that I'd have to testify, wore away most of the fat I'd had left. Tonight I was in all white. Winter white pants, and a high-collared wrap blouse. My only jewelry was a modest gold cross from my communion, and Tom's ring, of course.

"I'm back down to my fighting weight. Isn't that good?"

"Not if your stress and cortisol levels are through the roof."

"That's Jason talking. Tell him when he gets off his shift that the bad stress is over. What's left is good stress."

"Good stress?" Greg looked dubious.

"Planning a wedding. I finally get to look at bridal magazines for real, not just for kicks."

"Have you set a date?"

"Hopefully, I'll have something firm after tonight. Our parents are getting together for the first time to make plans."

"Your mom and dad never met Tom's parents?"

"In passing, maybe. Tom's met my mom a couple of times, and my dad, I think. We were broken up by graduation, so not then obviously." I batted away the memories of slinking to the dark corners of the auditorium with my parents while the Brody family basked in their son's accomplishments.

The buzzer rang. My mom and dad were scheduled a half hour early. "I better let you go," Greg said. I let them in.

I heard them come upstairs. First I prayed they were dressed like I'd asked. Then for long seconds I hated myself for feeling anything other than love or pride for my parents. Without them, I wouldn't be who I am.

"I'm so glad you came tonight," I said, hugging my dad then relieving my mother of her box of *windbeutel*. "Thanks for making this for me."

"Anytime—"

My dad owned a single suit, but it was solely for funerals and parish events that couldn't be avoided. It was black or nearly so. He hadn't worn it tonight. He'd simply worn a dark gray button down shirt whose creases matched those of the box it'd come out of this morning. The pants were jeans, pressed within an inch of their lives. Mom was in a deep purple silk dress. It was not her color, I thought uncharitably. I tried not to sigh. Before leaving, Greg took their coats and put them in my bedroom.

"You look so beautiful, honey."

"Thanks, Mom," I said. Before I could move away from the inspection I knew was coming, she'd caught hold of my collar.

"That blouse looks expensive." She flipped the tag in the back. "Eileen Fisher. Hmph. I think I saw something like it at Filene's Basement. Did you look there?"

"I didn't have time to bargain shop," I said. To my relief, she let it pass.

"I haven't seen you wear that necklace in so long. I didn't know you still had it."

The buzzer sounded again before I could respond to my mother that a cross wasn't the kind of thing you threw away.

"Dad, they're here." He'd disappeared as usual. I knew he was checking my bathroom pipes or making sure my screens were set in properly. It had taken me nearly thirty years to figure out that was how he showed love.

I arranged my parents on my couch then buzzed the Brodys in. The air was filled with kisses. I took everyone's coats and disappeared to the tiny hall closet where I'd made space for the Brodys. They got hangers while my parents had gotten space on the bed. But I wanted to treat them like true guests.

"Does anyone want anything to drink?" I asked when I came back to the room. No one took me up on that offer. My single couch and papasan chair weren't enough for this crowd. Grateful I at least had a dining room and chairs, I invited everyone to have a seat, and filled water glasses.

Except for dessert, my neighbors had designed the menu. I brought white wine to the table, then small salads with goat cheese, cranberries, and candied walnuts for garnish.

"This is a very cute apartment you have here," Eleanor said.

"Thanks. I like old buildings."

"Tom's moved into a place a lot like this one," she continued.

Tom's hand came under the table and squeezed the knee closest to him. "It was all part of my campaign to win her back."

That single sentence was why I was here. This man had seen the error of his ways and had picked me. I cleared the salads then brought out a chicken roasted with rosemary, garlic and onions. Potatoes had cooked with the bird, and carrots had glazed alongside. My dad stood from the head of the table and carved the chicken, giving the desired pieces to the Brodys first, and then serving the Corts.

Before I could lift a fork to my lips, my father rose again. "I'd like to propose a toast. To our soon to be blended families and to the happy couple, Casey and Tom."

We all clinked glasses.

"I've looked into it, and there are two weekends available in the fall at the club for the wedding. One in October and the other in November," Eleanor said.

"We thought a fall wedding would be best," Patrick said. "It's the best season in town, and the least chance of rain."

I knew I should have warned my parents. Deep grooves on the sides of his mouth and between his eyes lined my father's stricken face. "You're talking about the reception, right? You're going to get married at St. Ignatius like we did."

"You want them to get married in the church?" Eleanor's nose wrinkled a little.

"I'm lapsed, Daddy," I said, fiddling with the chain around my neck. Maybe I shouldn't have worn it. I'd wanted them to know that gaining a new family didn't mean I was leaving them.

"Once a Catholic, always a Catholic," he said.

"Patrick's a Catholic, but you're okay with the club, right honey?" Eleanor turned to her husband.

Patrick speared a potato and nodded. I was learning that while he may be the presiding judge for the entire county, he did not interfere in the domestic realm.

Eleanor took in a sharp breath. "We'll pay for the wedding, of course. If that's your concern."

My father turned a shade of red I'd never before seen. Damn. "My parents are more than happy to pay for the reception," Tom said. "They have lots of friends and family that we'll be obligated to invite. We could never put that on you. I think you're right, Mr. Cort." Then to me, Tom said, "Why don't we have the bride's family pay for the church wedding, and the groom's the reception?"

Still puce, my dad nodded agreement. If my parents couldn't help me pay for college or law school, they certainly had no money for a wedding reception bigger than one in the church basement.

"Maybe you can wear my dress," my mom added. "I'm sure it's in the attic somewhere. What do you think, *lieb*?"

My recollection of their black and white wedding photos was that my dad was in an indistinct dark suit, and my mother was in some kind of high waisted dress with lace on the top and satin on the bottom. It wasn't exactly how I saw myself at my wedding, but I didn't want to continue to upset the apple cart.

"Sure Mom, why don't we try it on this weekend?"

She beamed like the sun was lighting her up from the inside. I'd have to break it to her gently that lace and a train weren't exactly the look that I was hoping for. "I'll get the cream puffs," she said, rising and collecting plates before I had a chance to do it.

Eleanor was asking about how many people we'd have from our side and who would stand up for me when my mom came back with coffee and dessert.

"Is your uncle going to be at the wedding?" my dad asked Tom. I hadn't thought to warn him off the topic. He read the paper every day, and had opinions about nearly everything. In the silence that followed the question, I wanted the superpower to turn back time. As the kitchen clock ticked in the silence, marking the march of minutes forward, I didn't think that power was going to come to me anytime soon.

"Eamon is my brother. Of course he'd be at his nephew's wedding," Patrick said.

"Even though he's a rapist," my father said.

Appetite lost. The delicacy that had seemed so flaky and sweet and mouth-watering seconds ago, was an unappealing mess of congealed cream and pastry before me.

"Dad!"

"It's America. I'm entitled to my opinion. I don't want a man like that at any wedding for my only daughter."

"For your information," Patrick said, finally speaking up, "he is not a convicted rapist. He was tried under some vague federal statute. And he was acquitted. If he's guilty of anything, it's of having bad taste in women and poor timing."

"Wasn't one of your clients one of Brody's victims, honey?" My mom said congenially, like we were discussing a story from the paper, and not one that affected the people sitting right here at the table.

"Mom, I can't discuss my clients. There's attorney-client privilege."

"But she testified in open court about how the judge threatened to take her son away and made her wear red lingerie." My mother looked at me. "Isn't that right, Casey?"

"I don't think we should discuss this at the table. Why don't you tell the Brodys about how this recipe came straight from the old country?"

The look I gave my mom changed her gears and she was off talking about how her own mother had worked in a bakery, and the importance of high fat butter in making desserts that melted in the mouth.

Grudgingly, the Brodys complimented the puffs, and the tense dinner ended nearly twenty minutes later.

Tom's parents left first then my parents. My mom patted my arm and said something about young people needing time alone.

I closed the door behind them. Alone with Tom. That's something I hadn't been in a long time. My veins fizzed with nerves and my belly pooled with dread. I wanted us to be a normal couple, with normal excitement about the life they were going to spend together. But nothing about this felt normal.

Tom hooked his jacket on a dining room chair, loosened his tie, and disappeared into the kitchen. From the sound of the cork popping from the bottle, I assumed he'd helped himself to a glass of wine.

I took off my heels and arranged myself on the couch.

"I'm sorry about tonight," I said when Tom got back to the room.

"Not your fault," he said, sliding an arm along the back of the couch. His hand played with the strands of my hair. It felt familiar and almost relaxing.

"Are you okay with the church wedding? I know you're not religious—"

"If it'll make your parents happy."

I mustered up all the adult energy I could before I asked the next question. "Are you staying the night?" I tried to smile and look appealing, but I thought I could feel my lips tremble a little.

"I think it will be much more special if we hold off until the wedding night. What do you think?"

What did I think? A thousand conflicting thoughts filled my head. Did he want me? Was he attracted to me? I'd lost some weight. My clothes were better. I was going to tackle the nest of my hair next. But Miles wanted me the way I was. I closed my eyes and leaned against Tom. I needed to obliterate Miles from my memory. That was a once in a lifetime thing that wouldn't and shouldn't ever happen again.

Tom put the empty wineglass on the floor, and pulled my head toward his. The kiss was soft and kind. He tongue danced along my lips, not pushing down my throat. His other hand, not in my hair, smoothed down my neck and

along my shoulder. I took a deep breath, trying not to cata-
log everything that was happening, and instead melt into
the moment. It wasn't working. Fortunately, Tom didn't
seem to notice. He pulled away reluctantly.

"I think our honeymoon will be amazing if we can hold
off," he said.

"I'm game if you are," I said. He stood, shrugged into his
sport coat. "Are you leaving?"

"I promised I'd meet up with my brothers tonight. We're
going to shoot pool."

"Oh, okay," I said, walking down the hall to retrieve his
coat from the closet. I smoothed the khaki overcoat across
his shoulders, brushing stray lint from the lapels. Somehow
I doubt Eleanor had chastised him for buying the full-price
Burberry trench.

"You looked great tonight," he said, kissing me on the
forehead and grabbing my hand to finger the ring he'd put
on only months ago.

"I'll walk you down," I said, pulling my own cardigan
over my shoulders and sliding into my slippers just inside
the door.

"There's no need—"

"That's what couples do," I insisted.

I pulled his hand into mine, and we descended the three
stories to the ground floor. "Have a good night. Be safe," I
said. I watched him walk down the block toward his car.

"I didn't know you had company," Miles said.

I didn't hit my head on the trestle, though I felt like I'd
jumped a mile high. "What the hell?"

"I'm sorry to interrupt your domestic bliss, but you
weren't answering your phone."

"I was busy." I looked down North Moreland. Something wasn't right. "Where'd you park?"

"I'm right here," Miles said pointing to his Jeep.

"I need you to drive."

"What?"

"Now! Let's go. Follow that car."

37

I stuck the key in the lock and turned it. All four locks popped open and Casey was in the car before I could blink.

"Hurry up!" she shouted.

"What am I doing?" What was I doing? For at least two reasons I could think of, I shouldn't be here.

"See that blue Acura?"

I scanned the cars parked and driving along the street. There it was. The car's lights were on, the air filled with exhaust from its dual tailpipe, and the brake lights came on. "Yeah, what about it?"

"Follow it! You know how to do that, right?"

I pulled out carefully, keeping a car or two between me and the Acura. "Why are we doing this?"

"I don't want to say. Can you help me please? It may be nothing. Depends on where he turns."

In silence, I followed the car around Shaker Square, and then turned off where he did on Shaker Boulevard. There was very little traffic. At Lee, I waited in the right lane behind the car, trying to gauge if he was going to turn. No signal blinked.

"Why did you come to my place tonight?" she asked.

The light turned green, he turned, and I followed, pulling into the left lane, keeping my options open. He turned left this time onto Chagrin heading eastward. The traffic thinned. Keeping up with someone testing the limits of speed and power in a car was a challenge. Also, I didn't want to answer her. I had no business 'stopping by' the house of a woman who was about to walk down the aisle.

"Who are we following? I needed some excuse if the cops pull me over for speeding and weaving like this fool in front of us."

"Tom."

I nearly slammed on the brakes. "What?" We were at the five-way intersection at Chagrin and Warrensville Center Road. It would be a minute or two before we got our green light. Looked like Tom was heading southeast this time. The light turned quicker than I expected, and I was following him down a darker and emptier road. I wasn't too familiar with this side of town and needed to pay attention.

Ten minutes later, the car pulled into a single story stucco hotel pushed back from the road. Her fiancé appeared to make a call while in the car. Two minutes later a young black woman opened a door and beckoned. He locked his car door, looked around, then pushed the woman in groping her breast with one hand and shoving the door closed with the other.

"Oh, shit." I rounded on her. "Did you know where he was going?" Tears were streaming down her cheeks. "Ah, fuck. I'm sorry. I just...this was..."

"I know," she said on a shaky breath.

I turned the car back on. We didn't need to sit out here in the cold. I drove straight to my house. This woman needed hard liquor and I didn't want to take the chance that she didn't have any.

"Where are we?" she asked after I'd parked the car.

"My place."

"Oh."

"Come on, I'll warm you up."

I grabbed her shoulders, which I realized were thinner than before and bundled her into the living room. I hung her sweater in my closet, took her slippers. Why was she wearing slippers? I fished the brandy out of the cabinet.

"Have this," I thrust two fingers of liquor at her.

While she drank, I went to the bedroom and dialed Lulu. I liked Casey a lot, but this was beyond my scope. Way beyond. I wanted to take her out on a few dates, take her to bed again, see where this went...not console her about her prostitute-loving fiancé and his rapist uncle.

I ran back to the living room when the buzzer sounded.

"Who is that?" she asked. I pushed the button, unlocking the front door. "Who?" she asked again.

"Me," Lulu said, opening the apartment door and letting herself in.

"Why?"

Lulu jabbed a finger in my chest. "He said it was an emergency. Where's the fire? You're drinking on the couch. This looks very much like a date."

"She's engaged," I said. "This is *not* a date."

"The fire?" Lulu said, dropping her coat to the floor. "Get me one of those," she demanded, pointing at Casey's drink.

"One of my clients told me that Tom solicited prostitutes. That's why the oh-so beautiful and oh-so rich Lizzy Cofrancesco broke up with him."

"Why didn't you say anything?"

"I didn't know if it was true."

"Did you think to check him out?"

Casey looked at her best friend, disbelief etched on her face. "How was I supposed to do that? Hire an investigator? Ask around." She paused a long time. It looked like she was trying not to cry at her own willful blindness. "I didn't know...for sure."

"Now you do," I said putting an end to Lulu's twenty-twenty hindsight. I got myself a glass of water. Someone needed to stay sober here.

"What...how...?" Lulu asked

"She asked me to follow his car. We trailed Tom right to a hotel and into the arms of some woman who couldn't be more than twenty."

"Je-sus." Lulu downed her drink. "When are you going to give the ring back?"

Casey looked down at her hand like she'd never seen the ostentatious ring before. "He met my parents tonight. We made plans for the fall. Wedding at St. Ignatius. Reception at the Lakewood Country Club. Maybe wear my mom's dress, maybe find something I actually liked. You're supposed to be my maid of honor. Tom was going to ask his brothers tonight to be best man and usher. They're supposed to be playing pool right now."

"But they're not?" Lulu cringed while asking the question.

"No, not unless they're in the hotel room too." Casey squeezed her eyes shut tight, shaking her head vigorously. "I don't even want to imagine that."

38

The knock that pounded at my door nearly scared the living daylights out of me. My mother's bedtime tales of the Gestapo had made me wary of police, German shepherds, and heavy fists beating upon my door.

Pulling my robe together and taking a deep breath, I pulled the heavy wood open.

"What?" It was Miles. I lay a hand on my chest to calm my rapidly beating heart. "It's not even seven in the morning. What are you doing here?" He ignored me, pushing his way in. Tucked into fur-lined boots, I saw flannel pajamas peeking out of the oversized coat. Cold air radiated from him as he tossed the coat aside. "Don't you think you should have dressed before visiting?"

It was like I wasn't there. Miles fished through the piles of papers on my coffee table and sifted through the mail on my mantle. "Where is it?"

"Where is what? Can I help you find something in *my* apartment first thing Saturday morning?"

"The damned remote control."

I pulled the hard black plastic from under the pillow on the couch. "Here. Happy?" I retreated to the kitchen. Something told me I was going to need fuel for this.

The TV came on and the rat-a-tat-tat mixture of percussion and music signifying a special report filled the living room.

"Casey. It's on now!" Miles called.

I hurried back as fast as I could with a full cup of hot coffee, and Miles pulled me down to the couch.

"To reiterate, we have breaking news. Judge Eamon Brody is still at large. CNN received an anonymous box of cassette tapes late last night. Reporters listened to each and every recording and made transcriptions before turning the damning evidence over to local police. Before we play a portion of a recording, we ask that you take your children out of the room."

I looked at Miles, mute. There were a thousand questions I wanted to ask. But he pointed at the screen. It filled with a video of a reel-to-reel tape spinning on one half, and the other half was split further—a picture of Judge Brody on the top, and subtitles on the bottom.

Over the hiss of audiotape, there was heavy breathing.

"Down on your knees, girl." A male voice.

A woman's sniffling and crying momentarily drowned out the tape's hiss. "Do I...Can you...is there any other way?"

"Do you want your little girl to come home?" The male voice was gruffer than at first.

"Yes, please, but…"

"I could bury her so far in the system that you'd never be able to find her."

"Please don't…not to my baby. I'll do whatever you want."

The rasp of a zipper came next. I knew it was the black robe coming apart. "Open wide."

The camera cut to the newscasters who were as quiet as I'd ever seen them. In the silence I injected what I, and every other viewer over the age of consent, knew had happened. The split screen came up again. Papers rustled. "Here."

Through loud sniffles, the woman thanked Judge Brody, then the sound of a door slam.

"What you just heard was an unidentified woman being asked to perform sexual favors in order to keep custody of her child.

"Action News has learned that when this case was brought to Liam Brody in his role as Cuyahoga County's prosecutor, he declined to prosecute. His handpicked successor Lori Pope had also refused to charge Judge Brody. Instead, Brody's brother, Patrick orchestrated Judge Eamon Brody's move from probate to juvenile. In his role as Attorney General for the state of Ohio, Liam Brody refused the case again when FBI agents brought the case to the CBI.

"As viewers may remember from earlier coverage, the U.S. Attorney's office was unable to get a conviction under an obscure federal law that had never been tested before. After CNN broke the news of this previously hidden evidence, Attorney General Liam Brody issued a statement." The reporter picked up a sheaf of papers then read from the teleprompter. "'A special prosecutor will be appointed to review the evidence. Charges will be brought if warranted.' Attorney General Brody has recused himself in this matter.'"

As the anchors switched from sexual assault to dog adoption at the local shelter, Miles muted the TV.

"Judge Brody's going to jail this time," Miles said with conviction.

I sat back and took a long drink of coffee. If the sun hadn't just come up, I might have spiked the coffee with whisky. Triumph at justice prevailing mixed with worry about Tom. What would happen to his family?

"They knew all along, didn't they?" Miles' voice was full of accusation.

"We don't know that. Maybe they didn't want to see what was right in front of them." I knew my defense of the Brodys was weak. But the feeling of loyalty hadn't disappeared in a week.

"Are you serious? This is a cover up, pure and simple."

"Tom said—"

"You believe it? Everything that comes from anyone's mouth in this family smacks of pure self-preservation."

"It's hard to think the worst of someone you love."

"Is that why you haven't dumped him? You *love* him?"

"Miles!" I guessed Lulu had filled him in. I hadn't had the guts to confront Tom yet. I needed to do it. But the dream was a powerful thing. I twisted the diamond toward my palm.

"Don't Miles me." He opened his palm and started ticking through his fingers. "He solicits prostitutes. He's using you as a beard. You watched him sit by while his family planned the destruction of the Cofrancesco clan. Did you see what was in front of you on national television, no less, not five minutes ago? They've been covering up Eamon's crimes. All of them. The Brodys are as guilty as sin."

I drained my coffee, got up and placed my mug in the kitchen sink. Tightening the belt on my robe, I armored myself and came back to the living room.

"You have to go."

"Me? What in the hell did I do?" Miles paused, deliberated, lowered his voice. "I'm sorry. I like you, Casey. I really do. This is not how I wanted to start a relationship, but I need you to see that you have to disentangle yourself from the Brodys. I don't want you to go down with the ship."

39

"Why we fightin'?" Darius asked me. I looked at him curiously as I let him in the front door.

"Luke's not here."

"I know. I wanted to talk to you."

"In a suit?" I looked him up and down. His hair was what my mama would call fried, dyed, and laid to the side. The blue double-breasted suit had been pressed within an inch of its life. Was that a pocket square? This man looked like he was on his way to church, but it wasn't Sunday.

"Can we sit?"

I led him to the dining room. Didn't want him to get a crease from sinking into the leather couch. He sat at the chair nearest the door. I took a place at the other end of the table.

"I don't have cooties, Claire. You can come a little closer." With a pout, I shuffled a couple of chairs down. "Drop the case, Claire."

"You've got to be kidding me. After all I went through."

"After all you went through is the reason you should do it. I'm sorry for Luke's arm. I'm really very sorry," Darius said softly.

"My baby got hurt." I tried to keep the tears at bay, but the thought of the pain my little man must have been in, nearly broke my heart.

"I know, baby. I know. If I could take it back, I would. I was being stupid. But I...the guys."

"Why is it always some woman or the guys with you? Luke and I were never enough. And even with me out of the picture, your son isn't enough to capture your attention."

"I'm a change," he said, contrition in his eyes.

"How? You've been singing that tune for nearly ten years. What changed your mind?" I could hear the bitchiness in my voice, but couldn't extract it.

"Judge Brody."

My head snapped back as if I'd been slapped. If I never heard that man's name again, it wouldn't be too soon. "Could we not—"

"I'm sorry you had to go through that. How that man thought he could use black women that way. And the fact that you thought you'd have to be that man's plaything to keep Luke away from me. I'd a bowed out if I'd known what was going on."

"But you got Dinwiddie. He ain't cheap."

"You were going for full custody. I wasn't just going to stand there."

"How'd you get the money, anyway? Some woman?"

"I know I didn't go to Morehouse or some fancy school. But I did finish my classes this winter. I got hired on at Cleveland Clinic in the radiology department. They're paying eighteen plus an hour."

"What made you finally do it?"

"I need to support my son. And not by paying fifty dollars a month."

I did a quick calculation in my head. He'd be making nearly as much as me. A good private school and music lessons didn't seem so far out of reach. I wanted to say I'd believe it when I saw it, but that probably would have trampled on his sincerity. "Your son will appreciate this."

"Will you?"

My head snapped up. Was he? Nah, couldn't be. "Darius, the time for you and me is long past."

"Why? I still love you. I never stopped. It was you who decided we were over."

"We're from different worlds."

"Baby, we're both from planet earth."

"My mom—"

"This isn't about what your parents think is best. I'm from East Cleveland and you're from Hyde Park. Those two things will never change. But we got along real good. We had a great kid together. I've got some growing up to do, I know that. But so do you. I think we can do it together. It would be best for Luke. I didn't like growing up without a dad. Luke shouldn't have to."

With a little peck on the cheek, Darius left after his speech. Instead of calling my parents to get their opinion, I picked my son up early from his play date. When I told him his dad had stopped by, he had a million questions. Maybe

I could give Darius one last chance. My son deserved his father.

40

If anyone had told me last year I'd be the one calling the shots with Tom Brody, I wouldn't have believed it. But this time I knew exactly how the day was going to end with Tom.

I looked down at my white sweater and white corduroy pants. I wasn't nearly as fat as I had been in August, but I think monochromatic dressing suited me. Never again would I shop at Chicos or Norm Thompson, shrouding myself in hideous jewel toned clothes. I'd looked at those catalogs and thought I'd looked soft, floaty, ethereal. But looking back at pictures of me and Lulu over the years, I just looked like I was in a Technicolor dreamcoat, without the chorus.

I watched my leg jiggle a moment before standing. I looked at the clock above the mantle. It was six. Tom should be here by now. I walked to the living room door, fiddling with the knob. I resisted the urge to go see Greg and Jason. They'd tell me what I had to do. It still warred with what I wanted to do.

My heart leapt to my throat when the buzzer sounded. I swallowed hard then went to the hall and pressed unlock. I skipped the step where I asked who it was. There was no need. I was only expecting a single person. The faint sounds of a door slamming and locking were followed by footfalls that got heavier with every step. I opened the door for my fiancé.

"Here, let me take your coat," I offered. Then wrapped him in a hug. He was so very warm, despite the cool spring air outside. The smell was like a combination of basil, pepper and musk. It was him. I inhaled deeply. Damn.

"Casey," he said, holding the embrace longer than I would have. "You've been my rock."

I pulled back. "I can't believe what happened with Judge Eamon."

"Just Eamon now. I don't think he'll ever be Judge Brody again."

"Is he okay? What about Moira?"

"She's moved in with Mom and Dad. They brought over her full-time live-in caregiver. So she's comfortable, I think. Uncle Eamon used to care for her at night. And despite what he's been accused of, I think she misses it, him, their time together. To hear Uncle Patrick tell it, they had the greatest love story."

"Tell me." For the next hour we talked about Eamon and Moira, how they'd met as teenagers in the fifties at a dance, then couldn't find each other for a single long year. I had to smile at that. In today's internet era, we'd be able to find someone in an instant. "That sounds so romantic," I said. "Nothing like us."

"What do you mean? We're together, having found our way back to each other after a long break."

He sounded like a character from television reciting a monologue, not a real person.

"Why did you break up with me?"

With a sharp intake of breath, he let me know he hadn't seen that one coming. "What? When?" He was stalling.

"You know when. Nineteen ninety-five."

Tom looked away. Following his gaze, I could see nothing more than newly leafed trees swaying in the wind. A bus drove by, the sound of its diesel engine loud even on the fourth floor.

"Dad thought it was best."

"Why?"

"The Strohmeyers were significant campaign donors. They controlled the dollars of a lot of people in Cleveland. I loved you, but Dad thought the livelihood of three elected officials was more important."

"What about now? Aren't you worried about the Strohmeyers pulling support?"

"Uncle Liam's probably not going for the senate. Depends on how this shakes out. But you're not on the Strohmeyers' radar anymore, anyway." I hit the imaginary buzzer in my head. Wrong answer. Now that the Strohmeyer scion was a partner at the second largest law firm in Cleveland, his position was safe. No one cared about his youthful indiscretions.

"Why'd you break up with Lizzy?"

Tom hesitated a beat too long. "Why are you asking about all this today?"

"Please can you answer the question?"

"Can I have some water? Do you have any juice? Cranberry would be good."

He was starting to sweat. I got up and poured him a tall glass of juice with ice and a slice of lime. If he wasn't driving, I'd have thrown in a stiff shot of vodka.

"Where's all this coming from, Casey?"

"The upside of all the referrals I've gotten from your family is that I have a lot more genuinely paying work, and my bank account's a lot healthier." Tom tilted his head, lost first by my questions, then by this segue. "The downside. The rumor mill."

"What do you mean?"

"I got an earful on why you broke up with Lizzy."

Tom blanched. Any ruddiness from the cool spring air left his cheeks in an instant. "What did you hear?"

"That Lizzy broke up with you because of your penchant for young, black prostitutes."

Tom's head swung from side to side. His lips were poised for a full denial. I held up my hand. "Please...don't. I'm not a gossip. People's motives are too suspect for me to take anyone's word for it. But it did start to niggle at me. When we were in law school, you were too tired for sex a lot of the time. I thought it was me.

I took money I didn't have to buy lingerie. I got everything waxed. I took advice from Cosmo, for God's sake. But nothing changed. And we're back here again. This time you're saying you want to wait for marriage to have sex. But you're not religious. You're a red-blooded man. And unless you're on the asexual end of the spectrum, I was struggling to buy it. But I looked in the mirror. I knew I was fat. My thin face didn't match my body. But other men have shown an interest."

"That Miles guy, right? He's been all over you since that night in the wine bar. Always looking at you. Probably filling your head, talking shit about my family."

"It doesn't matter who it was, Tom. After your celibacy declaration, I followed you. Straight to that hotel. Straight into the arms of someone else."

Tom's eyes widened in fear. I'm not sure what he was afraid of, me telling the truth to the world. Me dumping him once and for all.

He sputtered for a long time before he could speak a full sentence. "It's just that I respect you so much, Casey, that—"

"Cut the bullshit. The older I get, the smarter I get." I fingered the diamond one last time then slipped it off my finger. I opened his palm and placed it there. "I don't think there's any point to my keeping this."

Tom's voice was incredulous. "You're breaking up with me?" What about the last ten minutes of conversation had made him think I was staying? I'd been a doormat for Tom, for judges, for clients for too damn long. I was done with everyone walking all over me. For once, I was going to stand up for myself and what I wanted.

"I can do a lot of selfless things, but playing second fiddle to prostitutes is not one of them."

He pushed the ring back in my hand, holding mine closed with his. "But this could work. Sex isn't the most important part of a marriage. Not in the end, anyway. We want the same things, a Catholic family, children, respectable careers."

"You break the law on one hand while pretending to up-hold it," I jabbed my finger at his chest. I may not stand up for myself, but I did know the difference between right and wrong.

"You'd always have your pick of cases," Tom continued like I'd never spoken. "Do you want to work in a firm like Lulu? You can do that. Part-time hours while the kids are young shouldn't be a problem."

"What about my sex life, Tom?"

"Women don't need sex as often as men. I promise to always use a condom. I'd never bring home a disease, I swear."

"No."

"I need you, Casey. Please don't leave me."

I looked into those brown eyes I'd loved for so long, and the warmth I used to see there had been replaced by calcu-lation. He needed *me*. *I* was the respectability. Everyone ex-pected a little corruption at the top. But if he married a girl from the wrong side of the tracks, it would show how mag-nanimous and accepting he and his family were. Everyone thought the handsome prince far better for choosing Cin-derella over all the rich and spoiled girls he could have picked.

"I have some demands," I said, letting the prongs hold-ing the stone press into my flesh.

"Name them."

"I'll keep your secret."

He closed his eyes. "Thank you."

"I get to stay on your family's referral list, so to speak. I need to make a living here."

"I'm sure that won't be a problem."

"And except for social occasions, we never speak to each other again."

41

"You look really good," I said, joining Casey at the restaurant table. I accepted a menu from the host, but laid it on the white tablecloth unopened.

"Thanks. Can I ask you a favor?"

"Sure," I said, not at all sure what she was going to ask, but knowing I was going to give her whatever she liked.

"Can I have a ride home?"

"Of course. You didn't drive?"

"My car died this afternoon. Lulu and I spent the last four hours with the mechanic. She dropped me off."

"You could have called—"

"I didn't want to miss dinner." The matter-of-fact way she said that shot straight to my heart, speeding it up mercilessly. Maybe there was still a chance for us.

I picked up my menu to hide the telltale heat I could feel suffusing my cheeks. "What would you like?"

"Do you want to split the mussels and fries?"

I wanted to tell her that she looked great. That she'd looked great before and now. Her weight made no difference to me. But I'd lived with my mother long enough, and had dated my fair share of women. I knew that I should stay far away from the topic. "Sure. I'll have short ribs. You?" I gave our order to the waitress, including Casey's half order of squash ravioli.

"How's work?" we both asked at the same time. Laughter broke the tension, and dinner got better. Especially after I ordered that bottle of white wine I'd been eyeing on the beverage list. Casey's frizzy blonde hair was everywhere after she'd raked her hand through it a few times, but I thought she looked adorable.

At ease was how she seemed these days. I'd seen her from afar at the Lincoln Inn and at the wine bar. She'd seemed happy, but distant. Removing the stress of Tom from her life had been the best thing she'd ever done. I'd never asked how she did it, but her practice seemed to still be thriving, so the sword of Damocles hadn't fallen on her head a second time.

I must have sounded forlorn on the phone with my parents, because they pried my crush on Casey out of me and urged me to call her.

"You only live once," my mother had said. "The worse she could say is no. But at least you'd have an answer." My father better understood the constant rejection men face, but he'd agreed with Mom. So I'd steadied my nervous index finger and dialed her number. She'd said yes, to meet her here at Moxie.

"Things are going well," she said. "I'm out of juvenile court altogether. Don't think I'll ever go back there."

"What are you doing now?"

"Only divorce, post-decree stuff, and felonies."

"You think we'll ever go up against each other?"

"Nah. I'm staying my butt out of federal court. Those sentencing guidelines are no joke. Between life imprisonment and forfeiture of the defendant's stuff, it's not a fair fight. I wouldn't go into a gun battle with a knife."

If I were a better bad-ass prosecutor, I'd defend the way the federal court worked, but I'd seen too many brothers go down for twenty-five years for non-violent drug offenses. Prisons were literally full to bursting with men who could otherwise be productive members of society. While it took dozens of people and two prosecutions to get one judge who was using his power to hurt women. The loss of the Brody case still stung, hard.

"Earth to Miles," Casey said.

"Sorry. I was thinking about Judge Brody."

"Yeah, well, he's fighting that tooth and nail. Claiming double jeopardy."

"We tried our best," I said, sounding defeated even to my own ears. The Brodys plum wore me out.

"Do you wanna get out of here? Why don't you come back to my place?"

I knew that look. I gave silent thanks to my parents then banished them from my mind. After tonight, maybe I could convince Casey to give us a try.

I paid the bill while she made a run to the ladies room. I was about to get our jackets from the check, when my phone buzzed. Who in the hell was calling on a Saturday night?

"Miles Siegel."

"Valdespino," the voice said.

"Lou," he'd finally let me use his first name. "What's up? I'm with Casey. We've finished up dinner and I'm about to take her home." I didn't normally kiss and tell, but whatever he was calling me about had better have been damned important.

"I know you're not on call, but I can't reach Rachel."

"So?" Unless this was the bust of the century, and I was going to be on television with guns, drugs, US currency, and pornography, I wasn't interested.

"I can't get into it over the phone. Do you know where the Sleepy Time Motel is on Northfield Road?"

The restaurant's doors were closed, but a chill went down my back nonetheless. "Yeah, I know where that is. I'll be there in fifteen."

"What's up?" Casey's eyebrows drew together as she scrutinized me and the Blackberry I held in my palm.

"Slight detour. Do you mind coming with me for a few minutes?"

"I have no car, so I'm at your mercy," she said with a small smile.

The drive to the hotel was much shorter this time. "Are we at—"

"Yeah. Don't know. FBI called me in. I don't think I'll be long."

I rolled down my window and followed the directions of an agent, driving around the back of the single story motel.

There were a couple of long storage containers in back. I wondered if it was meth or marijuana, or even guns. I'd never seen any quantity of cocaine large enough to fill shipping containers. Whatever was there, this was going to be huge. I could feel it in my bones.

We got out of the car. I badged my way forward, telling everyone that Casey was with me. Lou looked at both of us, but didn't admonish me for dragging her along. Silently, he lifted a metal bar. It reminded me of the iron post we'd had on our subterranean basement door when I was a kid.

"Brace yourself," Lou said.

The iron on iron gave a protesting squeak; then one of the doors was open. It took a moment for my eyes to adjust. People? Women? There were about a dozen women and children inside, blankets, a space heater, a few belongings.

I grabbed for Casey's hand, squeezing it hard. I wanted to apologize with that squeeze because it looked like this date was the last vestige of normalcy we'd have for a long time.

ABOUT THE AUTHOR

Aime Austin is the author of the Casey Cort Legal Thriller Series. Casey is almost always in trouble. Aime's full time job? Rescuing her. Good thing Aime's got experience. She practiced family and criminal law in Cleveland, Ohio for several years—so she has the skills for the job.

When Aime isn't rescuing Casey from herself, she's raising her son or traveling between Budapest and Los Angeles.

Made in the USA
Las Vegas, NV
21 July 2023

75068724R00187